'Please,' the main man —
'You've got to understand why I – I came in here.
I had to find some people I could talk to . . .'

Garvin twitched a corner of his mouth. He could
picture an attempt at communication with the
deadly silence and armed withdrawal that lurked
through the apartments beyond his own walls.

'Can't you say something?' the panic-stricken
man demanded.

'No! Think! How much food can there be left,
where we can get to it? There are whole gangs in
the warehouses, and they won't let anybody near
them. The rifle ammunition's getting low already.
How long can we go on this way – fighting over
every can of peas, killing each other over a new
shirt? We've got to organize ourselves – get a
system set up, try to establish some kind of
government. It's been six years since the plague
and nothing's been done.'

The unsteady voice was on the point of breaking.
'I want to be friends . . .'

ALGIS BUDRYS

Some Will Not Die

A Methuen Paperback

A Methuen Paperback

SOME WILL NOT DIE

British Library Cataloguing in Publication Data

Budrys, Algis
    Some will not die.
    I. Title
    813'.54[F]   PS3552.U349

    ISBN 0-413-42190-2

First published in United States 1978
by Starblaze Inc
Magnum edition published 1980
Reprinted 1986
by Methuen London Ltd
11 New Fetter Lane, London EC4P 4EE

Made and printed in Great Britain
by Hunt Barnard Printing Ltd, Aylesbury, Bucks.

The author owes special thanks to Ed Gorman for his help with the original edition.

Writing is a craft, and for teaching me most of what I know of it, for keeping me at it, and for never letting me forget my obligation to it, this is for

Lester del Rey and
Evvie,
and for my wife,
Edna.

"We are not considering a man. We are considering men; if no man is an island in a world of nearly four billions, then how can any man be independent of others when the population is one-tenth that figure? Men who would have been lost and insignificant in the world before the plague now had their slightest whims and quirks magnified by a factor of ten. The ripples of any one man's personality spread ten times as far, ten times as effectively. A man with nineteen neighbors need not consider any of them too much. A man with one neighbor has either a brother or an enemy, or both.

"So to understand the history of the world after the plague, we have to understand that no man—not even Theodore Berendtsen—could possibly serve as the single focus of that time.

"We are studying a man, yes. But we are considering men."

—Harvey Haggard Drumm,
A Study of the Effects of Massive Depopulation on Conventional Views of Human Nature. Chicago, 2001 AD, mimeographed.

SECTION ONE

PROLOGUE:

This happened many years after the plague, at about the same time there was already talk of reviving the American Kennel Club in the east and south. But this happened farther to the northwest:

Night was coming down on the immense plain that stretched from the Appalachians to the foothills of the Rockies. The long grass whispered in the evening wind.

Clanking and whining, a half-tracked battlewagon snuffled toward the sunset. Behind it lay the featureless grass horizon, almost completely flat and with no life visible in it. The empty grass fell away to either side. Ahead, the first mountains lay black and blended by distance, a brush-stroke lying in a thick line just under the sun.

The car moved forward at remorseless speed, a squat, dark, scurrying shape at the head of a constantly lengthening trail of pulped grass. Its armor was red with rust and scarred by welds. The paint was a peeling flat dark green. On the side of the broad double turret, someone had painted the Seventh North American Republic's escutcheon with a clumsy brush. The paint was bad here, too, though it was much

11

more recent. Another badge showed through from underneath, and, under that, someone else's.

Joe Custis, with the assimilated rank of captain in the Seventh Republican Army, sat in the car commander's saddle. His head and shoulders thrust up through the open hatch; his heavy hands were braced on the coaming. His broadbilled cap was pulled down low over his scuffed American Optical Company goggles, and crushed against his skull by an interphone harness. His thick jaw was burned brown, and the tight, deep lines around his mouth were black with dust and sweat that had cemented themselves together. His head turned constantly from side to side, and at intervals he twisted around to look behind him.

A speck of white, off to his left, became a freshly painted, well-maintained signboard nailed to a post planted at the top of a low, rounded rise. He dropped his goggles around his neck, and looked at it through his binoculars. It was a hand-lettered sign in the shape of a skull—not a new sign, but one kept renewed—reading:

NO FOOD—NO
FUEL—NO WO-
MEN

Custis picked up his command microphone. "Lew," he said to his driver, "you see that thing? Okay, well ease toward it. Get set for me telling you to stop altogether."

He jacked down the command saddle until his face was level with the turret periscope eyepieces, and raised the scope until its slim, stiffly flexible length was fully extended above the turret, looking, with its many joints, like the raised and quivering antenna of something that bred and went to outrageous combat on the red plains of Mars.

"Slow, now, Lew . . . slow . . . hold it."

The car stopped, its motors idling, and the periscope searched over the rise. Joe Custis reached up and pulled the turret hatch shut, close over his head as he sat awkwardly bent down, peering into the scope.

On the other side of the rise was a valley—what had been a valley, geologic ages past, and was now a broad, shallow bowl into which ten thousand centuries of rain had washed the richest topsoil—and in the valley were fields, and here and there low, humped, grass-grown mounds. There were no lights showing. The fields were empty of movement, but one was half-harrowed—the ground freshly turned, the surface still rich and greasy, until suddenly the marks of the spike harrow turned out of their course and swayed away toward one of the mounds, which was in fact a sod hutment. A farmer had interrupted his work and driven his horse—and the precious, hand-built harrow—into shelter.

The driver's voice cut into Joe Custis's headphones. "Want me to move in for a better look?"

"No. No, circle around this and let's get back on the old heading. Don't want to go no closer. Might be traps or mines."

As Custis lowered the periscope, the car backed away. When it had back-tracked to where it had first turned off course, it swung around and began rolling forward again. The whine of the bogey motors built back up its original pitch. Joe Custis threw the hatch back again, and raised the seat to its old position. The signboard began to dwindle as the car left it behind.

Back on the car's turtledeck, the AA machinegunner's hatch crashed open. Custis turned and looked down. Major Henley, the political officer, pulled himself up, shouting above the dentist's-drill whine of the motors: "Custis! What did we stop for?"

Joe cupped one hand to his ear, and after a moment Henley kicked himself higher in the hatch, squirmed over the coaming, and scrambled forward up the turtledeck. He braced a foot on the portside track cover and took hold of the grab iron welded to the side of the turret. He looked up at Custis, swaying and jouncing. Custis wondered how soon he was going to slip and smash out his teeth on the turret.

"What did you stop for?"

"Fortified town. Independent. Wanted to look it over. Gettin' to be a few of those places up this way. Interestin'."

"What do you mean, independent?"

"Don't give a damn for nobody. Only way to get in is to be born there. Or have somethin' it would take a cannon to stop. I don't think they got cannon. Would of hit us, otherwise, instead of buttonin' up the way they did."

"I thought you said this was outlaw-controlled territory."

Custis nodded. "Except for these towns, it is. Don't see any more open towns, do you?"

"I don't see any outlaws, either."

Custis pointed toward the mountains. "Watching us come at 'em."

Henley's eyes twitched west. "How do you know?"

"It's where I'd be." Custis explained patiently: "Out here on the grass, I can run rings around 'em, and

14

they know it. Up there, I'm a sitting duck. So that's where they are."

"That's pretty smart of them. I suppose a little bird told them we were coming?"

"Look, Henley, we been pointin' in this direction for a solid week."

"And they have a communications net that warns them in time. I suppose someone runs the news along on foot?"

"That's right."

"Rubbish!"

"You go to your church and I'll go to mine." Custis spat over the side, to starboard. "I been out on these plains all my life, workin' hired out to one outfit or another. If you say you know this country better, I guess that's right on account of you're a major."

"All right, Custis."

"I guess all these people out here must be stupid or somethin'—can't figure out how come they're still alive."

"I said all right."

Custis grinned without any particular malice, giving the needle another jab under Henley's city-thin skin. "Hell, man, if *I* thought Berendtsen was still alive and around here someplace, I'd figure things were being run so smart out here that we ought to of never left Chicago at all."

Henley flushed. "Custis, you furnish the vehicle and I'll handle the thinking. If the government thinks it's good enough a chance to be worth investigating, then that's it—we'll investigate it."

Joe looked at him in disgust. "Berendtsen's dead. They shot him in New York thirty years ago. They pumped him full of holes and dragged his body behind a jeep, right down the main street at twenty miles an hour. People threw cobblestones at it all the way. That's all there is left of Berendtsen—a thirty-year-old streak of blood down Broadway Avenue, or whatever they call it."

"That's only one of the stories you hear. There are others."

"Henley, a lot more people have heard that one than have heard he's still alive. And 'way out here. Maybe we should look around for Julius Caesar, too?"

"All *right*, Custis! That'll be enough of your kind of wisdom!"

Custis looked down at him steadily, the expression on his face hovering at the thin edge between a grin and something else entirely. After a moment, Henley blinked and broke the conversation off into a new direction. "How soon before we reach the mountains?"

"Tonight. Couple more hours, you'll get a chance to see some bandits." Now Custis smiled.

Henley said "Well, let me know when you come across something," and gingerly crawled back to the AA hatch. He dropped out of sight inside the car. After a moment he remembered, reached up, and pulled the hatch shut.

Custis went back to keep an eye out. At rest, his face was impassive. His hands motionlessly held the thick metal of the armor. But now and then, as his eyes touched the mountains in his constant scan around the horizon, he frowned. And at those times, his fingers would flex, as though it were necessary for him to reacquaint himself with the texture of wrought steel.

Custis had no faith in Henley's hopes. Berendtsen's

name was used to frighten children—real children or politicians; it was all one—all over the Republic. It had been the same during all the Republics before it. Somebody was always waving the blue-and-silver flag, or threatening to. A handful of fake Berendtsens had been turned up, here and there all over the Chicago hegemony, trading on a dead man's legend these past thirty years. Some of them had been laughed down, or otherwise taken care of, before they got fairly started. Some hadn't—the Fourth Republic got itself started while the Third was busy fighting a man who'd turned out to be merely a better liar than most. Through the years, the whole thing had turned into a kind of grim running joke.

But the fact was that the politicians back in Chicago couldn't afford to have the ghost walking their frontiers—or what they thought were their frontiers, though no one could truly say whose word was Law south of Gary. The fact was that somehow, in some way, the tale of Berendtsen had come drifting over the eastern mountains and contaminated the people with impatience. The fact was that Berendtsen was a man who had been able to take hold, after the plague scoured the world clean of ninety percent of its people in six howling months.—Or so the leegnd said; Custis had not much faith in that, either.

The fact you had to live with, in any case, was that Berendtsen had put together *something* called the Second Free American Republic—meaning probably the old American East and the eastern half of old Canada—and made it stand up for ten years before he got his. And nobody else had ever been able to do as well—at least not here, where the Great Lakes and Appalachians kept Berendtsen from ever being much

17

more than a name and an occasional banner. But between the times his name frightened them, with its promise of armed men coming over the mountains someday, and ordering things to suit a stranger someday, people still thought of ten whole years with no fighting in the cities. It made them growl with anger whenever the local politicians did something they disliked. It made them restless; it left no peace in the minds of the politicians as they tried to convince themselves the cities were almost back to normal—that soon enough, now, the cities and the people of the plains would become part of a functioning civilization once more, and the scar of the plague would be healed over at last.

It was not a comfortable thing, being haunted by a man nobody knew. You could say, and say with a good part of justice, that Berendtsen was behind every mob that rolled down on Government House and dragged the men inside up to the dark lamp posts.

Thirty years since Berendtsen died—the story went. Nobody was sure of exactly who'd been behind the shooting; the politicians or the people. But it was a sure thing it had been the people who'd multilated his body. And six months later the mobs'd killed the men they said killed Berendtsen. So there you were—try and make sense out of it, in a world where the towns went without machinery and the cities went without more than the barest trickle of food. A world where it was still worth a city man's life to approach farm country alone.

You couldn't. The man's name was magic, and that was that.

Custis, up in his turret, shook his head. If he didn't find this ghost for Henley, it was a cinch he'd never get paid—contract or no contract. But at least he'd gotten his car re-shopped for this job. Sourly, Custis weighed cutting the political officer's throat right here and reporting him lost to bandit action. Or cutting his throat and not reporting back at all.

The battlewagon was a long way from Chicago at this point. The only drinking water aboard was a muddy mess scooped out of one of the summer-shrunk creeks. The food was canned army rations—some of it, under the re-labeling, might be from before the plague—and the inside of the car stank with clothes that hadn't been off their backs in three weeks. The summer sun pounded down on them all through the long day, and the complex power-train that began with a nuclear reactor and a steam turbine, and ended in the individual electric motors turning the drive wheels and sprockets, threw off more waste heat than most men could stand.

Henley was just barely getting along. For Custis and his crew, any other way of life was too remote to consider. But it had been a long run. They'd stretched themselves to make it from the marginal, inexpert captive farmlands at the Chicago periphery, and they still had the worst part of the job to do. Maybe it would be easier to simply turn bandit himself.

But that meant cutting himself off from the city, at least until the next Republic needed the hire of the battlewagon. That was something Custis wouldn't have minded—if oil and ammunition, replacement barrels for his guns, pile fuels, and rations for his crew grew on the plain as thick as the grass.

"Bear 340, Lew," he said to his driver through the command microphone, and the car jinked slightly on

19

its tracks, heading on a more direct course for the nearest of the dark foothills.

And so, Joe Custis thought, there's no help for it—you have to chase after a ghost no matter what you'd rather do.

He looked back across the grass, with its swath of crushed, matted leaves, forever stretching away behind the car. Here and there, he knew, there were flecks of oil and dried mud that had dropped from the battle-wagon's underside. Here and there lay discarded ration cans, their crude paper labels already curling away from the flecked tin or enamel plating. Back along that trail lay campsites, each with its pits for the machineguns dismounted from the car to guard its perimeter. The ashes were cold. Rain was beginning to turn them into darker blotches on the bared black earth. The gun pits were crumbling. Who came to search these sites—what patient men came out of their hiding places to investigate, to see if anything useful had been left behind, perhaps to find some clue to the car's purpose?

There were such men, even outside the independent towns and the captive farms on the cities' borders. Lost, wandering hunters—mavericks of one kind or another—men like Joe Custis, but without his resources. Half-bandit, but unorganized and forever unorganizable. Rogue males, more lost than anything else that roamed the plains, for the bandits at least had their organization, and the independent towns had safety along with their inbreeding.

But the men on the plains would die, and their children would be few, and dying. And the bandits couldn't go on forever. There was no weapon of their own manufacture that could stand up to a farmer's shotgun. And the independent farmer would die, buried in the weakling seed he spawned, afraid to reach out across the miles of empty grass toward where other independent farmers would give him short welcome, scratching the ground with deteriorating tools, trying to raise food here on the prairie where there were no smelters—not even any hardwood trees—to give him implements.

And the cities—. It was different, elsewhere. So the Berendtsen legend said of the tightly packed East where an army could march from one city to another and establish one Law. And so also said the persistent legends of some kind of good living down in the agricultural southern plains.

But in the East the cities could reach out and control the farmlands—could send their citizens out to grow food, or could trade machinery to the farmer and so, gradually, make one society.

Out here, it couldn't be done. Or it hadn't been done, either Berendtsen's way or in whatever way the middle South was doing it. The first wave of refugees out of Chicago after the plague had set the pattern, and nothing had broken it. Without readily available fuel, or replacement parts for their machinery, and without harvesting and planting crews, the surviving farmers had soon learned to shoot on sight. It was either that or be robbed and then starve, for farming was back to the point where one man and his family could grow as much food as would feed one man and his family.

Some city refugees had organized into bandit groups and managed to get along, killing and robbing—kidnapping women; no man wants to die without leaving sons.

Most city refugees—those who lived—went back into the cities. There was ten times as much room as they needed. But even with all the warehouses in a city, there was not ten times as much food.

The cities scraped along. Momentary governments subjugated bits of farmland here and there. Measures of one kind and another enforced various kinds of rationing and decreed various sources of protein; there were rat farms in Chicago, and other things.

One way or the other, Chicago scraped along. But it dreamed of legends.

Custis stared at the mountains. He wondered if he would ever be coming back this way again. And how many men before him, he wondered, had set out on the road toward Berendtsen?

Seven republics in Chicago. Bandits in the mountains, raiding across the plains, forcing the surviving farmers into a permanent state of siege.

Night was falling. In some parts of the world, the sun rode high in the sky, or the first ripples of morning lapped the fabric of the stars. But here, now, night was falling, and Joe Custis searched the edges of his world.

CHAPTER ONE:

I

Matthew Garvin was a young, heavy-boned man who had not yet filled out to his mature frame. His grip on his automatic shotgun was not too sure. But he had been picking his way through the New York City streets for two days, skirting the litter and other obstructions left by the plague, and the shotgun made him feel a great deal more comfortable—for all that he still half-expected a New York City policeman to step out from behind one of the slewed, abandoned cars, or from one of the barricaded doorways, and arrest him for violating the Sullivan Act.

His picture of the world's condition was fragmentary. Most of it was gleaned from remembered snatches of the increasingly sporadic news over the TV. And he had heard those only while lying in delirium, on a cot beside the room where his dying father kept death watch over the other members of his family. He had not truly come back to alertness until well after his father was dead and the TV was inoperative, though it was still switched on.

All he could remember his father telling him, in all those days. was "If you live, don't forget to go armed." He was certain, now, that his father, probably delirious himself, had repeated it over and over, clutching his arm urgently and slurring the words, the way a man will when his rationality tries to force a message out through an almost complete loss of control.

And when he had finally wakened, and known he was going to live, Matthew Garvin had found the Browning lying on the floor beside his cot, together with a box of shells still redolent of woodsmoke and old cleaning solvent. His father's old hunting knapsack had been there, too, stocked with canned food, waterproof matches, a flashlight, a compass, and a hunting knife, almost as if Matthew and he had been going to leave for the North Woods together. They had been doing that every deer season for the past four years. But this time it was his father's gear that Matthew would be carrying; and it was the big Browning, instead of the rifle.

He had not questioned his father's judgment. He had strapped the knapsack on, and taken the shotgun, and then he had left the apartment—he could not have stayed, though he did his best to leave his family in some semblance of decent repose.

At first, he had not quite known what he was going to do. Looking out the window, he could see nothing moving on the streets. A pall of gray mist hung over Manhattan—part fog, part smoke, from where something was burning and had not been put out. He had gone and taken the heavy binoculars from his father's closet and studied the two rivers. They were almost clear of floating debris of various kinds, and so he assumed the great wave of dying was over—those who still lived, would live. He had probably been one of the last to be sick.

The streets and the waterfronts were a jumble of

abandoned and wrecked equipment—cars, trucks, boats, barges—much as he had last seen them, on the night when he had realized he, too, was at last growing feverish and dry-mouthed. That had been after the government had abandoned the continual effort to keep the streets clear and people in their homes.

Here and there, some of the main avenues had been opened, with cars and buses towed out of the way, lying as they had been dropped on the sidewalks. He could see one crane—a Metropolitan Transit Authority company emergency truck—where it had stopped, with a bright blue MG sports car still dangling from the tow hook. So there had not been time after he fell ill for anything to litter up the opened streets again.

He tried the radio—he had read enough novels of universal disaster to know nothing would come of it, and for a while he had been undecided, but his human nature had won out—and there had been nothing. He listened for the hum he associated with the phrase "carrier wave," and did not hear that, either. He looked down at the baseboard, and saw that someone—probably his father—had ripped the line cord out of the wall so savagely that the bared ends of the wire dangled on the floor while the gutted plug remained in the socket.

But he had not repaired it. The dead TV was good enough—in the end, he remembered, the final government announcement had been quite explicit—the President's twanging, measured voice had labored from phrase to phrase, explaining calmly that some would surely survive—that no disease, however impossible to check, could prove fatal to all human beings everywhere—but that the survivors should not expect human civilization to have endured with them. "To those of you who will live to re-make this world," the President had said, "my only promise is this: That with courage, with ingenuity, with determination—above all, with adherence to the moral principles that distinguish Man from the animals—the future is one of hope. The way will be hard. The effort will be great. But the future waits to be realized, and with God's help it shall be realized—it *must* be realized!"

But that had not been much to go on. He had put the binoculars back—if someone had asked him, he would have replied that certainly he planned to come back to the apartment; he would not have stopped to think about it until he had actually heard his positive words—and he had left, climbing down flight after flight of stairs.

He was on his way to Larry Ruark's apartment, he had realized at some point on his journey. Larry lived about fifty blocks uptown—by no means a difficult walk—and was a close friend from the time they had gone through the first two years of college together, before Larry had gone on to medical school. He had no way of knowing whether Larry had survived or not. But it seemed to him the chances were reasonably good. In part, they seem so to him because he was associating immunity with the word "doctor," and because he needed to find a friend alive; an undergraduate medical student to whom he gave an inappropriate title because that made his friend likelier to have lived. But in part, he knew, his reasoning was sound. Larry had been young, and in excellent health; that was bound to have improved his chances.

Matthew Garvin had thought that surely he might find out more about the world, on his way to Larry's.

He had expected to meet other survivors, and talk to them.

He had expected that, between them, he and the other young, generally sound people could piece together an accurate idea of what the world's condition was. There was nothing to fear from contact with each other, after all—either they had the plague, and would die, or had successfully resisted it, and would not. The time of the Carrier Panic—before it had been proven the disease agent, whatever it was, did not need to be transmitted from human hand to hand— that ugly time was over.

But he had begun to wonder whether the other survivors were aware of that. And he had begun to wonder whether some of them might not have become insane. For though he sometimes heard quick footsteps whose direction was disguised by echoes, he had been able to meet no one face-to-face, and when he had stood and shouted, no one answered. He knew he had come late to the inevitable sickness. He wondered what it was the more experienced survivors might have found out that would make them act like this.

Once he turned a corner and found someone who had survived the plague. It was a young man, canted awkwardly against a subway railing, dead, with fresh blood congealing around the stab wounds in his chest, and a torn grocery bag, empty, trampled at his feet.

The streets were badly blocked in places, and he had been moving more and more slowly, out of the same caution that made him hole up and lock himself in a truck cab overnight. So it was the next day when he saw the placards.

He was only a few blocks from Larry's then. The placards were Civil Defense Emergencly Posters, turned around to expose their unprinted backs. Hand-lettered on them now were the words "Live Medic," and an arrow pointing uptown.

After that, Matthew Garvin hurried. He was sure Larry Ruark had survived, now. And the placards were the first trace of some kind of organization. He had begun to think of the world as a place much like a locked museum at night . . . except for a sporadic, distant hint of sounds that were too much like isolated gunshots. He had heard the sounds of police machine-guns, during the Carrier Panic, and the deep thud of demolition as the Isolation Squads tried to cordon off the stricken areas—that had been quite early in the game—but this was different. This was like the sound of foot-snapped twigs in a forest infested by Indians.

The trail of placards led to Larry Ruark's apartment house. The barricade in the doorway had been pulled aside, and the front door stood open.

It was the first open barricade he had seen since he had set out on his journey, though he had caught occasional glimpses of motion behind the windows of barricaded houses. He wondered if those inside had yet made their first ventures outside. It had begun to occur to him that perhaps they had—perhaps they had pulled down the barricades and then, after a day or so, put them back up. They were a defensive measure, of course—in the last days of the plague the sick, the drunk, and the stupid had roamed the streets wherever the diminishing police could not turn them back. Matthew Garvin himself had gone through a bout of hysteria in which he had laughed, over and over again, "Now there won't be any war!" and the urge to go out—to get drunk, to smash something, to break loose and kick out at all the things society had erected in the expectation of war—the Shelter signs, the newspaper kiosks, the television stores, the motion picture theaters—all the things that battened on desperation—that need to show that suddenly he, too, understood how miserably frightened they had all been under the shell of calm—all that had boiled and shaken inside him, and if he had been just a little bit different he, too, would have been roaring down the flame-lit streets, and there would have been a need of barricades against him.

He moved tentatively up the steps to the foyer of Larry Ruark's apartment house. The foyer and the stairs up were clean—swept, mopped, dusted. The brass handle on the front door had been polished. In the foyer stood another placard: "Live Medic Upstairs."

There was nothing else to see, and there were no sounds.

He padded up the stairs, using only the balls of his feet to touch the treads. Yesterday he would not have done that. He did not entirely understand why he did it now. But it was appropriate to his environment, and he was young enough to be quite sensitive about conforming to the shape of the world around him.

Larry's apartment was at the head of the stairs. The sign on the door said: "Medic—Knock and Come In."

It *was* Larry! Matthew rapped his knuckles quickly on the paneling and pushed the door in the same motion. "Lar—"

The thin, hard arm went around his throat from behind. He realized that in another moment he was going to be pulled backward, off balance and help-less. He jumped upward, and that broke the hold

29

enough for him to turn around, still inside the circle of the arm. He and Larry Ruark stared into each other's eyes.

"Oh, my God!" Larry whispered. He lowered the hand with the butcher knife in it.

Matthew Garvin stood panting, still in his friend's embrace. Then Larry let his other arm sag, and Matthew stepped back quickly.

"Matt . . . Jesus, Dear God, Matt!" Larry pushed back against the door and sagged on it, his eyes round. "I saw somebody coming, and I figured—and it turned out to be you!"

He was emaciated; his hair, always speckled with early gray, was wild and grizzled. His eyesockets were the color of dirty blue velvet. His clothes were stained and shapeless on his bones. Matt's nostrils were still singed with the old, mildewed smell of them.

"Larry, what the hell is this?"

Larry rubbed his face, the butcher knife dangling askew between his fingers.

"Listen, Matt, I'm sorry. I didn't know it was you."

"Didn't know it was me."

"Oh, God damn it, I can't talk. Sit down someplace, will you, Matt? I've—I need a minute."

"All right," Matt said, but did not sit down. The room was furnished with an old leather couch, two shabby armchairs, and a coffee table on which sooty old magazines were laid out in a meticulous pattern. Very little light filtered through the cracks between the window drapes.

"Listen, Matt, is there any food in that knapsack?"

"Some. You hungry?"

"Yes. No—Anyway, that can wait. I just almost *killed* you—is this a time to talk about food? We've got to work this out—you've got to—look, do you know I can see the George Washington Bridge from my bedroom window?"

Matt cocked his head and frowned.

"I mean. I watched the people going out across the bridge. It went on for days, after the plague died down. They went climbing over the old Isolation Squad barricades. and all the cars and cadavers. I timed it. Something like twenty or thirty an hour. And they weren't going in groups. Twenty or thirty people an hour in Manhattan each got the idea of getting out into the country.

"They were hungry, Matt. And I saw a lot of them coming back—some of them were crawling. I'm sure they had gunshot wounds. Something over there is turning them back. You know what it's got to be? It's got to be the survivors on the Jersey side. They don't have any spare food, either. And that means the surviving farmers are shooting them when they try to go for food."

"Larry—"

"Listen, food shipments into Manhattan stopped seven weeks ago!"

"Warehouses," Matt said, like a man trying to deliver an urgent message in the depths of a nightmare, watching the knife swing back and forth between Larry's fingers.

"There are people in them. Holed up during the plague. I was just coming out of it, then—I couldn't get down the stairs yet, but there was still a little bit of radio, on the Police band—and the warehouses were full of them. Dead, dying, and live ones. They won't let anybody in. You've got to remember Manhattan is full of crowd-control weapons and am-

31

munition. You could pick 'em up anywhere—all you had to do was pry the dead fingers away. They're all gone now, of course—they've all been picked up. Anybody who has a food supply is armed. He has to be. If he isn't, some armed man has killed him for it by now."

"There's got to be food. There were two million people on this island! There were food stores on every block. They had to have some source of ready supply! You can't tell me there still isn't enough here to keep people eating for a while, at least. How many of us are there left?"

Larry shook his head. "Two hundred thousand, maybe. If the national average held good under urban conditions. I don't think it did. I think maybe there's really a hundred fifty thousand." Larry shook his head exhaustedly and walked away from the door with a clumsy, stiff-jointed gait. He dropped into one of the armchairs, and let the knife fall on the footworn carpet beside him.

"Look, you're all right." He motioned toward Matt's gun. "You fall into this place naturally. But what about me? Look—you think about it. Sure, there's got to be food around. But who knows where? The people who'd know are keeping it for themselves. All the obvious places are being emptied. And even when you have it, you have to get it home. And if you get it home, how long is it before you have to go out again? You can't even have water, unless you carry it in!"

"All right, so you carry it." Matt tapped his canteen. He had filled it from the water cooler in an abandoned office, this morning, and purified it with a halazone tablet from the kit in his pack. "And you have to go look for food because there aren't any more delivery boys. So what? There's plenty of time, every day. And there's time to think, too. You know what this is—what you're doing? It's panic."

"All right, it's panic! It's panic when an animal chews its leg off in a trap, too—you trying to tell me it didn't need to?"

"Larry, we're not animals!"

Larry Ruark laughed.

Matt watched him. Very gradually, he was calming, but there was still a sound like a riptide in his ears. He knew he would remember this conversation, later, better than he was hearing it now. He knew he would act, now, in ways that later thinking would improve on. But for the moment he could not stop his eyes from trying to watch Larry and the knife at the same time. And he could not keep from trying to settle it now—right now—before it became intolerable.

"You can't tell me anybody who can move is anywhere near starving to death in Manhattan. It'll be years before the last food is gone."

"What do I care, if I can't get it? I've got to think my way!" Larry's eyes jerked down toward where the knife lay, near his hand as it dangled over the arm of the chair. "You—you can go hunt for it. Listen, you know what they'd do to me, if I went outside? If they found out I was a med student? You know why I put those signs out all around this neighborhood? It's not for the people with the gunshot wounds and the inflamed appendixes and the abscessed teeth—sure, some of 'em may be desperate enough to come here for help. But you know how I get most of my protein? I get it from people who come up here looking to kill me. You know why? Because we lied to 'em. The whole medical profession lied to 'em. It told them it would lick the plague. It told them that a world full of medical scientists couldn't miss coming up with the solution.

"And what happened? You remember the last days of the plague—the Isolation Squads, the barricades, the machineguns and flamethrowers around the hospitals? Sure, we *told* 'em we were only protecting the research facilities from the mobs, when we fortified the hospitals. But they know better. They know their mothers and their wives and kids died because we wouldn't let 'em in. What do they care about things like a plague that hits the whole world, from end to end, inside three days? A plague everybody gets. A plague that forces a delirious fever on your body, so you can't see into the barrel of your microscope or hold two beakers steady? All they know is the biggest piles of corpses were lying around the aid stations and the research centers. And I was there, all right. I didn't have the training to do any good on the research side, so they gave me a Thompson submachinegun, and that's how I did my part, until I wore it out. And by then nobody minded if I went home. There wasn't much of anybody to mind.

"I know what they want, when they come up here. They want the dumb Medic who's idiot enough to advertise. Well, they don't get him. No, sir. And that's how I get my protein. 'Cause it's all protein, you know—I mean, you wouldn't eat a mouse or an earthworm, would you, Matt? But it's all protein. Your body wouldn't care where it came from. It would take it, and use it to keep alive, and be grateful. All your body wants to do is live another day.

"But I'm not doing too well, lately. They're getting

wise to me, in the neighborhood, and all I'm getting now is transients. I'll have to think of something new, pretty soon.

"You and me." Larry's eyes darted toward Matt. "You and me—we'd make out together. You can go out and forage, and I'll stay here and make sure nobody takes it away. How about that?"

Matt Garvin took a step toward the door.

Larry's hand moved aimlessly toward the knife. He pretended not to see what his hand was doing.

"Please, Larry," Matt said. "I just want to go."

"Listen, you can't go now. We've got plans to make. You're the only guy I can trust!"

"Larry, I just want to get out that door; me, and my shotgun, too."

"I'll throw the knife at your back on the stairs, Matt. I will."

"I'll walk down backwards."

"That won't be easy. If you slip, you're a loser."

"I guess so."

Matt Garvin opened the door, and backed out. He backed all the way down the stairs, without tripping, and watched the silent, motionless door of Larry Ruark's apartment. Down on the street, he ran—silently, ripping down placards as he went.

II

Fourteenth Street lay quiet under the dawn. From the East River across to the Hudson, it ran its blue-gray length between the soundless buildings. Except for a flock of lean, restless pigeons that circled momentarily above Union Square and then fluttered back to earth, it was sucked empty of life and motion like a watercourse running between dry banks. The wind of Autumn swept down the width of the paralyzed street, carrying trash.

East of First Avenue, lines of parked cars bleached at the flank of Stuyvesant Town. Here, finally, something moved. The creeping edge of sunlight touched Matt Garvin's eyes as he lay asleep in the back of a taxi.

Garvin was instantly awake, but, at first, only a momentary twitch of his eyelids betrayed him to the day. Then his hand closed on the stock of his shotgun, and he raised his body slowly. His eyes probed at the streets and buildings around him. He smiled in thin satisfaction. For the moment, he was all that lived on Fourteenth Street.

He slid his legs off the folded backs of the lowered jump seats, and sat up. The cab was safe enough, with the windows up and the doors locked—no one could have forced them silently—but there could have been men out there, waiting for the time when he had to come out.

He bent over, unstrapped his knapsack, and took out his canteen and a tin of roast beef. He opened the roast beef and began to eat, raising his head from time to time to be sure that no one was slipping toward him along the line of parked cars. He ate without waste motion, taking an occasional swallow of the flat-tasting but safe soda water in his canteen. He had run out of halazone long ago. When the roast beef was finished he repacked his knapsack, strapped it on his upper back, and, after one more look at his surroundings, clicked up the latch on the taxi door and silently moved out onto the cobblestoned island that was one of a series separating Fourteenth Street from the peripheral drive around Stuyvesant Town.

Cars were parked on both sides of the narrow island, their bumpers almost touching. The big red buildings towered upward on Garvin's left as he moved eastward along the housing project's edge, but the cars on that side protected him from any kind of accurate fire from the lower floors. In order to aim at him from the upper stories, a man would have had to lean so far out of his window as to expose himself to fire from the opposite side of the street. Garvin himself was protected from the south side of Fourteenth Street by the line of cars on his right Moreover, one man and his knapsack were not generally a worthwhile target, any longer.

Still, worthwhile or not, he picked his route carefully, and held to a low, weaving crouch. Holding the shotgun at high port, he moved rapidly eastward between the twin lines of cars, his eyes never still, his feet in their tennis shoes less noisy than the wind, his head constantly turning as he listened for what his eyes might miss.

And it was his ears that warned him at the corner of Avenue A. He heard the quiet sound of a store's latched door, which was bound to snap its lock no matter how carefully eased into place, and then there was the friction of leather shoes on a sidewalk.

He stopped, sheltered by an automobile's curved flanks, and the shotgun's muzzle swung almost automatically toward the source of the sound. He straightened his back cautiously and looked across the street through the car's rear windows, his breath sucking in through his teeth as he saw her.

The girl was slim; sprinting across the sidewalk in nervously choppy strides as she left the drugstore. Her face was white, and her eyes were terrifiedly wide. Obviously panicked at being out in the street during daylight, she was running blindly, straight for where Garvin was crouched, trying to reach the comparative safety of the island before she was seen.

He took two rapid steps backward before he realized there was no place for him to hide, and the girl was across the street before he could think of anything else to do. Then she was on the island, ducking into the shelter of the double row of cars, and it was too late to think.

She hadn't seen him yet. She was too intent on safety to see danger until he straightened out of his instinctive crouch, letting the shotgun's muzzle drop. Then her mouth opened, her eyes becoming desperate, and he saw the unexpected gun in her other hand.

"Hey!"

He shouted in surprise as he charged forward, throwing his arm out. He felt the shock of his forearm deflecting her wrist upward, and then the gun jumped in her hand, the echoes pattering like a hard-shoe dance down the empty street. His charge threw their bodies together, and his arm hooked like a whip and pinned her gun-arm out of the way. His thighs snapped together in time to take the kick of her driving knee, but he could only dig his chin into her shoulder and try to shelter his face against the side of her head as her other hand clawed at his ear and neck. Then his momentum overcame her balance, and they were safely down on the island's cobblestones.

"Stay down!" he grunted urgently as he twisted around and slapped the gun out of her hand, catching it before it could be damaged against the stones. She sobbed an incoherent reply, and her nails drew fresh blood from his face. He fell back, but threw his shoulder into her stomach in time to keep her from forcing her way back to her feet.

"Haven't you got any sense?" he cursed out hoarsely as she tried to break away. He flung an arm out and kept her scrambling fingers from his eyes. "Every gun in the neighborhood's waiting for us to stand up and get shot."

"Oh!" She stopped struggling immediately, and this unexpected willingness to believe him was more surprising than his first glimpse of her. As her arms dropped, he rolled away, wiping the blood off his stinging face.

"For *Christ's* sake!" he panted, "What did you think I was going to do?"

Her face turned color. "I—"

"Don't be stupid!" he cut her off harshly. "Do you

39

have any idea how many women were left alive by that damn virus, or whatever it was?" She winced away from the sound of his voice, surprising him again. How did she manage to stay alive, this naive and sensitive? "Raping a girl sort of ruins your chances for striking up a permanent acquaintance with her," he went on in a gentler voice, and was oddly pleased to see a smile lightly touch her face.

"Here." He tossed her gun into her lap. "Reload."

"What?" She was staring down at it.

"Reload, damn it," he repeated with rough persistence. "You're one round short." She picked the weapon up gingerly, but snapped the cylinder out as if she knew what she was doing, and he felt free to forget her for the moment.

He pulled his legs up under him and got into a squat crouch, turning his upper body from side to side as he tried to spot the sniper he was almost sure the sound of her shot had attracted. One man was a doubtful target, but the two of them were worth anyone's attention, and he did not trust that anyone's eyesight to save the girl.

The windows of Fourteenth Street looked blankly back at him. For some reason, he shuddered slightly.

"Do you see anyone?" the girl asked softly, surprising him again, for he had forgotten her as an individual even while adding her as a factor to the problem of safety.

He shook his head. "No. That's what worries me. Somebody should have been curious enough to look out. Probably, somebody was—and now he's picked up a rifle."

Apprehension overlaid her face. "What're we going to do? I've got to get home." She fumbled in her jumper pockets until she found a tube of sulfa ointment. "My father's hurt."

He nodded briefly. At least that explained why she'd been outside. Then he grimaced. "Gunshot wound?"

"Yes."

"Thought so. That stuff's no good. Not anymore."

"There were so many kinds of things in the drugstore," she said uncertainly. "This was the only one I was sure of. Is it too old?"

He shrugged. "Way past its expiration date, that's for sure. And I've got a hunch we're up against whole new kinds of bacteria that won't even blink at the stuff. Every damn antibiotic in the world was turned loose, I guess, and what lived through that is what we've got to deal with. These days, my vote's for soap and carbolic acid.

"Bad?" he asked suddenly.

"What?"

"Is he hurt bad?"

Her lip trembled. "He was shot through the chest three days ago."

He grunted, then looked back at the blank windows again. "Look—will you stay here until I get back? I want to see you home. You need it," he added bluntly.

"Where are you going?"

"Drugstore."

Her lips parted in bewilderment. The innocence of her did not belong on this deadly street. Her simple acceptance of everything he told her—even her failure to shoot him when he gave her back the gun—reacted in him to create a baseless but deep and sudden anger.

"To make a phone call," he added with brutal sarcasm. Then he managed to smooth his voice. "If something happens, don't you do anything but turn around and go home, understand?"

The anger fading, but still strong, he jumped to his feet and began to run without waiting for an answer.

Stupid kid, he thought as he weaved across the street. She had absolutely no business running around loose. He crossed the white center-line, and no one had fired yet.

If the snipers had any brains, they'd wait until he came out. They'd be able to judge whether his load was worth bothering with.

How had she managed to live this long? His sole slammed into the curb, and he drove himself across the sidewalk.

Just my luck to get shot by somebody stupid.

He tore the door open and flung himself into the drugstore, catching one of the fountain stools for balance as he stopped. He leaned on it for a moment while he waited for his breath to slow.

They were probably figuring the smart percentage. One man with his pack wasn't temptation enough. He and the girl definitely were, once they were close together again, where a simple dash under cover of night would reach their bodies. But the girl by herself was safe from all but the myopic, and he, separated from her, was also moderately safe. A handful of packages from the drugstore might tip the scales against him—until you stopped to consider that the best thing to do was to wait until he had rejoined the girl, in which case, if the potential sniper already had a woman . . . .

Sick with calculations, he slammed his palms against

42

the edge of the Formica counter-top and pushed himself away from the fountain.

Among the jumbled shelves, he found a bottle of germicide, some cotton swabs, and bandages. He packed them carefully into his knapsack, cursing himself for not asking whether the bullet was still in the wound. He shrugged as he realized that surgical forceps were an unlikely instrument to encounter here, drugstore or no. Then he turned toward the outline of the doorway, light in the store's darkness, and stopped.

The store was safe, he found himself thinking. The girl had proved that for him by coming out alive. He had reached it, and now that he was in, it was an easily defended place.

Outside lay Fourteenth Street—a gray band of sidewalk, swept partially clean by the wind, and the dusty blue-black of the street's asphalt. Beyond it hunched the sheer, blank-windowed brick buildings, and beyond these, the ice-blue sky. There were no waiting rifles—not where he would be likely to see them.

He looked about him. There must be something else he could find that might be useful. If he looked around, he was pretty sure to stumble across something. If he looked around long enough. If he waited.

He laughed once, shortly, at himself, and stepped out into the street, breaking into a run as frantic as the girl's had been, his chest pumping, his stride off-balance from the shifting weight of the pack, the sweat breaking out on his face and evaporating icily.

He realized that he was afraid, and then he was across the street and safely on the island, sprawled out on his panting stomach, between the cars. He looked up at the girl and suddenly understood that his fear had been of losing the future.

He waited a few moments for the pumping of his lungs to slow. The girl was looking at him with some incomprehensible expression shining on her face.

Finally he said, "Now, let's get you home. You start, and I'll cover you from behind."

The girl nodded wordlessly, putting aside whatever it was that she had been going to say, and turned up the island in the direction from which he had come. He followed her, and they worked their way back toward First Avenue, neither of them speaking except for his occasional growled monosyllable whenever her crouch grew dangerously shallow.

Moving quietly, they reached a point opposite the entrance to the Stuyvesant building on the corner of First Avenue. The girl stopped, and Garvin closed the ten-yard interval between them, crouching beside her.

He felt his left hand's fingers twitch as the indecisive restlessness of his muscles searched for an outlet. The girl could simply leave him at this point, and it might be years before he saw another woman, particularly one who was free. At least, he assumed she was free. What kind of man would let his woman go out alone like this? If she had one, he didn't deserve to keep her.

Garvin laughed at himself again, disregarding her surprise at the short, sharp bark.

"It was still dark when I went down to the drugstore," she said, her voice betraying her helplessness. "But it took me so long to find anything. How are we going to get back across to the building?"

Once more, Garvin's trained habits of thought protested their momentary shock at her foolhardiness. She had already betrayed the fact that her home was virtually undefended. Now she seemed to have unquestionably assumed that he was going home with her.

He shook his head, even while he jeered at himself because he was appalled at the girl for doing what he had feared she would not.

The girl was looking at him questioningly, and again there was something else in her glance, as well. A flicker of annoyance creased his cheeks at his failure to understand it completely.

He repeated the head-shake. "Going to have to run for it. It'll be easier with two of us, though," he said. "You'll go first. I'll cover you, and then you'll keep an eye out when I try it. If you see anything, shoot at it." He hefted his shotgun, grimacing. It was a good defensive weapon, suited to fighting in stores or houses, but its effective range was pitifully short. He wished now that he had a rifle instead.

He shrugged and made sure the shotgun was off safety. He jerked his head toward the building. "Let's go."

"All right," she said huskily. She turned and slipped between two cars, put her head down, and ran blindly across the drive and sidewalk, down the short flight of steps to the terrace, and into the building's doorway, where she stopped and waited for Garvin.

He took a quick look around, saw nothing, and followed her, running as fast as he could, his legs scissoring in long, zig-zagging strides, his back muscles tense with his awareness of how exposed he was.

He reached the steps, his momentum carrying him sideward, and had to catch himself against the rail, while a sudden spray of bullets from across the street crashed into the concrete steps, raising an echo of hammer-blows to the flat, wooden sounds of gunfire.

Lead streaks smeared across the concrete, and puffs of dust drifted slowly away.

Then he was under the rail and in the shelter of the sunken terrace, his hands and face bleeding from the laceration of the hedge, while his breath panted past the dirt in his open mouth and his heart pumped rapidly and loudly.

The girl began firing back.

He twisted violently, breaking free of the thousand teeth the hedge had sunk into his clothes, and stared at the girl in the doorway, one leg folded under her, the other bent and thrust out, her left hand gripping her knee and the muzzle of her revolver supported at her left elbow. As if she were firing at a paper target set up on the opposite rooftop. She squeezed off two shots and waited.

"Get out of that doorway!" he shouted. "Inside the building!"

The girl shook her head slightly, her eyes on the rooftop. Her lower lip was caught between the tips of her teeth, and her face was expressionless. There was no answering fire from the rooftop.

"I can't see him anymore," she said. "He must have jumped behind a chimney."

Sweating Garvin squirmed his legs into position. "Try and keep him pinned down," he shouted across the terrace, and, jumping to his feet, sprinted for the doorway in a straight line, trying to cover the distance as rapidly as possible. He threw one glance across the street, saw no movement on the roof, and pulled the girl to her feet with a scoop of his arm. He flung the lobby door open, and they stumbled through together, into shelter.

* * *

46

He slumped against the lobby wall, his ribs clammy with the perspiration streaming down the sides of his chest. He looked at the girl, his eyes shadowed by the darkness of the lobby, while his breathing slowed to normal.

Once again, she was neglecting to reload the gun. And yet she had squatted in that doorway and done exactly the right thing to keep them from being killed. Done it in her own characteristic way, of course, exposing herself as a sitting target not only to the attacker but to anyone else as well. Somewhere, she had learned the theory of covering fire, and had the courage to apply it in spite of her woeful ignorance of actual practice.

Thus far, he had simply thought of her as being completely out of place on the street. Now he found himself thinking that, with a little training, she might not be so helpless.

She looked up at him suddenly, catching his glance, and he had to say something rather than continue to stand silent.

"Thanks. You take your chances, but, thanks."

"I couldn't just let him . . ." She trailed the sentence away, and did not start another.

"Pretty dumb guy, whoever he was," Garvin said.

"Yes." She stared off at nothing, obviously merely filling time, and the thought suddenly struck Garvin that she was waiting for something.

"I can't understand him," she said abruptly.

"Neither can I," Garvin said lamely. Perhaps she had not meant to let him in the apartment. It was quite possible—and logical—that she would ask him to help her get into the building, but would leave him then. Was she waiting for him to give her the supplies and leave? Or didn't she know what to do now, with the sniper waiting outside? He cursed himself for not taking the initiative, one way or the other, but plunged on. "Exposing himself on a roof like that. Somebody's sure to pick him off."

"I didn't mean . . . But you're right. He *is* being foolish."

No, of course she hadn't meant what he meant. Garvin cursed himself again. To the girl, it was incomprehensible that anyone would want to kill someone else. He, to whom it was merely stupid to expose oneself to possible fire, had completely misunderstood her. He was a predator, weighing every move against the chance of becoming prey. She was a fledgling who had fallen out of her nest into his hungry world.

He caught himself sharply, derision in his mind. But, maudlin or not, he nevertheless did not want to leave her now, with no one to protect her.

She looked at him again, still waiting. He did not say anything, but kept his eyes away from her face, waiting in turn.

"You can't go back out there now," she said finally, hesitating.

"No—no, I can't." He tried to keep his voice noncommittal.

"Well, I. . . . You *can't* go out. You'll have to stay here."

"Yes."

And there it was. His fingers twisted back into his damp palm and curled in a nervous fist. "Let's get going," he said harshly. "We have to see about your father."

Her expression changed, as though some cryptic apprehension had drained away in her—as though she, in her turn, had been afraid that he would not do what she hoped he would. Her voice, too, was steadier, and her lips rose into a gentle smile.

"I'll have to introduce you. What's your name?"

He flushed, startling himself. A gentle, remembered voice chided him from the past. *Matthew, you were impolite.*

"Matt—*Matt* Garvin," he blurted.

She smiled again. "I'm Margaret Cottrell. Hello."

He took her extended hand and clasped it awkwardly, releasing it with abrupt clumsiness.

He wondered if he'd been right—if she had not wanted him to leave, and had not known what she could do to stop him if he tried. The thought was a disquieting one, because he could not resolve it, or reach a decision. He followed her warily as she turned toward the stairway behind the lifeless elevators. Just before she became no more than a darker shadow in the stairwell's gloom, he caught the smile on her lips once more.

The apartment was on the third floor. When they came out of the stairway, she went to the nearest door, knocked, and unlocked it. She turned to Garvin, who had stopped a yard away.

"Please come in," she said.

He started forward uneasily. He trusted the girl to some extent—more than he trusted anyone else, certainly—but for two and a half years, he had never opened any closed door before completely satisfying himself that nothing dangerous could be waiting behind it.

Yet, he could not let the girl know that he distrusted the apartment. To her, it would probably seem foolish, and he did not want her to think him a fool.

He stepped into the doorway, trying to hold his shotgun inconspicuously.

"Margaret?" The voice that came from inside the apartment was thin and strained. Worry flickered over the girl's face.

"I'll be right there, father. I've got someone with me." She touched Garvin's arm. "Please."

The second invitation broke his uncertainty, and he stepped inside.

"He's in the back bedroom," she whispered, and he nodded.

To his surprise, he noticed that the place was heated. A kerosene range had replaced the gas stove in the kitchen, beside the front door, and there was a space heater in the living room. Both had their stovepipes carefully led into the apartment's ventilation ducts, and the hall grille had been masked off to prevent a backdraft. Garvin pursed his lips. It was a better-organized place than he'd expected.

They reached the bedroom doorway, and Matt saw a thin man propped partially up in the bed, the intensity of the eyes heightened by the same fever that paled his lips. His chest was bandaged, and a wastebasket full of reddened facial tissues sat beside the bed. Garvin felt his mouth twitch into a grimace. The man was hemorrhaging.

"Father," Margaret said, "This is Matt Garvin. Matt—my father, John Cottrell."

"I'm glad to meet you, sir," Garvin said.

"I rather suspect that I'm glad to see you, too." Cottrell said, smiling ruefully. The pale eyes, sunken deep in their dark sockets, turned to Margaret. "Were you the cause of all that firing outside?"

"There's a man up on the roof across the street," she said. "He tried to kill Matt as he was bringing me home."

"She pulled me out of a real mess," Garvin put in.

"But Matt went back into the drugstore, after he met me and I told him you were hurt," Margaret said.

Cottrell's gaze shifted back and forth between them, his smile growing. "After he met you, eh?" He coughed for a moment, and wiped his mouth. "I'd like to hear about that, while Matt's looking at this." He gestured toward his bandaged chest, wincing at the pull on his muscles. "Meanwhile, Margaret, I think I'm getting hungry. Could you make some breakfast?"

The girl nodded and went out to the kitchen. Garvin slipped the pack off his back and took out the supplies from the drugstore. As he walked toward the bed, he caught Cottrell's look. The man was too sick for hunger, and Matt had eaten, but neither of them wanted the girl in the room while they were appraising each other.

"A typical day in our fair city," Cottrell said when Matt filled him in on what had happened this morning.

Matt grunted. He had washed the caked blood off Cottrell's chest, and swabbed out the wound, which was showing signs of a mild infection unimportant in itself.

The bullet was deep in Cottrell's chest—too deep to be probed for. And there was a constant thin film of blood in the old man's mouth. Garvin re-bandaged him and threw the dirty swabs and bandages away. Then he put the bottle of germicide down on the table beside the bed, together with the rest of the supplies. He strapped his knapsack shut, testing its balance in his hand. He picked up his shotgun and took the shells out of it.

"Being busy won't accomplish very much, Matt," Cottrell said quietly.

Garvin looked up from the gun, his breath gusting out in a tired sigh. The blood in Cottrell's throat and bronchial tubes made him cough. When he coughed, the wound that bled into his respiratory system tore itself open a little farther. And more blood leaked in and made him cough harder.

"I don't know very much medicine," Garvin said. "I've read a first aid manual. But I don't think you've got much time."

Cottrell nodded. He coughed again, and smiled ruefully. "I'm afraid you're right." He threw the newly bloodied facial tissue into the wastebasket. "Now, then, what are your plans?"

The two men looked at each other. There was no point to hedging. Cottrell was going to die, and Margaret would be left defenseless when he did. Garvin was in the apartment—a place he never could have reached without Margaret—and Margaret could not now survive without him. On the level of pure logic, the problem and its answer were simple.

"I don't know, exactly," Garvin answered slowly. "Before I met Margaret, I was going to find myself someplace to hole up with a couple of years' worth of supplies, if I could gather 'em. There's more in this town than most people know."

"Or are expert enough to get away from other people?"

Garvin looked at Cottrell with noncommittal sadness. "Maybe. I've come to my own way of looking at it. Anyhow, I figure if I can hold out long enough, when they start getting desperate and break into apartments—if I can make it through that, then somebody's bound to get things organized sooner or later, and I can join 'em. I figure we're in for a time of weeding-out. The ones who live through it will have brains enough to realize turning wolf doesn't cure hunger.

"Anyway—now that I'm here, I guess I'll do what I was intending to. Carry in all the stuff I can, and just hope. It isn't much," he finished, "but it's the best I can think of." He did not mention the obstacle he was most worried about, but it was one over which he had no control. Only Margaret could say what her reaction would be.

Cottrell nodded thoughtfully. "No, it isn't much." He looked up. "I think you're probably right in theory, but I don't think you'll be able to follow it."

Garvin frowned. "I don't see why not, frankly. It's pretty much what you've been doing."

"Yes, it is. But you're not I." Cottrell stopped to wipe his lips again, and then went on.

"Matt, I'm part of a dead civilization. I believe the last prediction was that ten percent of the population might survive. Here, in Manhattan, under our conditions, I'd estimate that only half that number are alive today. Under no circumstances is that enough people to maintain the interdependence on which the old system was based. Despite the fact that we are surrounded by the generally undamaged products of

53

twentieth century technology, we have neither power, running water, nor heat. We are crippled."

Garvin nodded. There was nothing new in this. But he let the old man talk. He had to have been a tough man in his day, and that had to be respected.

"We have no distribution or communication," Cottrell went on. "I found this place for Margaret and myself as soon as I could, equipped it, and armed myself. For I knew that if I had no idea how to produce food and clothing for myself, then neither did the rest of my fellow survivors. And the people who did know—the farmers, out on the countryside, must have learned to look out only for themselves, or die.

"And so I took to my cave-fortress. If you don't know how to produce the necessities of life, and can't buy them, then you have to take them. When they become scarce, they must be taken ruthlessly. If you have no loaf, and your neighbor has two—take them both. For tomorrow you will hunger again.

"I am a hoarder, yes," he said. "I carried in as much food as I could, continually foraged for more, and was ready to defend this place to the death. I moved the kerosene stoves in, and pushed the old gas range and the refrigerator down the elevator shaft, so no one could tell which apartment they'd come from. I did it because I realized that I—that all of us—had suddenly returned to the days of the cavemen. We were doomed to crouch in our little caves, afraid of the saber-toothed tigers prowling outside. And when our food ran low, we picked up our weapons and prowled outside, having become temporary tigers in our own turn."

"Yes, sir," Matt said politely. He couldn't see why

old bones, raked over now, had any effect on him and his plans.

Cottrell smiled and nodded. "I know, I know, Matt. . . . But the point is, as I've said, that you are not I. It was my civilization that ended. Not yours."

"Sir?"

"You were young enough, when the plagues came, so that you were able to adapt perfectly to the world. You're not what I am—an average American turned caveman. You're an average caveman, and you haven't turned anything—yet. But you will. You can't escape it. Human beings don't stay the same all their lives, though some of them half-kill themselves trying to. They can't. There are other people in the world with them, and, try as each might to become an island unto himself, it's impossible. He sees his neighbor doing something to make life more bearable—putting up window screens to keep the flies out, say. And then he's got to have screens of his own, or else walk around covered with fly-bites while his neighbor laughs at him. Or else—" Cottrell smiled oddly, "his wife nags him into it."

Cottrell coughed sharply, wiped his mouth impatiently, and went on. "Pretty soon, everybody wants window screens. And some bright young man who makes good ones stops being an island and becomes a carpenter. And some other bright young man becomes his salesman. The next thing you know, the carpenter's got more orders than he can handle—so somebody else becomes a carpenter's apprentice. You see?"

Matt nodded slowly. "I think so."

"All right, then, Matt. My civilization ended. Yours is a brand new one. It's just beginning, but it's a civilization, all right. There are thousands of boys just like you, all over the world. Some of them will sit in their caves—maybe draw pictures on the walls, before their neighbors break in and kill them. But the rest of you, Matt, will be doing things. What you'll do, exactly, I don't know. But it'll be effective."

Cottrell stopped himself with an outburst of coughing, and Matt bit his lip as the old man sank back on his pillows. But Cottrell resumed the thread of his explanation, and now Matt understood that he was trying to leave something behind before he was too weak to say it. Cottrell had lived longer and seen more than the man who was going to become his daughter's husband. This attempt to pass on the benefit of his experience was the old man's last performance of his duty toward Margaret.

"I think, Matt," Cottrell went on, "that whatever you and the other young men do will produce a new culture—a more fully developed civilization. And that each generation of young men after you will take what you have left them and build on it, even though they might prefer to simply sit still and enjoy what they have. Because someone will always want window screens. It's the nature of the beast.

"And, it is also in the nature of the beast that some people, seeing their neighbor with his window screens, will not want to make the effort of building screens of their own. Some of them will try to bring their neighbor back to the old level—by killing him, by destroying his improvements.

"But that doesn't work. If you kill one man, you may kill another. And the other people around you will band together in fear and kill *you*. And someday, after it's been demonstrated that the easiest way, in the long run, is to build rather than to attempt to destroy—after everyone has window screens—some bright young man will invent DDT and a whole new cycle will begin."

Cottrell laughed shortly. "Oh, what a nervous day for the window-screen-makers that will be! But the people who know how to make spray-guns will be very busy.

"The plague was a disaster, Matt," he said suddenly, veering off on a new track. "But disasters are not new to the race of Man. To every Act of God, Man has an answer, drawn from the repertoire of answers he has hammered out in the face of the disasters that have come before. It's in his nature to build dams against the flood—to rebuild after the earthquake. To put up window screens. Because, apparently, he's uncomfortable with what this planet gives him, and has to change it—to improve on it, to make himself just a little more comfortable. Maybe, just for the irritated hope that his wife will shut up and leave him alone for a few minutes.

"Who knows? Man hunted his way upward with a club in his hand, once. You're starting with a rifle. Perhaps, before your sons die, the world will once again support the kind of civilization in which a young man can sit in a cave, drawing pictures, and depend on others to clothe and shelter him.

"But not now," Cottrell said. "Now, I wouldn't entrust my daughter to anyone but a hunter.

"And I'm *making* you a hunter, Matt. I'm leaving you this dowry: responsibility, in the form of what my daughter will need to make her happy. In addition, I leave you the apartment as a base of operations, together with the stove, the water still, and the fuel oil.

The First Avenue entrances to the Canarsie Line subway are on the corner. That tunnel connects with all the others under the city. They'll be a relatively safe trail through the jungle this city has become. You'll be able to get water from the seepage, too. Distilled water is easily restored to its natural taste by aeration with an eggbeater.

"Last of all, Matt, you'll find my rifle beside the door. It's a mankiller. There's ammunition in the hall closet.

"That's your environment, Matt. Change it."

He stopped and sighed. "That's all."

Garvin sat silently, watching the old man's breathing.

What would Cottrell have done if his daughter hadn't brought a man home? Probably, he would have found comfort in the thought that, across the world, there were thousands of young men and women. His personal tragedy would have been trivial, on that scale.

Yes, doubtless. But would it have made the personal failure any less painful? Cottrell's philosophy was logical enough—but, once again, in the face of actual practice, logic seemed not enough. Just as now, with all the philosophy expounded, there was still the problem of Margaret's reaction.

Sweat trickled coldly down Garvin's chest.

"By the way, Matt," Cottrell said dryly, "For a young man who doubtless thinks of himself as not being a cave dweller, you're apparently having a good deal of trouble recognizing the symptoms of shy young love, American girl style."

Garvin stared at the old man, who went on speaking as though he did not see his flush, smiling broadly as he savored the secret joke he had discovered in his first glances at Margaret and Matt.

"And now, if you'll call Margaret in here, I think we ought to bring her up to date." He coughed violently again, grimacing at this reminder, but when he flung the bloody tissue into the wastebasket, it was a gesture of victory.

Five months later, Matt Garvin padded silently through the dark of Macy's, his magnum rifle held diagonally across his body. He moved easily, for his knapsack was lightly loaded, even when stuffed full of the clothing he'd picked up for Margaret.

Though he made no sound, he chuckled ruefully in his mind. First it had been one thing Margaret needed, and then another, until finally he was going farther and farther afield. Well, it was the way things were, and nothing could be done about it.

A shadow flitted across the lighter area near a door, and he stopped in his tracks, wishing his breath were not so sibilant. Damn, he'd *have* to work out some kind of breathing technique! Then the other man crossed the light again, and Garvin moved forward. There was a cartridge in the magnum's chamber, of course, and he was ready to fire instantly. But he could almost be sure there was someone else down here, prowling the counters, and he didn't want to fire if it could be avoided.

On the other hand, if he waited much longer, he might lose the man in front of him.

With a mental shrug, he threw the rifle up to his shoulder and shot the man down, dropping instantly to the floor as he did so. The echoes shattered through the darkness.

Another man fired from behind a display and charged him, grunting. Matt sprang to his feet, the magnum swinging butt-first, and broke his neck. He stopped to listen, ready to fire in any direction, but there was no sound. He grinned coldly.

He stopped to strip the packs from both corpses before he vanished into the darkness. He thought to himself, not for the first time, that a rifle was too clumsy for close-in combat—that if the man had been able to block the magnum's swing, things might easily have worked out another way. What you needed for this sort of situation was a pistol.

But he was still reluctant to think of himself as a man with much occasion for one.

CHAPTER TWO:

Three years went by.

His boots full of frigid water, and his rifle securely strapped to his pack, Matt Garvin was picking his way through the trash in the drainage channel between the subway rails. A hundred feet ahead of him, dim light from a roof grating patched out the darkness, and he ran his thumb over the safety catch of the 9mm Mauser he had looted out of a littered pawnshop drawer on Eighth Avenue. He stopped for a moment, opened his mouth to quiet the sound of his breath, and listened.

Water dripped from a girder to the concrete of the station platform ahead of him. Behind him in the tunnel—at about the Third Avenue entrance, he judged—someone else was moving. That was all right. There were two long blocks between them, and he'd be out of the tunnel by the time the other man was within dangerous distance.

He listened again, disregarding the faint splash of water on the platform, the different but equally unimportant slosh up the tunnel.

He heard nothing, and his eyes, probing as much of the First Avenue station platforms as he could see, found nothing but dim gray, bounded by the converging lines of platform and roof, broken by the vertical thrust of girders.

Moving forward cautiously, he reached a point near the beginning of the north side platform, and stopped to listen again. Nothing moved.

He pulled himself up on the platform and lay flat, the Mauser ready, but there was no scrape of motion, either on this platform or on the one across the tracks, and none of the indistinct shadows changed their shapes as he watched them. Nevertheless, as a final if somewhat inconclusive check, he listened to the water droplets as they fell steadily from the girder to the platform. Sometimes a man got careless and let such a drop hit him, interrupting the beat.

But there was nothing. He pushed himself up off his stomach, crouched, and padded quietly to the tiled wall beside the foot of the stairs.

A few months ago, he had tried putting up a mirror there, in order to see up the stairs without exposing himself. It had been smashed within a few days, and he had been especially cautious for a while, but no one had ever been waiting for him at the head of the stairs. He had finally come to the conclusion that someone else must have solved the problem ahead of him. A fresh corpse at the street entrance had tended to confirm this—the possibility that it was only a decoy had been discarded as an overcomplication.

It had been good to feel that he had an ally—if only in this vague, circumstantial way. It was no indication that the very man responsible might not be his killer tomorrow, but there was enough of an idealist left in Garvin to allow him a certain satisfaction at this proof that there was at least one other man somewhere near who could draw the distinction between self-protection and deliberate trap-setting. However, he had never tried to replace the mirror.

He listened again as a matter of routine, heard nothing, and waited. After ten minutes, there had still been no sound, and knowing that his own approach had been silent, he broke suddenly and silently for the opposite wall, gun ready to fire in his hand.

There was no one at the head of the stairs. He crept upward cautiously, found no one at the turnstile level, and reached the foot of the stairs to the street.

It was unlikely that there would be anyone up there, exposed to the daylight. Moreover, if he made his passage into the building fast enough, he was unlikely to have any trouble. Lately, there had not been any considerable amount of sniping from windows. Ammunition was running low, and the possible rewards of nighttime scavenging from the corpses were not usually worth the expenditure.

Shifting the straps of his pack into a tighter position, he moved carefully up the steps, took a sweeping look at the deserted length of Fourteenth Street, and zig-zagged across the sidewalk at a run. His beating footsteps were a sudden interruption in the absence of sound. As he reached the entrance to his building and slipped inside the door, silence returned.

In the darkness of the lobby, Garvin's shoes whispered on worn rubber matting, for it had been raining on the last day the building staff had functioned. The firedoor on the stairwell clicked open and shut, and his steps on the cement stairs were regular taps of leather as he climbed. He was not completely relaxed—above the sound of his own footsteps, he listened for the noise that might be made by someone else in the stairwell. Nevertheless, though there were other people scattered throughout the fifty-odd apartments in the building, no one had ever attacked anyone else within the building itself. There had to be a sort of mutual respect between the families. The thought of fighting within the twists and corridors of the building, with every closed door a deathtrap, was not an attractive one. The stairwell, in particular, was the only means of passage to the world outside. Only a psychopath would have risked obstructing it.

He reached his floor and stepped out on the landing with only a minimum amount of precaution. He crossed the corridor to his own door, unlocked it, and stepped inside, holstering his gun. The shot roared out of the hallway leading from the bedrooms and crashed into the metal doorframe beside him.

Garvin leaped sideward, landing on the kitchen floor with a thud. His fingers slapped against his gun butt, hooked around it, and the gun was in his hand, his feet under him in a slash of motion as he rolled and flung himself backward behind the stove. The breath whistled out of his nostrils and back in through his mouth in an uneven gasp.

There was no sound in the apartment. He turned his head from side to side, trying to find some noise—a hand on a doorknob, a footstep on linoleum—that would tell him where his attacker was.

There was nothing.

The kitchen was beside the apartment door. Beyond it was the dining alcove and the living room, and beyond that were two bedrooms opening on a hall that ran the remainder of the apartment's length. The bathroom was at the end of the hall, its door facing the apartment entrance. The man could have fired from either bedroom, or from the bathroom itself.

Where was the man—and where was Margaret? Garvin's knuckles cracked as his hand tightened on the gun's butt, and his face became almost stuporous in its lack of overt expression.

Keeping his gun ready, Garvin moved forward until he was barely hidden inside the kitchen doorway. His mind was busy searching out and separating the remembered impressions of the attack.

The shot had been fired in the hall. It was impossible to decide how far back. Had the man moved after firing? He tried to remember if there had been any other sound. No, he decided. Wherever the shot had come from, there the man still was.

What had happened to Margaret? His jaw tightened as he considered the possibilities.

If she had seen the man come in, she might have tried to shoot him—if she had been near her gun. If not, she might still be hiding somewhere in the apartment, waiting for Garvin to come home. If the man had gotten in without her knowing it. . . .

The possibilities were indeterminate, he told himself savagely. Whatever had happened, in any case, there was nothing he could do about it now. If she were still hidden, it was up to her to handle that part of the situation as her judgment dictated.

There was still no sound in the apartment.

How long had the man been here? If Margaret was still alive and undiscovered, would the hidden man stumble on her if he was forced to move on to another room? Her gun was probably in the larger bedroom. Was she there, waiting for a chance to get a shot in?

He could count on nothing to help him. He and Margaret had both learned all the tricks that life in New York demanded. He would have to act as though he could be sure that she would know how to take care of herself. But he was not sure.

The silence continued. He had to get the man moving; had to get some idea of his location. And he needed freedom of movement. He unstrapped the magnum and carefully set it aside.

Backing up noiselessly, Garvin reached behind him and opened the casement window, pushing the panel slowly. The guide rod slid in its track with a muted sound.

"Please!"

The voice, distorted by the echoes of the hallway, was frightened and anxious. Garvin snatched his hand away from the window.

It was quiet again. The man had stopped, but the quavering print of his voice was still playing back in Garvin's mind.

And suddenly he understood how he would feel, unexpectedly trapped in a strange apartment. Every corner would have its concealed death, each step its possible drastic consequence. Was the pitiful hope of whatever goods could be brought away worth the stark terror of unknown deadliness?

He opened the window a bit farther.

"Please! No! I . . ." The words rushed out of the shadowed hallway. "I'm—I'm sorry! I was frightened. . . ."

Garvin's lips stretched in a reflex grin. If the man

66

actually thought Garvin was somehow going to cross from window ledge to window ledge along the building's sheer outside wall, he had to be in a room where he was open to such an attack.

He couldn't be in the bathroom. The large bedroom was in the corner of the apartment. By the time a man inching along the building's face could possibly reach it, it would be easy to take any number of steps to handle the situation. The man had to be in the smaller bedroom, the one nearest the living room. And he had to be standing at the door.

The door to the small bedroom was set flush with the wall, and opened to the left. In order to defend the room or fire down the hallway, the door would have to be completely open. Therefore, the man's hand and arm were exposed, and, most probably, his face as well.

The man had to maintain his position in command of the hall. If Garvin could once get a clear lane of fire down the hallway, it was the other man who was trapped in an exitless room.

But the hall was dark, while the living room had a large window, the light of which would have made it suicidal for Garvin to step out.

Once again, he thought of Margaret. He fought down the urgency of the impulse to cry out for her. If the other man didn't know about her, it was so much more advantage on Garvin's side.

Grimly, Garvin worked the slide on the Mauser as noisily as possible. The sound, like the slip of the window's guide rod, was designed only to make his unknown adversary go into a deeper panic. There had already been a bullet in the chamber. He ejected it carefully into his palm and put it in his pocket. He pushed the window completely open, thudding the guide rod home against its stop.

"Please! Listen to me!" The panicked voice began again. "I want to be friends."

Garvin stopped.

"Are you listening?" the man asked hesitatingly.

There was no accompanying sound of movement from the bedroom. The man was maintaining his position at the door. Garvin cursed silently and did not answer.

"I haven't talked to anybody for years. Not even shouted at them, or cursed. All I've done for six years is fight other people. Shooting, running. I didn't dare show myself in daylight.

"It isn't worth it. Staying alive isn't worth it. Grubbing through stores for food at night. Like an animal in a garbage can!" The trembling voice was filled with desperate disgust.

"Are you listening?"

Unseen, Garvin's eyes grew bleak, and he nodded. He remembered the odd touch of kinship he had felt with the man who had killed the stalker at the subway entrance. The mirror at the turn of the steps had been an attempt to make at least that small part of his environment a bit less dangerous. When the stalker smashed it, it meant that there were still men who would kill for the sake of a knapsack that might or might not contain food.

"Please," the man in the bedroom said. "You've got to understand why I—I came in here. I had to find some people I could talk to. I knew there were people in this building. I got a passkey out of the Stuyvesant Town offices. I wanted to find an apartment

68

for myself. I was going to try to make friends with my neighbors."

Garvin twitched a corner of his mouth. He could picture an attempt at communication with the deadly silence and armed withdrawal that lurked through the apartments beyond his own walls.

"Can't you say something?" the panic-stricken man demanded.

Garvin scraped the Mauser's barrel against the window frame, as though an armed man were beginning to clamber out on one of the nonexistent window ledges.

No! Think! How much food can there be left, where we can get to it? There are whole gangs in the warehouses, and they won't let anybody near them. The rifle ammunition's getting low already. How long can we go on this way—fighting over every can of peas, killing each other over a new shirt? We've got to organize ourselves—get a system set up, try to establish some kind of government. It's been six years since the plague, and nothing's been done."

The man stopped for a moment, and Garvin listened for the sound of motion, but there was nothing.

"I—I'm sorry I shot at you. I was frightened. Everybody's frightened. They don't trust anybody. How can they?"

Talk, talk, talk! What have you done with Margaret, damn you?

"But please—please trust me." The unsteady voice was on the point of breaking. "I want to be friends."

Despite his fear, the man obviously wasn't going to move from his position until he was absolutely sure that Garvin was out on the window ledges. Even then. . . . Garvin pictured the man, trembling against the

69

door, not sure whether to run or stay, keeping watch on the hallway, ready to spin around at the sound of breaking glass behind him.

He was frightened, now. But had he been? Was it only after that one shot had missed, and the self-made trap had snapped home, that the terror had begun to tremble in his throat?

What had happened to Margaret?

Garvin moved back to the kitchen doorway.

"Come out," he said.

There was a sigh from the bedroom door—a ragged exhalation that might have been relief. The man's shoes shuffled on the linoleum of the bedroom floor, and his heel struck the metal sill. He moved out into the hall, thin, his hollowed eyes dark against his pale face.

Garvin pointed the Mauser at his chest and fired twice. The man held his hands against himself and fell into the living room.

Garvin sprang forward and looked down at him. He was dead.

"Matt!" The door of the hall closet rebounded against the wall, and Margaret clasped her arms around Garvin. She buried her teeth in his shoulder for a moment. "I heard him fumbling with the key. I knew it wasn't you, and it was too far to the bedroom."

Garvin slipped his gun into its holster and held her, feeling the spasmodic shake of her body as she cried. The hall closet was almost directly opposite the door to the small bedroom. She hadn't even dared warn him as he came in.

He looked down at the man again, over Margaret's shoulder. One of the man's hands were tightly clasped around a Colt that must have been looted from a policeman's body.

"You poor bastard," Garvin said to the corpse. "You trusted me too far."

Margaret looked up, as pale as the man had been when he stepped out to meet Garvin's fire. "Matt! Hush! There wasn't anything else you could do."

"He was a man—a man like me. He was scared, and he was begging for his life," Garvin said. "He wanted me to trust him, but I was too scared to believe him." He shook himself sharply. "I still can't believe him."

"There wasn't anything else to do, Matt," Margaret repeated insistently. "You didn't have any way of knowing whether I was all right or not. You've said it yourself. We live the way we have to—by rules we had to make up. He was in another man's house. He broke the rules."

Garvin's mouth shaped itself into a twisted slash. He couldn't take his eyes off the dead man. "We're good with rules," he said. "The poor guy heard somebody—so he took a shot at me.

"And what could I do? Somebody tried to kill me in my own home. It didn't really matter, after that, what he said or did, or what I thought. I had to kill him. Anyway at all."

He pulled away from Margaret and stood beside the corpse for a moment, his arms swinging impatiently as he tried to decide what to do. Then he moved forward, as though abruptly breaking out of an invisible shell. His footsteps echoed loudly in the hall, and then he was back from the bedroom, a sheet dangling out of his clenched hand.

"Matt, what're you going to do?" Margaret asked,

her voice almost a whisper as her puzzled eyes tried to read his face.

He bent and caught the dead man under the arms. "I'm putting up a 'No Trespassing' sign." He dragged the corpse to the living room window, knotted one end of the sheet to the metal centerpost, and slung the remainder of the sheet around the dead man's chest, leaving just enough slack so his lolling head would hang out of sight. Then he lowered the corpse through the open window.

Garvin turned. Suddenly, all his muscles seemed to twist. "I hope this keeps them away! I hope I never have to do this again." Even with the distance between them, Margaret could easily see him trembling.

"I'll do it again, if I have to," he went on. "If they keep coming, I'll have to kill them. After a while, I'll be used to it. I'll shoot them down with children in their arms. I'll use their own white flags to hang them up beside this one. I'll ignore the sound of their voices. Because they can't be trusted. I know they can't be trusted, because I know I can't be trusted."

He stopped, turned, and looked at Margaret. "You realize what that poor guy wanted? You know who he sounded like? Like *me*, that's who—like me, Matt Garvin, the guy who just wanted a place to live in peace."

"Matt, I know what he *said* he—"

"Hey! Hey, you, in there!" The muffled voice came blurredly into the apartment, followed by a series of sharp knocks on the other side of the wall that separated this apartment from the next.

Margaret stopped, but Garvin slid forward, his boots making no sound on the floor as he moved quietly over to the wall.

72

The knocking started again. "You! Next door. What's all that racket?"

Garvin heard Margaret start to say something. His hand flashed out in a silencing gesture, and he put his ear to the wall. His right hand came down and touched the Mauser's holster.

"I'm warning you." He could hear the voice more clearly. "Speak up, or you'll never come out of there alive. I'm mighty particular about my neighbors, and if you've knocked off the ones I had, I'll make damn sure you don't enjoy their place very long."

Garvin's mouth opened. He'd known there was someone in there, of course, but, up to now, there had never been any break in the silence.

"Well?" The voice was impatient. "I've got the drop on you. My wife's in the hall right now, with a gun on your door. And I can get some dynamite in a big hurry."

Garvin hesitated. It meant giving the other man an advantage.

"Hurry up!"

But there was nothing else he could do. "It's all right," he finally said, speaking loudly enough for the other man to hear. "There was somebody in here, but we took care of it."

"That's better," the other man said, but his voice was still suspicious. "Now let's hear your wife say something."

Margaret moved up to the wall. She looked at Garvin questioningly, and he reluctantly nodded. "Go ahead," he said.

"This is Margaret Garvin. We're—we're all right." She stopped, then seemed to reach a decision and went on with a rush. "My husband's name is Matt. Who are you?"

That wasn't right. Garvin frowned. She was getting too close to an infringement on the silent privacy that had existed for so long, now. Men were no longer brothers. They were distant nodding acquaintances.

Surprisingly, the other man did not hesitate a perceptible length of time before answering. "My name's Gustav Berendtsen. My wife's name is Carol." The tone of his voice had changed, and now Garvin thought he could make out the indistinct trace of a pleased chuckle in Berendtsen's voice. "Took care of it, did you? Good. Damn good! Nice to have neighbors you can depend on." The voice lost some of its clarity as Berendtsen obviously turned his head away from his side of the wall. "Hey, Toots, you can put that cannon down now. They straightened it out themselves."

Out in the hall, a safety catch clicked, and no-longer-careful footsteps moved back from the Garvins' door. Then Berendtsen's door opened and shut, and, after a moment, there was a shy voice from beside Berendtsen on the other side of the wall.

"Hello. I'm Carol Berendtsen. Is—" She stopped, as though she too was as unsure of herself as Margaret and Garvin were, here in this stange situation that had suddenly materialized from beyond the rules. But she stopped only for a moment. "*Is* everything all right?"

"Sure, everything's all right, Toots!" Berendtsen's voice cut in from behind the wall. "I've been telling you those were damn sensible people living in there. Know how to mind their own business. People

74

who know that, know how to make sure nobody else tries minding it, either."

"All right, Gus, all right," Garvin and Margaret heard her say, her low voice still carrying well enough to be heard through the masonry. "I just wanted to hear them say it." And then she added something in an even lower voice. "It's been a long time since I heard people just talking," and Garvin's hand tightened on Margaret's as they heard her.

"Sure. Toots, sure. But I kept telling you it wasn't always going to be that way. I—" His voice rose up to a louder pitch. "Hey, Garvins! I gotta idea. Also got a bottle of Haig and Haig in here. Care for some? We'll come over," he added hurriedly.

Garvin looked at Margaret's strained face and trembling lips. He could feel his own face tightening.

"Please, Matt?" Margaret asked.

She was right. It was too big a chance not to take.

"Sure, Hon," he said. "But get my rifle and cover the door from the hall," he added softly.

"All right," he said, raising his voice. "Come over."

"Right," Berendtsen answered. "Be a minute."

The words were jovial enough, Garvin thought.

He heard Margaret move back into the hall, and his mind automatically registered the slight creak of the sling's leather as she lifted the rifle to cover the door.

And then he heard Carol Berendtsen's voice faintly through the wall.

"I—I don't know," she was saying to Gus, her voice uncertain. "Will it be all right? I mean, I haven't talked to another woman in. . . . What'll she think? I haven't got any good clothes. And there's a strange man in there . . . Gus, I look so—I'm *ashamed!*"

And Gus Berendtsen's voice, clumsy but gentle, its

power broken into softness. "Aw, look, Toots, they're just people like us. You think they've got any time for frills? I bet you're dressed just fine. And what's to be ashamed of in being a woman?" And then there was a moment's silence. "I'll bet you're prettier than she is, too."

"You'd *better* think so, Gus."

Something untied itself in Garvin. "I think you can put that rifle away, Hon," he said to Margaret. He saw her look of uncertainty, and nodded to emphasize the words. "I'm pretty sure."

Garvin poured out another finger of the Scotch. He raised his glass in a silent mutual toast with Berendtsen, who grinned and lifted his own glass in response. Gus chuckled, the soft, controlled sound rumbling gently up through his thick chest. The glass was almost out of sight in his spade of a hand, huge even in proportion to the rest of his body. He sat easily in the chair that should have been too small for him, the shaped power of his personality reflected in his body's casual poise.

"Ought to be able to set up a pretty good combo," he said. "One of us stays home to hold the fort while the other one goes out for the groceries. Take turns. Might try knocking a hole through this wall, too. Be easier." He slapped the plaster with his hand.

Garvin nodded. "Good idea." They both smiled at the drift of women's voices that came from one of the bedrooms. "Make it easier on the baby-sitter, too."

"My gal was a little worried," Berendtsen agreed. He grinned again. "You know, we may have something here." He raised his glass again, and Garvin, catching his train of thought, matched the gesture. "To the Second Republic," Berendtsen said.

"All six-and-two-halves rooms of it," Garvin affirmed. Then his glance reached the living room window, and he realized that there was still something undone. He got up to loosen the sheet and let the body fall to join the others that lay scattered among the dark buildings.

But he stopped before his hand touched the sheet. No one would know, now, how much honesty there had been within the fear of the intruder's voice. But it was time somebody in the world got the benefit of the doubt. They'd carry him down to the ground, Gus and he, and give him a burial, like a man.

CHAPTER THREE:

It was winter again, and seven years since the plague. December snow lay deep between Stuyvesant's buildings, under the frosty night, while Manhattan raised its blunt stone shoulders up and, here and there, silent figures in the department stores took time from their normal foraging and climbed the prostrate escalators to the toy counters.

A delegation from the next building in the block made a gingerly meeting with Matt Garvin and Gus Berendtsen, out on one of the windswept playgrounds.

Garvin watched the delegation leader carefully. It was an older man, fat and small-eyed—a man who'd been somebody before the plague, he guessed.

Matt knew he was being nervous for no clear reason. But he didn't like dealing with older people. There was no telling how much they had time to learn—how many little tricks they remembered from the old days.

The man smiled affably, proffering his hand. "Charlie Conner," he boomed. "I guess I run that she-bang back there," he said deprecatingly, jerking his thumb back over his shoulder toward his own building. But the young, wolfish riflemen with him did not twitch their eyes to follow the gesture.

"Matt Garvin. And this is Gus Berendtsen," Matt noticed Gus was looking at Conner the same way he'd looked over each member of each new family they'd found in the apartments of their building. "I guess between us we do your job for our building."

Conner grinned. "Tough, isn't it? What'd you do—just spread out gradual, sweating it out every time you made contact with a different family?"

"Something like that," Gus cut in. "Make your point."

Conner's eyes shifted. "Don't get jumpy," he soothed. "All I am is figuring now we've got our whole buildings organized, it's time we joined up together. The more people we've got, the more we can control things. The idea is to make sure your own rules get followed in your own territory, right? Nobody wants any wild hares fouling things up. You want to be sure that as long as you follow the rules, everything's all right, right? You want to know your family's protected while you're out someplace. You want to be sure there's a safe store of food, right? Well, the bigger the community, the more sure you can be. Right?"

Garvin nodded. "Uh-huh."

Conner spread his hands. "All right. Now, I've got my place organized nice as pie. Ought to. Fifteen years District Captain in this ward. Lots of experience. Now, I'm sure you boys have things going pretty well, but maybe there's one or two things you could stand to have better. Okay, here I am. My people're real satisfied. Right, boys?" he asked his riflemen.

"Right, boss."

Gus said: "What you mean is, we should join you."

Conner chuckled. "Well, now, look, I'm not likely to want to join you, now, am I?"

He leaned negligently against the crudely-painted sign Gus and Matt had seen planted through the playground's asphalt: "Meet me here tomorrow, and we'll talk joining up together.—Charlie Conner."

Gus and Matt exchanged glances. "We'll think about it," Gus said.

"You do that," Conner said. "Oh, look, I know you think you've been doing all right. And you have—no question about it. But now you're ready to spread out into more than one building, and you've got to figure sooner or later you have to meet somebody with more experience, running things. It just figures, that's all. You didn't hope you could start a whole city government, did you? I mean, you boys weren't going to run one of you for Mayor or anything, were you?" Conner chuckled uproariously.

"We'll think about it," Gus repeated. "You'll hear from us."

Conner's eyes narrowed. "When?"

Matt said: "When we're ready."

Conner looked thoughtfully at the two of them. "Don't stall me too long, now."

"You worried you might die of old age?" Gus asked. They turned around and walked away. Conner looked after them, turned, and stalked back toward his own building. The rifle parties of both sides waited until everyone else was gone, and then they backed away from each other. Finally, the playground stood empty again.

In their apartment, Matt put his rifle down softly. "Well, now we know," he said. "I thought we'd been running into too many rival foraging parties. They had to come from someplace nearby."

"What do you think about Conner?"

"I think he's lost more people than we have, or he would have let things go on the way they have been, with his foraging parties and ours leaving each other alone unless they were both set on picking up the same thing."

"So what do we do?"

"I think we've got the upper hand. I think we can stick it out without him longer than he can without us."

"And meanwhile we keep losing people?"

Garvin looked up sharply. "Not as many as he does. That's the key. He's hurting worse than we are."

"You tell that to our widows."

"I don't have to tell our widows anything. All anybody can promise a woman these days is that her man's safe as long as he stays inside his own four walls. Of course, that way they both starve, and so do their kids. "

"Look, if we make a deal with Conner, nobody dies."

"You're sure. You're sure Conner means all he wants is to be the big frog in a bigger puddle. He's not looking for extra women, or extra food for his own people. He keeps those gunmen of his in line by promising them no more than new friends to play gin rummy with."

"All right—maybe. We can't be sure."

"We don't have to be sure of anything. We just have to keep as alive as we can. Look, Gus—I'm not saying we should forget Conner. Or his offer, I'm saying that two or three weeks from now, he may not be so bossy. If we're going to trade something with him, I want a 50-50 chance of an even deal. Right now, we don't have that."

"So we wait."

"Well, we can try breaking into his building. How many widows do you figure that'll make for us?"

"Okay. We'll let it ride."

A week later, the sign in the playground said:

NOTICE! Anyone Not A Member Of The East Side Mutual Protective Association, (Charles G. Conner, Pres.) is Hereby Declared An Outlaw, and is subject to trial under due authority. By The Authority Invested In Me By The Democratic Party Of The State Of New York, United States Of America.

(signed) Charles G. Conner

"Oh, yeah, huh?" Matt Garvin said.

The little group of men returned to Stuyvesant from the east, cutting across the playground and access drives in the courtyards. As he led them back home, Matt Garvin shivered and hunched up his heavy collar to protect his ears. The wind was light, just strong enough to cover the quiet crunch of footsteps with its whispering, but he and the men had been out all afternoon, and the chill was beginning to sink deep into their bones.

He looked up into the moonless sky, wishing there were clouds to cover the light that filtered down from the stars.

And a new star burst into searing life between the buildings.

"Scatter!" he shouted, while the parachute flare drifted slowly down, etching each man's shadow blackly against the white of snow, and the first fingers of rifle fire reached out.

Garvin stumbled for cover behind a car parked at the side of one of the access drives, his feet floundering in the wet snow. He was almost blind from the sudden explosion of light into his eyes, but he skidded somehow into shelter, slamming against the cold metal. His eyes snapped reflectively shut while fire pinwheeled across his retinas, but he forced them open and aimed his rifle as best he could, trying to cut up the flare's parachute. He missed, but it made no difference, for there was a triple pop from the roof of one of the buildings, and three more of the flares hung swaying and slowly dropping above the frantically running men. He cursed and huddled beside the car, snapping almost futile shots at the windows where the red sparks were winking.

The crash of rifle fire was like nothing he had heard since the height of the plague. There was never a complete break in the echoing hammer. He judged that there were at least thirty snipers, if not more, and they were all emptying their clips as fast as possible, reloading at top speed, and pouring out ammunition at a rate no one could possibly afford.

There had been twelve men in his group, counting himself. He saw three of them lying in the snow, two of them with their rifles pinned under their bodies. Those men had simply folded forward in their tracks. The third had possibly fired once. He had been looking up, at any rate, for his upper body had fallen back, and he lay stretched out, his rifle beside him, with his legs bent under him. The rest of the men had reached cover of some kind, for there was no movement in the courtyard. Most of them were not firing back, and not even Garvin could tell where they were.

He swore steadily, the words falling out in a monotone. The trap had sprung perfectly. One man had stationed himself on the roof of the opposite building with his flares, and had simply illuminated the court when he picked out the shadows of Garvin's party. The riflemen had been waiting at their windows.

The sniping fire cut off abruptly, and when Garvin realized why, a savage laugh ripped briefly out of his throat. The first flare was almost on the ground, and the men in the buildings were looking down at it, as blind as he had been.

He jumped to his feet instantly, shouting.

"Break for it!"

There was a flounder and the sound of running footsteps in the snow as the remaining men burst out of bushes and from behind cars. Garvin ran jerkily across the driveway, hunting fresh cover, and now he saw some of the other men running with him, like debris tossed by an explosion, nightmare shapes in the complexity of wheeling light and lurching shadow thrown by the flares as they oscillated under their parachutes.

He threw a glance over his shoulder and stopped dead. One of his men had stopped beside one of the bodies, and was trying to carry it away.

"Drop him!" Garvin shouted. The flare fell into the snow, silhouetting the man. "Come on!"

The three other flares, high in the air and drifting down slowly, were only a little below the tops of the buildings, still well above most of the snipers. The man tugged at the corpse once more, then gave up. But he was starkly outlined by the flare on the ground, burning without any regard for the snow's feeble attempt to quench it.

The man began to run. Garvin and the other seven men, swallowed up by a trick of the complicated shadow-pattern, stood and watched him, silent now.

When he was finally shot down, Garvin and someone else cursed once, almost in unison, and then the eight men slipped around a corner of the building, ran across a final courtyard, and into Garvins' building, while the three flares settled down among the four corpses, and a triumphant yell broke out from the snipers.

"This is the worst yet," Berendtsen said, his face taut and his eyes cold as he sat at the table in Garvin's living room. "I never thought of flares. This tears it— it's no longer a question of competing with them for forage. They're cutting off our supply route."

Garvin nodded. "We were lucky. If they hadn't fouled up with their flares, it wouldn't have been just four." He turned in his chair and let his glance sweep over the other men in his living room. They represented all the families in the building. He saw what he expected in their faces—grim concentration, indecision, and fear, in unequal but equally significant mixtures. He turned back to Gus, one corner of his mouth quirking upward. There was nothing in these men to mark a distinction between them and the snipers. In a sense, they were afraid of themselves. But they had reason to be.

"All right," Berendtsen said harshly, "we were lucky. But we can't let it go at that. This is just the beginning of something. If we let it go on, we'll be starved right out of here."

"Anybody got any ideas?" Garvin asked the men.

"I don't get it," one of them said in a querulous

voice. Garvin checked him off as one of the frightened ones. "We weren't bothering them."

"Smarten up, Howard," one of the other men cut in before Garvin could curb his own exasperation. Matt recognized him. His name was Jack Holland, and his father had been one of the three men who were cut down at the attack's beginning. He carried a worn and battered toy of a rifle that was obviously his family's second- or third-best weapon, but even with his teen-age face, he somehow invested that ridiculous .22 with deadliness. Garvin threw a quick glance at Berendtsen.

Gus nodded slightly, in the near-perfect communication that had grown between them. As long as Holland was speaking for them, there was no need for their own words.

"We're the richest thing in this neighborhood," the boy went on, his eyes and voice older than himself. "What's more, those guys have kids and women going hungry on account of us cleaning out all the stores around here. We've been doing plenty to them."

Garvin nodded back to Berendtsen, and there was a shift in the already complex structure of judgments and tentative decisions that he kept stored in his mind. In a few years, they would have a good man with them.

He found himself momentarily lost in thought at the plans which now were somehow far advanced in his mind, but which had first had to grow, bit by bit, over the past years. The Second Republic—he still smiled as he thought of it, but not as broadly—had expanded, and as it grew to encompass all of this building, so he and Gus had more experience to draw from, more men to work with and assign to the constantly diversifying duties.

Strange, to plan for a future, in the light of the past. But somehow good to plan, to shape, to hope. Even to know that, though the plan had to be revised from minute to minute as unexpected problems arose, the essential objective would never change.

He cut through the murmur of argument that had risen among the men. "Okay. Holland's put it in a nutshell. We're an organized outfit with a systematic plan for supplying ourselves. That's fine for us, not so good for anybody that isn't with us. We all expected something to happen when we started. Some of us may have thought our troubles with Conner these last few trips were the most we could expect. We should have known better, but that's unimportant now. Here it is, and we're stuck with it. Once again, now—what do we do?"

"We go in there and clean the sons of bitches out," someone growled.

"You going first?" another man rasped at him.

"Damn right, boy," a third said, leaving it a moot point as to whom he was supporting.

"That's what I thought." Berendtsen was on his feet, towering over the table as much as his voice crushed the babble. He waited a moment for the last opened mouth to close, his bleak eyes moving surely from man to man, his jaw set. Garvin, drawing on the thousand subtle cues that their friendship had gradually taught him to recognize, could catch the faint thread of amusement in the big man's attitude—perhaps because he, too, had recognized the wry spectacle of the no-longer-quite-uncivilized afraid of the still-savage. But the men swung their glances hurriedly at Berendtsen, and only a few held sly glints in their eyes as they did so.

"You're acting like a bunch of mice when a flashlight spots 'em," Gus went on. "And don't tell me that's exactly what happened to you, because there's supposed to be a few differences between us and mice."

Matt grinned broadly, and a few of the men twitched their mouths in response. Berendtsen went on.

"This thing's suddenly become serious, and it's like nothing we've run up against before. When people start knocking on walls all around you, telling you the building's being organized, it's one thing. But those birds are off by themselves. We can't *make* them do anything."

He stopped to sweep the men with his glance once more. "And we're not going to try to go into those buildings and take them room by room. It can't be done to us. We can't do it to them."

"We can't lick them, and they can't lick us. But we can chop each other up little by little, and we can all stare while we're doing it. Because we sure as hell can't forage and fight a war at the same time. There's plenty of other people out there to make sure it takes a strong party to bring home the bacon.

"There's one way out. We can join up with each other. If we can get Conner to settle for something less than us being his slaves. It's not the most likable idea in the world, but I don't see any other way to save what we've got. Conner's no prince. He'll try and make it as tough on us as he can. But maybe we can work something out. I say it needs trying, because it's a cinch we lose too much, any other way."

The argument broke loose again, and Garvin sat letting it wear itself out. He didn't think Gus was right. It meant somebody would have to stick his neck out, and that went against all his grain.

But he couldn't think of anything else to do. Gus was right about that part, at least. Matt had been hoping that giving it time would show some way out. Now he didn't know what to do, so, again by instinct, he was willing to let somebody else move. He looked across the table at Gus, who sat brooding at the blacked-out window, as if he could see the other buildings huddled in the night outside.

"Well, if we don't do *something*," Jack Holland's sharp voice emerged from the tangle of words, "we can go down in history as a bunch of people who almost got things started again but didn't make it."

"I don't give no damn for history," another man said. "But I got five kids, and I want 'em to eat."

And that about settled it, Garvin thought. But none of them could honestly call it anything except a bad bargain. Especially Gus and he, for it would be they who would have to go out and talk to Conner.

"Almost Christmas," Gus said in a low, brooding voice. He and Garvin stood at the window, the blankets pulled aside now that the men were gone and the lamps were out. "Peace on Earth, good will to men. Oh, little town of Stuyvesant, how still we see thee . . ." He snorted. "A hundred years from now, they'll have Christmases. They'll have trees, and tinsel, and lights. And I hope the kids play with toy tractors."

"I got Jim a stuffed bear," Garvin said. "What'd you get for Ted?"

Gus snorted again. "What do you get any four-year-old? Books with lots of pictures—Carol wants to start his reading pretty soon. A wooden toy train—stuff like that. That's for a four-year-old. When he's a year or two older, we can start explaining how come the books don't mean anything, and the train's a toy of something that just isn't, anymore. It's the question of what you get him then that bothers me."

Matt, too, found himself staring dull-eyed at the cold city as Berendtsen's mood communicated itself and seeped into his system.

Tomorrow would be better. Tomorrow was always better, for someone. The difficult task lay in ensuring that the someone was one of yours.

He had Jim, and one-year-old Mary. Moreover, Margaret was almost certain she was pregnant again. Gus and Carol had Ted.

The weight that rode Berendtsen's shoulders slumped Garvin's own.

"Think it'll work?" Gus said expressionlessly.

"Up a pig's tail, maybe," Matt answered.

Dawn slipped through the weave of the blankets over Garvin's bedroom windows, and he shook his mind free of sleep. He swung off his side of the mattress, shivering.

"Stove's gone out again, dear," Margaret mumbled sleepily from under the blankets.

"I know. I guess I forgot to fill it before I went to bed. Go back to sleep," he whispered, dressing hastily. She turned over, smiled, and buried her face in the pillow again. By the time he finished lacing his boots, she was asleep once more, and he chuckled softly at her faint snores.

He stopped to look in on the children before he went out to the kitchen to heat shaving water, and he lit the burner absently, staring down at the flame for a long while before he put the pan on. He walked quietly back to the bathroom with the pan in his hand, still bemused—less lost in thought than busy avoiding thought—washed, and shaved with a steady but automatic hand. He flushed the toilet with a pail of dishwater, filled and lit the stove, had breakfast, and finally sighed, pushed his dishes away, and stood up. He went over to the rough doorway that had been cut in the wall, and rapped on it lightly.

"Yeah, Matt," Gus answered from inside. "Come on in. I'm just knocking off another cup of coffee."

Garvin stepped inside, and sat down at Berendtsen's table. Gus was leaning on his elbows, his neck drawn down into his shoulders, both hands on the big cup of yellowishly weak coffee that he held just below the level of his chin, raising it to his mouth at intervals. They sat without speaking until Gus finally put the emptied cup down.

"Cold day," he said.

"Damn near froze in bed. Forgot to fill the stove," Matt answered.

Berendtsen sighed from far back in his throat. He got to his feet and picked up his rifle. He pulled a square piece of white sheet out of his jumper pocket and tied two of the corners to the rifle barrel.

"Got yours?" he asked.

"Inside," Matt nodded back toward his apartment. "Carol know what you're doing?"

Berendtsen shook his head. "Margaret?"

"No."

"I think now we should have told them," Gus said.

"I started to tell Carol—I don't know. The way I suddenly figured it, before I really said anything, was that it wouldn't make any difference in what happened. Figured she might as well get a good night's sleep, instead." He grinned wryly. "Turned chicken."

Matt nodded. "Yeah." He moved toward the doorway. "Me too. Well, let's get it done."

They went out through Matt's apartment, and made sure the other men were set at their covering positions in the windows that overlooked the next building. Then the two cowards went out into the cold.

They stepped out into the middle of the drive that separated the building from theirs, stopped, and looked up at the blank wall.

Garvin exchanged a glance with Gus. "What do we do now?" he asked.

Berendtsen shrugged. He held his white-flagged rifle more conspiciously, and Matt did the same. Finally, Gus threw his head back and shouted.

"Hey! Hey, you, in there!"

The echoes died on the air, and nothing moved.

"Hey! Conner! We want to talk to you!"

But somewhere in those banks of glass, there must have been a slowly opening window.

Behind them, in their own building, someone fired first, but it no longer mattered. It did not cause, but was a desperate attempt to prevent, the fire that suddenly burst from behind a half-dozen windows.

Because Matt had been half afraid it would come, the crash of fire was as shocking as the sudden collapse of his right leg. He fell on his side in the drive, his head cracking against the asphalt, and was completely unable to move for a frantic time that seemed fatally long. Then, finally, while the sniping from the enemy building was diverted by the heavier fire of his own men, he was able to use Gus's body for cover, pushing it ahead of him until he reached the shelter of a car. He stayed there till nightfall, freezing and bleeding, with his eyes unwaveringly on dead Berendtsen's face, while the sporadic fire continued over his head between the buildings. And gradually, through the long, long day until his men were able to get to him and take him back to his building, his eyes acquired an expression which they never quite lost again, which, for the rest of his life blazed up unpredictably to soften the voices of those around him.

Through his spasmodic sleep, Garvin heard the sobs. They rose, broke, and fell, and the beat of his quasi-delirium seemed to follow them. At intervals, as he shivered or strained his clamped jaw against the pain in his leg, he heard Margaret trying to calm Carol. Once, he himself managed to say "Easy there, Ted. I'll explain later, when I feel better. Look after your mother meanwhile, huh?" to a bewildered and frightened child. But, most of all, he could not escape his mind's indelible photograph of Gus Berendtsen's sprawled body.

When he woke fully, after seventeen hours, the shock reaction had ended. His leg hurt, but the wound had managed to stay clean, and the bones were obviously unbroken. He sat up and looked around.

Margaret was sitting in the chair beside him, watching him silently. He took her hand gently. "Where's Carol?"

"She's asleep, back in her apartment. Mrs. Potter's

taking care of her. Ted's with Jimmy." Her expression was peculiarly set, her face unreadable.

"What are you going to do about those people?" she asked.

He looked at her blankly, his mind still fuzzy, not catching her meaning immediately.

"What people?"

She had kept herself under rigid control up to now. Now she broke—characteristically.

"Those *savages*." Her face was still rigid, flexing only enough to let her lips move, but her voice cracked like a piano wire whip. "People like that shouldn't be *alive*. People who'd *do* a thing like *that!*"

Garvin dragged a long breath, letting it seep out slowly. A wave of pain washed up from his leg, and he closed his eyes for a moment. What could he say? That people were not savage by option? Already she had forgotten what it meant to the unorganized people of the area, having to compete with armed foraging teams.

His own mind was clear now. He had thought of another solution to the Conner problem.

For Margaret's sake—possibly for Carol's as well, and for the sake of young Ted, who had to somehow grow up in this world, and do his man's work in it— he was grateful that his next step now would be what it would.

He squeezed Margaret's hand. "I'll take care of it," he said somberly.

Hobbled by bandages, Garvin ran clumsily across the driveway with his men. The narrow space between the two buildings roared and echoed with the sleet of gunfire between the enemy and the covering guard in his building. Ahead of him, he heard the spasmodic and much lighter fire of his advance men as they cleaned out the enemy in the building's basements. He lurched under the shifting weight of the sack of dynamite sticks that he, like all the other men in his party, was carrying.

Holland, running beside him, put a hand under his elbow. "You making it okay, Matt? We would have handled this without you coming along."

Garvin spat out a laugh. "I'll have to touch it off." He passed the corner of the building and limped rapidly toward the entrance that would take him into the basement, where some of the men must already be placing their charges against the girders and bearing walls.

Margaret stared at him incredulously. *"Matt! All* those people. You killed all those people just because I said . . ."

He stood wordlessly in his living room, his vision blurring with each new thrust of pain up his leg, his shoulders down, the empty sack dangling from his hand. He rubbed his eyes wearily.

"Matt, you shouldn't have listened to me. I was upset. I—"

He realized he was swaying, but he did not try to control himself as strongly as he would have if any of his men had been present.

"I didn't do it because of anything you said," he tried to explain, the words blurring on his tongue. "I did it because it was the only way left. I had to order it and do it myself because I've got the responsibility."

"You had to kill those people?"

"Because there are more people. Take a look out some other window—out some window that shows you the rest of this city, with the buildings still standing."

"No, Matt, I can't."

"Have it your way, then." He dropped into a chair, looking down at the gummy stain on his coverall leg, wishing in his weariness, that it had been Gus, of the two of them, who had happened to stand slightly behind the other.

Another night fell, and Garvin stood at a window and watched it.

"Christmas Eve, Jack," he said to Holland, who was watching with him.

"Yes, sir."

Matt grunted, half ruefully. "Can't see it, can you, Jack?"

Holland hesitated, frowning uncertainly. "I don't know, sir. I can see it—I can understand the reasons for it, all right. But it doesn't . . ." He looked quickly at Garvin, obviously wondering whether it was safe to go on.

Matt chuckled again, more freely. "I won't eat you just because you tell me that what we did doesn't feel right. This is still a free republic." He gestured at the dark buildings, and his face twisted with regret. "Out there, it isn't, yet. But it's the same as it was when Gus and I knocked on your father's wall and told him what *his* choice was, the same way Gus knocked on my wall. Gus was wrong, that night after the ambush. He was right, but he was wrong. We *can* make them do things our way—if we knock louder than Gus ever thought we could make ourselves do." He turned away from the window and put his hand on Holland's shoulder.

"Better go change the downstairs guard, Jack."

He looked down at the moonlit rubble that had been the next building. He could almost read the sign that surmounted the tumble of brick, metal, glass, and flesh. "LEARN YOUR LESSON—COOPERATE—Matt Garvin, President, Second Free American Republic."

"Yes, sir," Holland said. He turned to go. "Merry Christmas, sir."

SECTION TWO

SECTION
TWO

PROLOGUE:

The ground in the foothills was rocky, covered by loose gravel, and treacherous. The car heaved itself up over a sharp ridge with torturous slowness and pancaked down on the other side with a hard smash. The steering levers whipped back and forth just short of the driver's kneecaps, and the motors raced.

"No more seeing, Joe," the driver told Custis. "Lights?"

"No. Bed 'er down, Lew."

The driver locked his treads, and cut the switches. The damper rods slammed home in the power pile, and the motors ground down to a stop. The car lay dead.

Custis slid down out of the turret. "All right, let's button up. We sleep inside tonight."

The driver dogged his slit shutters and Hutchinson, the machinegunner, began stuffing rags into the worn gasproof seal on his hatch. Robb, the turret gunner, dogged down the command hatch. "Load napalm," Custis told him, and Robb pulled the racks of fragmentation shells he'd been carrying in the guns all day. He fitted new loads, locked the breeches, and pulled the charging handles. "Napalm loaded," he checked back in his colorless voice.

"Acoustics out," Custis said, and Hutchinson activated the car's listening gear.

Henley, standing where the twin .75s could pound his head to a pulp with their recoiling breeches, asked: "What're you going to do now, Custis?"

"Eat." Joe broke out five cans of rations, handed three to the crew and one to Henley. "Here." He squatted down on the deck and peeled back the lid of the can. Bending it between his fingers, he scooped food into his mouth. His eye sockets were thick with black shadow from the overhead light. His face was tanned to the cheekbones, and dead white from there to the nape of his recently shaved skull. The goggles had left a wide outline of rubber particles around his eyes. "We'll see all the bandits you want in the morning."

"You mean you've made us sitting ducks on purpose?"

"I mean if I was a bandit I wouldn't talk to nothin' but a sitting duck, and I'm under contract to let you talk to some bandits."

"Not from a position of weakness!"

Custis looked up and grinned. "That's life, Major. Honest, that's the way life is."

"There's somebody," Custis said at daybreak. He stepped away from the periscope eyepiece and let Henley take his look at the soldiery squatted on the rocks outside.

There were men all around the battlewagon, in plain sight, looking at it stolidly. They were in all kinds of uniforms, standardized only by black-and-yellow shoulder badges. Some of the uniforms dated two or three Republics back. All of them were ragged, and a few were completely unfamiliar. West Coast, maybe.

Or maybe even East.

The men on the rocks were making no moves. They waited motionless under the battlewagon's guns. At first glance, the only arms they seemed to have were rifles that had to be practically smoothbores by now— and it had taken Custis a while to find out why these men, who looked like they'd known what they were doing, were trusting in muskets against a battlewagon. There were five two-man teams spread in a loose circle around the car. Each team had an M-14 fitted with a grenade launcher. The men aiming them had them elevated just right to hit the car's turtledeck with their first shots.

"Black-and-yellow," Henley said angrily.

Custis shrugged. "No blue-and-silver, that's true," he answered, giving Henley the needle again. "But that was thirty years ago. It might still be Berendtsen."

Custis went back to the periscope eyepiece for another look at the grenadiers. Each of them had an open, lead-lined box beside him with more grenades in it.

Custis grunted. Napalm splashed pretty well, but it would take one full traverse of the turret to knock out all five teams. The turret took fifteen seconds to revolve 360 degrees, while a grenadier could pull a trigger and have a grenade lofting in, say, one second's time. A few seconds later the grenade would have covered the outside of the car with radioactive dust that would make it death to stay inside, or death to get out. Nor could the battlewagon get out of the grenade's way in time—the basis of an interdictory weapon like this was that it would be used as soon as you made the slightest move, but, you could believe, no sooner than that.

"Stalemate," Custis grunted. "But no worse than that. Generous of 'em." He unbuckled his web belt and took off his .45. He walked under the command hatch and undogged it.

"What're you doing?" Henley demanded.

"Starting." He threw the hatch back and pulled himself up, getting a foothold on the saddle and climbing out on top of the turret. He flipped the hatch shut behind him and stood up.

"My name's Custis," he said carefully as the men raised their rifles. "Hired out to the Seventh Republic. I've got a man here who wants to talk to your boss."

There was no immediate answer. He stood and waited. He heard the hatch scrape beside him, and planted a boot on it before Henley could lift it.

"What about, Custis?" a voice asked from off to one side, out of range of his eyes. The voice was old and husky, kept in tight check. Custis wondered if it might not tremble, were the old man to let it.

He weighed his answer. There was no sense to playing around. Maybe he was going to get himself killed right now, and maybe he wasn't, but if he played games here he might never get a straight answer to anything.

"Theodore Berendtsen," he said. "About him."

The name dropped into these men like a stone. He saw their faces go tight, and he saw heads jerk involuntarily. Well, the British had stood guard over Napoleon's grave for nineteen years.

"Turn this way, Custis," the same worn voice said.

Custis risked taking his eyes off the grenadiers. He turned toward the voice.

Standing a bit apart from his troops was a thin, weather-burned man with sharp eyes hooded under thick white eyebrows. He needed a shave badly. His marble-white hair was shaggy. There were deep creases in his face, pouches under his eyes, and a dry wattle of skin under his jaw.

"I'm the commander here," he said in his halting voice. "Bring out your man."

Custis stepped off the hatch and let Henley come out. The political officer gave him a savage look as he squirmed up and got to his feet. Custis ignored it. "Over there—the white-haired one," he said without moving his lips. "He's the local boss." He stepped a little to one side and gave Henley room to stand on the sloping turret top, but he kept watching the old commander, who was wearing a pair of faded black coveralls with that black-and-yellow shoulder badge.

Henley squinted up toward the thin figure. The back of his neck was damp, even in the chill morning breeze, and he was nervous about his footing.

"I'm Major Thomas Henley," he finally said, "direct representative of the Seventh North American Republic." Then he stopped, obviously unable to think of what to say next. Custis realized, with a flat grin, that his coming out cold with Berendtsen's name hadn't left the major much room to work in.

"You're out of your country's jurisdiction, Major," the commander said.

"That's a matter of opinion."

"That's a matter of fact," the commander said flatly. "You and Custis can come down. I'll talk to you. Leave the rest of your men here."

Henley's head turned quickly. "Should we go with him?" he muttered to Custis.

ALGIS BUDRYS

"Lord, Major, don't ask *me!* But if you're plannin' to get anywhere, you better talk to somebody. Or do you expect Berendtsen to plop down in your lap?"

Henley looked back at the thin figure on the hillside. "Maybe he already has."

Custis looked at him steadily. "They shot Berendtsen in New York City thirty years ago. They threw what was left of his body on a garbage heap. And a year later there was a tomb over where they threw it."

"Maybe, Captain. Maybe. Were you there?"

"Were you?"

Custis felt annoyed at himself for getting so exercised about it. He glared at the major. Then his common sense came trickling back, and he turned away to give Lew his orders about keeping the car sealed and the guns ready until he and Henley got back.

Thirty years dead, Berendtsen was. Judged for treason, condemned, killed—and men still quarreled at the mention of his name. Custis shook his head and took another look at the old, dried-out man on the hill, wearing those patched, threadbare coveralls.

Most of the commander's men stayed behind, dispersed among the rocks around the silent battlewagon. Ten of them formed up in a loose party around the commander and Henley, and Custis walked along a few yards behind the two men as they started off into the mountains.

It was turning into a bright but cool day. Looking up into the west, Custis could see the mountaintops pluming as high altitude gales swept their snow caps out in banners. The track they were walking on wound among boulders higher than Custis's head, and he felt vaguely uncomfortable. He was used to the sweeping plains where his father had raised him; where, except for the spindly trees along the sparse creeks, nothing stood taller than a man.

The commander's base was a group of low, one-room huts strung out along the foot of a butte, with a cook-fire pit in front of each one. Their outlines were broken by rocks and boulders piled around them. There were prepared slit-trenches spotted around the area, two machinegun pits covering the approach trail, and a few mortar batteries sited on reverse slopes. From the size of the place and the depth of the organization, Custis judged the commander had about four hundred people in his outfit.

Custis wondered how he could keep them all supplied, and the answer he got from looking around was that he couldn't do it very well. The huts were dark and dingy, with what looked like dirt floors. A few wan-looking women were carrying water up from a spring, balancing pails made out of cut-down oil cans. They were raggedly dressed, and the spindly-legged children that trotted beside them were hollow-eyed. Here and there, among the rocks, there were a few patches of scraggly garden. Up at one end of the valley, a small herd of gaunt cows was grazing on indifferent grass.

Custis nodded to himself. It confirmed something he'd been thinking for a couple of years; the bandits were still crossing the plains to raid into Republican territory, but they'd never dared set up their own towns on the untenable prairies. It was an impossible thing to have every man's hand against you and still try to make the change to a settled life.

But with women and children, the bandits needed

a permanent camp somewhere. So now they were pulled back all the way into the mountains, trying to make a go of it, but with their weapons wearing out. They were dying on the vine, something left behind, and by the time the cities started spreading out their holdings again, there'd be little here to stop them. If the cities could ever get themselves organized. Maybe everything was dying. The legendary East and South were too far away to count. Maybe everything that counted was dying.

"In here," the commander said, gesturing into a hut. Henley and Custis stepped inside, followed by two men with rifles and then the commander. The hut was almost bare except for a cot and a table with one chair, all made out of odd pieces of scrap lumber and weapons crates. The commander sat down facing them with his veined, brown-mottled hands resting on the stained wood.

Custis spread his feet and stood relaxed. Henley's hands were playing with the seams along his pant legs.

"What about Berendtsen, Major?" the commander asked.

"We've heard he's still alive."

The commander snorted. "Fairy tales!"

"Possibly. But if he's still alive, these mountains are the logical place for him to be." Henley looked at the commander meaningfully.

The commander's narrow lips twitched. "My name isn't Berendtsen, Major. I don't use his colors. And my men don't call themselves The Army of Unification."

"Things change," Henley answered. "I didn't say

you were Berendtsen. But if Berendtsen got away from New York, he'd have been a fool to stay near there, or use his own name anywhere. If he's in these mountains, he might not care to advertise the fact."

The commander grimaced. "This isn't getting us anywhere. What do you want from me?"

"Information, then, if you have it. We'll pay for it, in cash or supplies, whatever you say, within reason."

"In weapons?"

Henley paused for a moment. Then he nodded. "If that's what you want."

"And to blazes with what we do to the people in the independent towns? I suppose so. What about your own people in the outlying areas, once we're re-armed?"

"It's important that we have this information."

The commander smiled coldly. "There's no pretense of governing for anyone's benefit but your own, is there?"

"I'm loyal to the Seventh Republic. I follow my orders."

"No doubt. All right, what do you want to know?"

"Do you know of any groups in this area that Berendtsen might be leading?"

The commander shook his head. "No. There aren't any other groups. I've consolidated them all. You can have that news gratis."

"I see." Henley smiled for the first time Custis had ever seen. It was an odd, spinsterish puckering of the lips. The corners of his eyes twinkled upward, and gave him the look of a sly cat. "You could have made me pay to find that out."

"I'd rather not soil myself. A few rusty rifles pulled

out of the old armories aren't worth that much to me."

Henley's mouth twitched. He looked at the austere pride on the commander's face, gathered like a mask of strength and youth on the gray stubbled cheeks, and then he said: "Well, if I ever do find him, I'm empowered to offer him the presidency of the Eighth Republic." His eyes glittered and fastened like talons on the old commander's expression.

Custis grunted to himself. He couldn't say Henley had exactly surprised him.

And the old man was looking down at the tabletop, his old hands suddenly clenched. After a long time, he looked up slowly.

"So you're not really working for the Seventh Republic. You've been sent up here to find a useful figurehead for a new combination of power."

Henley smiled again—easily, blandly—and looked like a man who has shot his animal and only has to wait for it to die. "I wouldn't put it that way. Though, naturally, we wouldn't stand for any one-man dictatorships."

"Naturally." One corner of the commander's lip lifted, and suddenly Custis saw Henley wasn't so sure. Custis saw him tense, as though a dying tiger had suddenly lashed out a paw. The commander's eyes were narrowed. "I'm through talking to you for the moment," he said, and Custis wondered how much of his weakness had been carefully laid on. "You'll wait outside. I want to talk to Custis." He motioned to the two waiting riflemen. "Take him out—put him in another hut and keep your eyes on him."

And Custis was left alone in the hut with the old commander.

110

The commander looked up at him. "That's your own car out there?"

Custis nodded.

"So you're just under contract to the Seventh Republic—you've got no particular loyalty to the government."

Custis shrugged. "Right now, there's no tellin' who I'm hired out to." He was willing to wait the commander out and see what he was driving at.

"You did a good job of handling things, this morning. What are you—about twenty-nine, thirty?"

"Twenty-six."

"So you were born four years after Berendtsen was killed. What do you know about him? What have you heard?"

"Usual stuff. After the plague, everything was a mess. Berendtsen put an army together, took over the territory, made the survivors obey one law, and strengthened things out that way."

The commander nodded to himself—an old man's nod, passing judgment on the far past. "You left out a lot of people between the plague and Berendtsen. And you'll never imagine how bad it was. But that'll do. Do you know why he did it?"

"Why's anybody set up a government? He wanted to be boss, I guess. Then somebody decided he was too big, and cut him down. Then the people cut the somebody down. But I figure Berendtsen's dead, for sure."

"Do you?" the commander's eyes were steady on Custis.

Custis tightened his jaw. "Yeah."

"Do *I* look like Berendtsen?" the commander asked softly.

"No."

"But hand-drawn portraits thirty years old don't really mean anything, do they, Custis?"

"Well, no." Joe felt himself getting edgy. "But you're not Berendtsen," he growled belligerently. "I'm sure Berendtsen's dead."

The old commander sighed. "Of course. Tell me about Chicago," he said, going off in a new direction. "Has it changed much? Have they cleaned it up? Or are they simply abandoning the buildings that're really falling down?"

"Sometimes. But they try and fix 'em up, some-times."

"Only sometimes." The commander shook his head regretfully. "I had hoped that by this time, no matter what kind of men were in charge . . ."

"When's the last time you were there?"

"I was never there. But I've seen a city or two." The commander smiled at Custis. "Tell me about this car of yours. I used to be quite fond of mechanized equipment, once." Now he was an old man again, dreaming back into the past, only half-seeing Custis. "We took a whole city once, with almost no infantry support at all. That's a hard thing to do, even with tanks, and all I had was armored cars. Just twenty of them, and the heaviest weapons they mounted were light automatic cannon in demiturrets. No tracks—I remember they shot our tires flat almost at once, and we went bumping through the streets. Just armored scout cars, really, but we used them like tanks, and we took the city. Not a very large city." He looked down at his hands. "Not very large, no. But still, I don't believe that had ever been done before."

"Never did any street fighting," Custis said. "Don't know a thing about it."

"What do you know, then?"

"Open country work. Only thing a car's good for."

"One car, yes."

"Hell, mister, there ain't five cars runnin' in the Republic, and they ain't got any range. Only reason I'm still goin' is mine don't need no gasoline. I ran across it in an old American government depot outside Miles City. Provin' grounds, it was. My dad, he'd taught me about runnin' cars, and I had this fellow with me, Lew Gaines, and we got it going."

"How long ago was that?"

"Seven years."

"And nobody ever tried to take it away from you?"

"Mister, there's three fifty-caliber machineguns and two .75s on that car."

The commander looked at him from head to foot. "I see." He pursed his lips thoughtfully. "And now you've practically handed it to me."

"Not by a long shot, I ain't. My crew's still inside, and it's kind of an open question whether you're ready to get your troops barbecued just for the sake of killing us and making the car no good to anybody."

The commander cocked an eyebrow at him. "Not as open as all that."

"Open enough. You set it up so we can both pull back from each other if that turns out best; if we come to some kind of agreement."

"You're here. Your crew's down the mountain."

"My crew's just as good without me, Mister."

The commander let it ride, switching his tack a

little. "You'll admit you've come to a peculiar place for a man who only knows open country work."

Custis shrugged. "Car needed shopwork. Chicago's the only place with the equipment. If I use their shops, I do their work. That's the straight up and down of it. And it's one more reason why gettin' the car'd be more work than it was worth to you. Anything you busted on it would stay busted for good. And you know it. You're so fond of cars, where's yours? Wore out, right? So now you're walkin'."

"Horses."

"Horses!"

The commander smiled crookedly. "All right. It takes a good deal to budge you, doesn't it, Custis?"

"Depends on the spot I'm in. My dad taught me to pick my spot careful."

The commander nodded again. "I'd say so. All right, Custis, I'll want to talk to you again, later. One of my men'll stay close to you. Other than that, you're free to look around as much as you want to. I don't imagine you'll ever be leading any expeditions up here—not if Henley's plans work out. Or even if they don't."

He turned away and reached under the cot for a bottle, and Custis hadn't found out what the old commander was driving at.

Outside, they were cooking their noon meal. The camp women were huddled around the firepits, bent shapeless as they stirred their pots with charred, long wooden spoons, and the smell of food lay over the area near the huts in an invisible cloud that dilated Custis's nostrils and made his empty stomach tighten up. Whatever these people ate, it was hot

114

and smelled different from the sludgy meat in the car's ration cans.

Then he shrugged and closed his mind to it. Walking upwind, he went over to a low rock and sat down on it. One of the commander's riflemen went with him and leaned against a boulder fifteen feet away, cradling his rifle in the crook of one thin arm and looking steadily at Custis through coldly sleepy eyes.

A bunch of kids clustered around the fires, filling oil cans that had crude handles made out of insulated wire. When they had loaded up they moved out of the little valley with a few riflemen for escort, carrying food out to the men who were in position around the battlewagon. Custis watched them for a while, then ignored them as well as he could.

So Henley was working for a group that wanted to set up the next government. It wasn't particularly surprising that the Seventh Republic was financing its own death. Every government was at least half made up of men from the one before. They played musical chairs with the titles—one government's tax collector was the next government's chief of police—and whoever wasn't happy with the graft was bound to be figuring some way to improve it the next time the positions moved around.

It looked a hell of a lot like, however the pie was cut, Custis wasn't going to get paid. The Seventh wouldn't pay him if he didn't come back with Berendtsen, and if he did find him the Eighth wouldn't hold to the last government's contract.

Custis twitched his mouth. Anyhow, the car was running as well as you could expect. If he got out of here, Kansas City might have a job for him. He'd heard rumors things were happening down there. It wasn't familiar territory, and there were always rumors that things were better somewhere else, but he might try it. Or he might even head east, if the highways over the mountains were still any good at all. That could be a real touchy business all around, with God knew what going on behind the Appalachians, and maybe an organization that had plenty of cars of its own, and no use for half-bandit plains people. Going there wouldn't be the smart thing to do. As a matter of fact, he knew, inside, that he'd never leave the northern plains, no matter how he reasoned. It was too risky, heading for some place where they were past needing battlewagons.

He wondered how the boys in the car were making out. He hadn't heard any firing from over there, and he didn't expect to. But it was a lousy business, sitting cooped up in there, not knowing anything, and looking out at the men on the rocks as time went by.

When you came right down to it, this was a lousy kind of life, waiting for the day you ran into a trap under the sod and the last thing you ever did was try to climb out through the turret while the people who'd dug the hole waited outside with their knives. Or wondering, every time you went into one of the abandoned old towns on the far prairie, where supposedly nobody lived, if somebody there hadn't found some gasoline in a sealed drum and was waiting to set you on fire.

But what the hell else could a man do? Live in the damned cities, breaking your back in somebody's jackleg factory, eating nothing that couldn't be raised or scavenged right on the spot—and not much of that—

living in some hole somewhere that had twelve flights of stairs before you got to it? Freezing in the winter and maybe getting your throat cut for your coat in some back alley?

Custis shivered suddenly. To hell with this. He was thinking in circles. When a man did that, he licked himself before he got started.

Custis slid off his rock, stretched out on the ground, and went to sleep thinking of Berendtsen.

CHAPTER FOUR:

This is what happened to Theodore Berendtsen when he was young, having grown up in the shadow of a heap of rubble with a weathering sign on top of it. That was all he had in the way of a portrait of his father. And this is what he did with it:

Ted Berendtsen opened the hatch and shouted down over the growl of the PT boat's engines. "Narrows, Jack."

Holland nodded, typed the final sentence of his report with two bobbing fingers, and got up. "What's the latest from Matt?"

"Nothing new. I just checked with Ryder, on radio watch."

Holland scrambled up on deck, stretching his stiff muscles. "Man, next time Matt sends out a mission, somebody else can go. I've *had* PT's."

Ted nodded sourly. "I've had Philadelphia, too," he growled in conscious imitation of Jack's voice. For the hundredth time, he caught the faint smile on Jack's lips, and resolved, for the hundredth time, to stop his adolescent hero-worship. Or at least to tone it down. "Brotherly love. Wow!"

He flushed. Boyish excitability was no improvement.

Holland grunted and ran his eyes over the bright machine-gunned scars in the deck plywood. He shook his head. "That's a tough nut down there."

Ted nodded solemn agreement, instantly stabbed himself with the realization of solemnity, flushed again, and finally shrugged his mental shoulders and, for the hundredth time, gave up on the whole problem of being sixteen. Instead, he watched the shoreline slip by, but soon found himself unable to resist Manhattan's lure. The skyscraper city bulked out the horizon in front of him, windows flashing in the sun.

He knew Holland was watching the look on his face, and he cursed himself for being conscious of it just because Holland had gotten him his first man-size rifle and taught him how to use it.

"Damn, it's big," he said.

Jack nodded. "Big, all right. Wonder how much more of it's joined up since we left?"

"Not the West Side, that's for sure."

"Those boys aren't ever likely to budge," Holland said.

Ted nodded. Too solemnly, again.

Matt Garvin put the report down and sighed. Then he looked past Ted at Jack Holland with the quick sharpness of a man who knows that the other will understand him perfectly. "People in Philadelphia aren't any different, are they?"

Jack smiled thinly, and Ted felt envy, as he always did whenever Jack and old Matt communicated in these sentences and short gestures that represented paragraphs of the past. He ruthlessly stifled a sigh of his own. When he and Jack had boarded the PT boat, a month before, he had vaguely hoped that something—some uncertain ordeal by fire or inconcise overwhelming experience—would give him that intangible which he recognized in Holland as manhood. He had hoped, as the PT growled slowly down the Jersey coast, that some sort of antagonist would put out from the shore or rise from the sea, and that, at the conclusion of the harrowing struggle, he would find himself spontaneously lean of cheek and jaw, carelessly poised of body, with automatically short and forceful sentences on his lips. But nothing had changed.

"What do you think?" Matt asked him.

The question caught him unaware. He realized he must have looked ridiculous with his absent gaze snapping precipitously back to Matt Garvin.

"About Philadelphia?" he said hastily. "I think we'll have a hard time with them, Matt."

Garvin nodded. "Which would mean you think we're bound to run into those people sometime, right?"

"Ahuh." He caught the smile on Jack's lips again, and cursed inwardly. "Yes, I do," he amended. Damn, damn, *damn!*

"Any special reason why you think so?"

Ted shrugged uncomfortably. He thought about his father less than he should have, probably. He only vaguely remembered the big man—bigger than life-size, doubtless, in a child's eyes—who had been so friendly. If he had seen his death, perhaps, he would have that missing thing to fill out his inadequacy—a cause, passed down, to be upheld and to which he could dedicate himself. But he had not seen his father die. Of it all, he remembered only his mother's grief, still vaguely terrifying whenever too closely thought of.

He stood hopeless before Matt Garvin, with only reasoning to justify him. "I don't know exactly, Matt," he stumbled. "But they're down there with Pennsylvania and New Jersey in their laps whenever they need them. They're going to be crowding up this way in another twenty-five, thirty years. All we've got's Long Island, and it's not going to be enough to feed us by them. We're stuck out here on this island. They could pinch us off easy." He stopped, not knowing whether he'd said enough or too much.

Garvin nodded again. "Sounds reasonable. But this report doesn't show any organization down there. How about that?"

Ted glanced quickly at Jack. If Holland hadn't covered that in his report, it could only have been because he shared Ted's opinion that the true situation was self-evident. The thought occurred to him that Garvin was testing his reasoning.

He felt even more unsure of himself now.

"Well," he said finally, "I can't think of anything about Philadelphia that would make people down there much different from us. I don't see how they could have missed setting up some kind of organization. Maybe it works a little different from ours, because of some local factor, but it's bound to be basically the same." He stopped uncertainly. "I'm not making myself clear, am I?" he asked.

"It's all right so far, Ted. Go on," Garvin said, betraying no impatience.

"Well, it seems to me," Ted went on, some of his inward clumsiness evaporating, "that you'd have a tough time spotting our kind of organization if you just took a boat into the harbor, like we did in Philly. Chances are, you wouldn't run across our radio frequency. If you landed on the West Side, you'd run into the small outfits in the warehouses. Even if you happened to pick the organized territory—I don't know; if somebody came chugging up the river, I wouldn't be much likely to trust him, no matter what he tried to say. It's the same old story. You can't join up with anybody, anymore, unless it's on your own terms. There's been too much of our hard work and fighting done to keep our organization going. It doesn't really matter whether they've had to do the same for themselves. Each of us is in the right, as far as we're separately concerned. And it'd be a lot nicer, for us, if we were the ones who came out running things, because that's the only way we could be sure all that work of ours hadn't been for nothing."

He stopped, thinking he'd finished, but as he did, another thought came to him.

"It'd be different, if there were a lot of things to negotiate about. Then there'd be room to talk in. I guess, maybe, if we keep organizing, we'll work our way up to that point. But right now, it's a pretty clear-cut thing, one way or the other. Nobody's any better off than anybody else—if somebody was, we'd of heard from them by now. Looking at it from our viewpoint, then, it's a lot better for our organization if we do all the deciding on who joins up with us. So, if somebody from outside comes nosing around, the best thing to do is just discourage him." He broke off long enough to grin crookedly. "They sure discouraged us down at Philly.

"All we ever saw of Philadelphia itself was the waterfront. I'd say that almost anything could be going on down there, and we couldn't spot it. You'd have to go deep into the town itself, into the residential area. The same way that somebody coming into Manhattan would have to get to the lower East Side. And I guess we're pretty sure no stranger's going to get that chance."

"Hmmm." Garvin was grinning at Jack, and Holland was smiling back. Ted stood awkwardly, looking from one to the other.

"All right, Ted," Garvin said, turning back to him. "Looks to me like you kept your eyes open and your brain working."

Faintly surprised, Ted acknowledged to himself that he probably had. But he'd devoted no special effort to it, and he'd certainly done nothing else to distinguish himself. The brief engagement in Philadelphia's harbor had offered none of the many hoped-for opportunities to shed his adolescence. All in all, he didn't know how to answer Matt now, and he was deeply grateful that no answer seemed to be expected.

"I guess that's it, Ted. You might as well go home. Margaret'll have supper going by now. Tell her I'll be along in a while, will you? You and Jack take it easy for a day or two. I'll be giving you something else to do pretty soon."

"Right, Matt. See you tonight." That, too, he thought, had been too crisply casual. He noticed that Jack had started to say something himself—probably the same thing, in effect, and had stopped abruptly, with that same half-concealed, knowing smile at Garvin. Damn, damn, *God* damn!

* * *

"Well, that's that," Holland said outside Matt's headquarters. He stretched luxuriously, his eyes grinning. He slapped Ted's shoulder lightly. "I'll see you tomorrow," he said, and walked off, his stride catlike, easily holding his slung rifle straight up and down with the heel of his hand against its butt.

Ted smiled. Jack had been cooped up on the boat for a month. The adjective "catlike" was as easily applied to his frame of mind as to his walk. Ted smiled again. Ruefully.

He hitched his own rifle sling higher up on his shoulder and walked determinedly toward the Garvins' apartment.

Ever since his father's death, Ted and his mother had more or less been staying with the Garvins. Their apartments adjoined, and up to the time that Ted had earned the right to carry his own rifle, both families had been equally under Matt's protection. Ted had been raised with Jim and Mary Garvin—discounting Bob, who was five years younger than Ted, and therefore even more useless than Mary as a companion. Recently, of course, Mary had been acquiring greater significance, even if she was only thirteen. She seemed to him admittedly more mature of mind than other girls her age, most of whom Ted ignored completely.

He bent over and tightened the mounting screws on his rear sight with careful concentration.

"You mean they had a *machinegun?*" Mary asked breathlessly.

"Ahuh." He shrugged casually, and made sure the windage adjustment was traveling freely but precisely. "Had a bad time for a couple of minutes there." He pulled out the bolt assembly and squinted at the already immaculate walls of the chamber.

"What did you do then? I'd have been awfully scared."

He shrugged again. "Turned around and ran. It looked like only a couple of guys, but it smelled like more. No telling what they might have backing them up." He slipped the bolt back in and worked it a few times, spreading the lubricant evenly. "Tell you the truth, I kept thinking about those mortars Matt's got down by the river. No reason for them not to be set up the same way. Anyway, we pulled out. Ryder was on the portside turret—that's the left—and he hosed them down a little. Knocked them out, I guess, because we were still in range and they didn't do anything about it." He ran the lightly oiled rag over all of the rifle's exposed metal, set the safety, and slid in a freshly loaded clip. As he looked up, Jim caught his eye and winked, looking sidelong at Mary. Ted's cheeks reddened, and he shot a steely glance at his friend.

"Well, I guess I'll turn in," he said lightly. His mother had gone inside a few moments before. He stretched and yawned. He slung the rifle on his shoulder. "Good night, everybody."

"Good night, Ted," Mrs. Garvin smiled, looking up from her sewing. "G'nite, Ted," Jim said cuttingly.

"Good night, Ted," Mary said. He raised his hand in a short, casual wave to her and walked through the connecting doorway, the heel of his hand resting easily against his rifle's butt.

"Ted?"

He winced faintly as he closed the door behind

him. "Yes, Mom," he said quickly, before the apprehension in her voice could multiply itself.

She came into the room, standing just inside. "Of course it's you," she said with a nervous smile. "I don't know who I thought it'd be."

"Well, there's the bogeyman, and then there's ghoolies and ghosties . . ." He let his mock gravity trail off into a smile, and her face smoothed a little.

"Can I get you some tea or something?" he asked, putting the rifle up on the rack he'd hung beside the door.

"Why, yes, thanks. Are you going to sleep now?"

"I guess so. I'm pretty tired," he said on his way to the kitchen.

"I made your bed. Your room's just the way you left it."

"Thanks, Mom," he said, letting himself smile with tolerant tenderness, in the kitchen where no one could see him.

He brought the cupful of tea out to her, and she took it with a grateful smile. "It's good to have you home again," she said. "I rattled around in here, all by myself."

"There's all those Garvins next door," he pointed out.

She smiled lightly. "Not as many for me as there are for you. The kids get a little noisy sometimes, for my taste. Matt's busy all day, and he goes to sleep almost as soon as he eats. And Margaret's not as good company as she used to be." Her smile grew worried. She's getting awfully gloomy, Ted. Matt's in his forties, and he's still carrying his rifle with the rest of the men. What would happen if he died?"

126

"I guess he's got to, Mom. It's his responsibility. If he couldn't handle it, somebody else would be running things. He's doing a good job, too. I haven't heard many complaints about it."

"I know, Ted. Margaret knows too. But that doesn't help, does it?"

"No, I suppose not. Well, there isn't anything we can do about it, the way things are." He bent over and kissed her cheek. "Going to stay up for a while?"

She nodded. "I think so, Ted. Good night."

"Good night, Mom."

He went down the hall to his room, undressed, and blew out the lamp. He lay awake, his eyes closed in the darkness.

It was a hard life, for the women. He wondered if that was why Jack Holland wasn't married. He was twenty-nine already.

Damn. Thirteen more years.

Matt was either forty-two or three. Old Matt, who wouldn't be so old in any other time and place. Old Matt must have been young, nineteen-year-old Matt sometime, trying to stay alive in the first few months after the plague. The vague plague, that nobody knew much about because he could only know what had happened to him or those with him, and had no idea what it had been like all over the world.

All over the world. There must be thousands of places like Manhattan, scattered out among the cities, with men like Matt and Jack in them, trying to organize, trying to get people together again. And, more than likely, there were thousands of guys like Ted Berendtsen, who ought to cut out this pointless mental jabbering and get some sleep, right . . . now.

"Man, I'm not going to like this," Jim Garvin said as they loaded up their packs and jammed extra clips into their bandoliers.

Ted shrugged, smoking up his fore sight to kill glare. "Be crazy if you did. But it's got to be done faster than we figured, I guess."

"Pop say anything to you about it?"

Ted shook his head. "Nope. But that report Jack and I brought back from Philly is what did it. We've got to have this area squared away in case they move up on us. They know where we came from." He settled his pack snugly onto his shoulders, and twisted his belt to get the Colt's holster settled more comfortably. He didn't usually carry a pistol, but this was going to be close-range work, once they flushed their men out from cover. The thing weighed a ton.

"S'pose you're right," Jim admitted.

Ted frowned slightly. Jim should at least have thought of the obvious question, as long as he was in a questioning frame of mind. He'd wondered about it himself, until he realized that the attempt to take all of the lower West Side in one operation had to be made. Just perhaps, the slow process that had worked on the East Side could be modified to fit, and there was time enough, more than likely, but that territory had been completely impenetrable for twenty years. The men in it knew every alley and back yard. Any attempt to take it piecemeal would mean an endless series of skirmishes with infiltrators.

Of course, he had a year and some months on Jim.

"Set?" Jack Holland came up to them, his pack bulging with ammunition, dynamite, and gasoline bombs, his rifle balanced in his hand. Ted nodded shortly, and was vaguely surprised to hear Jim say, "Yes, sir." He looked from Jim to Jack, and barely twitched an eyelid. Jack grinned faintly.

"Okay, then, let's get formed up. Matt's taking the financial district, swinging up from the Battery. We go straight across town. Bill McGraw and another bunch are going in just below Forty-second Street." He grinned and gestured perfunctorily and ribaldly. "That's us—Lucky Pierre."

Jim laughed, and Ted chuckled, winking at Jack again. The kid had been showing his nerves a little.

The three of them crossed the street to where the rest of the men in their group were waiting, scattered inconspicuously among the cars and doorways from old, vital habit. Ted looked up at the sky. It was growing dark. They'd move out pretty soon.

Jack dropped back and walked beside him. "Make sure Jim sticks pretty close to you, huh?" he said in a low voice. "I won't be able to keep much of an eye on him myself."

"Sure," Ted answered. "I'll take care of him."

For two nights and three days, what had once been the lower half of Hell's Kitchen had been tearing itself open. From that first cold morning when they had come out of their positions and dynamited their way into a packing plant, the slap of rifle fire and the oc-casional bellow of heavy sidearms had swept and echoed down the cluttered streets and wide, deadly avenues. Building by heavy building, they had blown gaps in walls, smashed windows, and shot their way from room to room in the first rush of surprise. Here and there, a firebomb had touched off a column of smoke that twisted fitfully in the breeze and light rain that had begun falling on the second day and was still coming down. A steady stream of runners was carrying ammunition up to them, and they supplied themselves from whatever miserable little they found, while scavenger squads cleaned up the weapons and ammunition left behind by corpses.

Two days, three nights. They had started on the uptown side of Fourteenth Street, with covering squads to clean out the downtown side and leave them a clear supply route.

They had reached Eighteenth Street by nightfall of the third day.

Ted slumped his head back against a wall and fed cartridges into a clip. "How's it, Jim?"

Jim Garvin rubbed his hand over his face and shook his head in a vague attempt to clear out some of the weariness. "It stinks."

Ted put the full clip in his bandolier and started on another. He grinned faintly. "Yeah," he agreed. "You see Jack today?"

"Nope. Think he's still around?"

"Chances are. He was doing house-to-house when we were just tads, remember?" He opened his pack and threw Jim a can of meat. "Tie into this, huh? I've been saving some. The slop they've been eating here is enough to make you sick."

Jim shuddered and exhaled through his clenched teeth. "God, isn't it just? All these bloody warehouses around here, too." He opened the can and dug into it gratefully.

"A stinking set-up. Everybody just hung on to what they had, and to hell with you, buddy. Remember that bunch that'd been gettin' no vitamins except out of canned fruit?"

"No organization at all," Jim agreed. "What the hell's wrong with these people?"

Ted shrugged. "Nothing, I guess. But they had a bunch of forts all ready made for them. These freakin' warehouses were built to take it. And besides, they were warehouses. Up to the roof in supplies. Guess it looked like the simple way out."

"How long d'you think we'll be at this mess?"

"Depends. If Matt cleans up his end, we'll get a push from him. If McGraw comes down, we'll have 'em squeezed. I'd like it best if both happened, but I don't know—that Greenwich Village is a rat-trap, from what I hear, and McGraw's bound to be having it just as tough as we are. I wish I knew how this whole operation was going."

"So long as Pop's all right, I don't give a hoot and a whoop for the rest of the operation. The part I worry about is right here."

"Yeah, but the whole thing ties together," Ted explained.

"That's for somebody else to worry about," Jim said.

Ted looked at him thoughtfully. "Yeah. Guess you're right." For the first time, the thought struck him that it didn't look as if Jim was going to take over when his father left off. He was a good man with a rifle, and he never stopped after he started. But he didn't do his own worrying.

That jarred him, somehow. He didn't like the thought, because Jim was a friend of his, and because he was a first-grade fighting man, just like his father.

Only being a fighting man wasn't good enough any more. It was a bigger sphere of operations now. New factors were coming into the picture all the time. This entire move against the West Side was not a foraging expedition, or an organizing process, though both would result. It was primarily a strategic maneuver against the day when Philadelphia began to move up the coast. Matt had started out a rifleman and learned, bit by bit, at the same pace with which the world grew more complicated. But Jim wouldn't have that time to learn by practice what he didn't understand by instinct. He was too young, and Matt was too old to give him that time.

What the hell, this was supposed to be a republic, wasn't it? A republic lived by developing different kinds of leaders as it needed them.

But he didn't like the idea, nevertheless. He'd have to think it over, think it out, before he could accept it.

"Might as well get some sleep, Jim," he said. "Looks like we've closed up the big shop for the night. I'll take the first watch."

"Okay." Jim rolled over gratefully, and pillowed his head on his arms. Ted checked the action on his .45, which had jammed on him twice already. He handled the truckhorse of a gun distastefully. The only good thing about it was the same thing that was good about Matt's magnum rifle, which he wouldn't handle either. The things kicked like bombs, burned out their barrels, took nonstandard ammunition, were nuisances to maintain, and had all the subtlety of a club. But hit a man anywhere at all on his body with a bullet from one of them, and hydrostatic shock would knock him out, if not kill him. Which, to Ted's mind, was rarely an advantage. There was no point in killing a potentially good man if you could put him out of action some other way.

None of which instruction-manual thinking, Ted reflected, was really effective in keeping him from worrying about his big problem. He was beginning to understand why Jack Holland had never really teamed up with Jim on any job. Once you considered things in the proper light, all sorts of evidence began turning up.

Jack Holland. He hoped it would be Jack Holland who would be taking over from Matt, when the inevitable time came.

A week, now. Jack had finally had to abandon the planned straight-forward sweep, block by parallel block, and had sent his right flank out to clean up as many of the uptown blocks east of Ninth Avenue as it could. On that side of what had become the border of the warehouse gangs' territory, the Republic's men had made contact with McGraw's group—Ryder's now —which had executed a duplicate movement. But, effectively, as far as the warehouse gangs were concerned, Garvin's forces were bogged down at Nineteenth Street and Thirty-first Street, with only minor penetrations into the periphery west of Ninth Avenue. Matt's personal forces were moving slowly out of Greenwich Village, with isolated pockets still to be mopped up in the almost ideal defensive positions that twisted alleys and cross-streets provided. But there, too, the actual core of resistance had hardly been bruised, for almost all the heavily built docks, warehouses, and docked ships were still holding out.

Somehow, Ted had acquired a squad of his own from men who had fallen in with him. They were apparently willing to follow his suggestions without debating them, and, as long as he didn't seem to be making costly mistakes, he was perfectly willing to let it ride that way. They certainly weren't hindering him and Jim any. All of them were heavily stubbled and ragged by now, and none of them had had much sleep. The latter probably fogged their judgment, and the former operated in his favor as well, since his own beard, augmented by grime, was enough to hide the boyish roundness of his face.

But the ammunition was running low.

His head dropped forward and he jerked it up again, coming out of his doze. Jack twisted a grin at him. "Kinda tiresome, ain't it?"

Ted grunted. "What d'you hear on the box?" he said, motioning toward the radio.

"Ryder's coming down, Matt's coming up. We're going west. Speed: six inches per hour."

"They tried that stunt with the PT's?"

Holland snorted. "Ever try to torpedo a warehouse? They knocked out most of the freighters in the channel, which doesn't help us a goddamned bit."

"We've got to crack those birds soon, Jack."

"I know. We'll be firing Roman candles at them if this keeps up. You got any ideas?"

"No." He dozed off again, leaning on a garbage can.

Ten days, and he reached his conclusion. It was not an idea, he recognized, no more than Austerlitz or the shelling of Monte Cassino were ideas. It was a calculated decision based on the problem before him, reached in the light of the urgent necessity for the problem's solution. Again, as with many of his recent decisions, he did not like it when he came to it. But it was the product of logical extrapolation, based on rational thinking and personal knowledge which he could honestly believe he had analyzed completely. Once he recognized this last, he knew he had given himself no choice.

"Problem is to get in close enough to dynamite the warehouses, right?" he said to Jack.

"Ahuh. Been that way for some time, now. They've got those boys on the roofs of the houses all around them. They can cover them, and the lads in the houses keep us back. We clean out a house, they toss dynamite down and blow the house to shreds, leaving an exposed area we can't cross anyway. Can't go in at night, because this is their territory, booby-trapped. So?"

"Wait for an east wind. Get one, and burn the houses. Go in under the smoke. Blow your way into the first floor, sit back, and wait for them to come out. They don't come out, blow the second floor."

Holland whistled. He looked at Ted thoughtfully. "Kind of mean, isn't it? The guys in those houses get it either way—they come out while we're waiting in the street, or they burn."

"Jesus Christ!" Jim said, staring at Ted.

Berendtsen swayed wearily on his feet. Suddenly, he realized that he had done something neither Jack Holland nor Matt Garvin's son were capable of. He had reached a decision he hated, but would carry out, given the opportunity, because he knew that whether it was right or wrong on some cosmic balance scale, he believed it to be right. Or, not right—necessary. And he could trust that belief because he trusted himself.

"All right," he said, his voice calm, "let's get on that

135

radio and talk to Matt. We've got an old precedent for all this, you know," he added dryly.

He led his sooty, weary men back along the broad length of Fourteenth Street, his left hand lost in a bulbous wrapping of bandage, his empty pack flapping between his shoulder blades. He and Jim and the rest of his squad were lost in the haphazard column of Matt Garvin's men, but his mind's eye separated his own from the rest. All the men were shuffling wordlessly up the street, weary past the bone, but he tried to read the faces of his squad. There had been many more men in the firing and dynamiting parties, but these had been the ones he led.

He tried to discover whether the men who followed him thought he was right or wrong. But their faces were blank with exhaustion, and he could not let his own expression disclose the slightest anxiety. And then he realized what the hard part of being a man was.

When they reached Stuyvesant at last, he found Matt Garvin. They looked at each other, he with his wounded hand and Matt with a shoulder almost dislocated by the magnum's repeated detonations. He drew one corner of his mouth up crookedly, and Matt nodded and smiled faintly.

Now I know, Berendtsen thought.

Silently, Ted Berendtsen walked up the stairs while Jim hung back. He ran his hand over his jaws, and his cheeks, under their temporary gauntness, were just as soft. His feet stumbled on the steps.

Jesus Christ, I'm only sixteen! he thought. He grimaced faintly, at this last, illogical protest. Matt had a few more years.

CHAPTER FIVE:

Matt Garvin had grown old, for his time. His oldest son, Jim, was twenty-two, and his daughter, Mary, was twenty. His youngest son, Robert, was a little past fifteen. And the civilization he had seen re-established now held all of Greater New York.

It was enough. He could sit at his window, looking out over Stuyvesant Town where the building generators had put lights back in the windows, and nod slowly to himself. It was done. Up and down the coast, where his scouting boats had wandered, he knew there were other cities shining once more beside the broad ocean. In those cities there must be other men like himself, satisfied with what they had accomplished. Soon, now, the cities would spill over—the pocket civilizations would touch and coalesce, and the plague would be forgotten, the land and the people whole again.

Out in the inlands, each isolated by the broken strands of transportation and communication, there would be other cities, all flickering back to life. And in the farmlands between them, where life had not really changed, there would be other men waiting to join hands with them.

He spoke about it, hesitantly, during a meeting with

his most important lieutenants. And Ted Berendtsen looked up.

"You're right, Matt. It'll happen, and soon. But have you thought about what's going to happen when it does?"

Jim Garvin looked up sharply. No, his father hadn't thought about it. Not in detail. Neither had he.

Berendtsen was finishing his point. "We're not just going to puddle up by osmosis, you know. Somebody's going to have to build pipelines. And when we get that puddle—who's going to be the big frog? Somebody'll have to. We can't just all live happily ever after. Somebody still has to lead. What guarantee do we have that we'll enjoy it?"

Jim sighed. Berendtsen was right. They were not one people, separated, now reuniting. They were half-a-hundred, perhaps more, individual civilizations, each with its own society, each with its own way of life. It would not be an easy, or a happy, process.

Matt Garvin looked at Jack Holland and shrugged his shoulders heavily. "Well, what's your answer to it all, Jack?"

Jim Garvin saw Jack Holland's side-glance at Ted before he said anything, and nodded quietly to himself. It wasn't Holland who was really second in command, it was Berendtsen, young as he was.

"I don't know," Holland said. "Seems to me that it's about time for a lot of outfits like ours to be spilling over into the surrounding territory, yeah. But it's going to be a long time before whatever happens around Boston or Philadelphia makes itself felt up here. They're doing the same thing we are—pushing out and looking for land to grow food on. We're out on Long Island, busy farming. Philly'll be doing the same thing in its own corner. So will Boston and Washington. It'll be years before we grow up to the size where we'll need more territory. They're even smaller. They'll take more time. By then, we'll be farther along. We'll always be stronger than they are."

Berendtsen shook his head, and the gesture was enough to draw everyone's attention. "Not quite the whole problem," he said.

Matt sighed. "No, I guess it isn't. How do you read it?"

"Our scouting reports from Boston indicate that New England's having the same old problem. You can't farm that country worth a damn. There's a good reason why that was all manufacturing country up there—you can't feed yourself off the land. There's nowhere near the population up there that there used to be, of course, but they're still going to be spreading out faster than anybody else. They'll have to. They need four acres to our one.

"Now—Philly's in a bad spot. They're down on the coast with Baltimore, Washington, and Wilmington right on their necks. That's besides Camden. They won't move up here until they're sure of being safe from a push coming up from below. They can handle that three ways—lick the tar out of those people, bunch up with them in some loose alliance against us, or—and this is what I'm afraid of—start building up for a fast push in this direction *before* those other cities get set. Once they've got a lock on us, they can concentrate on holding off anybody else."

He leaned forward. "Now. We've already assumed that whatever happens, we want our side on top."

Something jumped in Jim Garvin's solar plexus.

They had, hadn't they? It had already become a question of "How do we get them to do things our way?" But what other way was there? A man worked for himself, for what was his. A society—an organization of men—did the same. You fought for what was yours.

"All right, then," Berendtsen said. "If Philly moved up here, and took over, I'd join them. So would everybody else. It wouldn't be our society any more, but at least it would be *a* society. We'd get used to it in time, if we had to.

"The same thing works in our favor. If we take over another outfit, their citizens'll join up with us. They may not like it. Some individuals will be holdouts to the bitter end. But, as a whole, that group will become part of us.

"Think it over."

Berendtsen's voice and expression had been completely neutral. He spoke as though he were reading off a column of figures, and when he stopped he settled back in his chair without any change of manner.

Matt nodded slowly. "I think you're right. In general, and about Boston and Philadelphia. Both those outfits are being pushed. They'll be moving faster than we will."

Jim looked around again. Holland was nodding softly, and he himself had to agree.

He looked at Berendtsen, once again trying to understand what made his brother-in-law tick. There didn't seem to be a fast answer, even though they had grown up together. He could guess what Ted would do in a particular circumstance, but he could never really get down to the basic motivation that made him do it. Somehow, he doubted if Mary could do any better. Both of them could penetrate his calm, withdrawn shell along certain fronts, but the whole Theodore Berendtsen—the man who lived in the whipcord body with the adding-machine mind —escaped them with unconscious elusiveness.

What does it? he thought. What was there hidden behind his brooding eyes that pulled each problem apart and allowed him to say "Hit it here, here, and there. Get that, and this part'll collapse and let you get at the rest of it," as coldly as though it were a piece of physical machinery to be stripped down and rebuilt until it functioned smoothly and without effort.

And now there was something new in the wind. Jim shot a fresh glance at his father. Matt was half-twisted in his chair, racked by arthritis. His right hand was almost completely useless. And if his mind was still clear, his eyes tired but alert, Ted's thinking was just as straight, and he was out in the city every day, directing Ryder in the absorption of the neighboring New Jersey cities, while he himself cleaned out the Bronx and lower Westchester.

Jim looked up and caught Jack Holland's eye. They grinned wryly at each other and then turned their attention back at Ted.

"There's only one thing to do," Berendtsen said, still not raising his voice. "No matter how fast they get set, down in Philadelphia, it'll be two years at least before they come up this way. There's no sign that Trenton's anything but an independent organization yet.

"We need supplies. We need heavier weapons, more tools, more machinery. We need men who're used to handling them. And we've got to nip Boston in the bud. We can't stand to get caught between two forces."

141

Holland stiffened in his chair. "You want to push up into New England now?"

Ted nodded. "We've got the men. They're used to the idea of fighting aggressively, instead of just defending their personal property. They've got it through their heads that the best security lies in putting as much distance as possible between our frontier and their families. They've learned that a cooperative effort gets them more food and supplies than individual foraging.

"We'll pick up more recruits as we go along. I don't care what kind of set-up they've had up to now, ours is bigger. We can feed 'em and take care of their families better than anyone else."

"That's an awful lot of fighting," Matt said.

"It doesn't have to be," Ted answered. "We'll make the usual try at getting them to join us peacefully."

Matt looked steadily at Gus Berendtsen's son and said nothing, but Ted nodded slowly back, with a crooked smile on his face. "We'll make the attempt, Matt."

Jim looked at Holland, and Jack looked thoughtfully back. He was right, again. They'd have to make examples of the first few local organizations, but after that they'd be able to progress smoothly until they reached Boston. And, by then, their forces would have grown large enough to carry out the plan. Once they had New England to back them up, Philadelphia was no menace.

They both looked up and saw Matt's eyes searching their faces. Jim saw Holland nod slowly, and then he nodded himself, because Ted was right.

Yes, Jim thought, he was right. Again. He had the answer, and there was no denying it.

"There's going to be a lot of killing," Jim said, but it was just for the record. What record, he didn't know.

Berendtsen's face softened, and for one moment Jim thought he had somehow managed to learn how to read minds. "I know," he said gently, and it took a few seconds for Jim's flash of irrationality to pass and for him to realize that Ted had been answering his spoken question.

"Well, what'd the great young white father come up with this time," Bob asked him, his voice sarcastic.

Jim looked at his younger brother wearily. "Just a couple of ideas on what we're going to do next."

But the vagueness of the answer didn't discourage Bob, and Jim realized that all he'd done was to offer him bait.

"Yeah? When's he taking over?"

"For Sweet Willie's sake, will you get off this kick and leave me alone!" Jim exploded.

"No," Bob said, "I will not leave you alone." The back of his own neck was red, but his eyes were snapping with some sort of perverse joy at having gotten under Jim's skin. "You may not enjoy thinking, but I'm going to force your daily quota down your throat anyway. Berendtsen's moving in on Dad as fast as he can, and you know it. He got his smell of power when he butchered his way through the West Side and he's been aching for a chance to repeat the performance on a bigger scale. And you and Jack just sit there and let him push Dad around as much as he damn well likes!"

Jim sucked in a breath and looked steadily at Bob

for a full minute before he trusted himself to speak. In the back of his mind, he admitted that he was a little afraid of these increasing verbal battles with his brother. Bob had read a lot of books, and he was constantly poking and prying around the city, camping in libraries for weeks at a time, or bringing the books home in his pack, carefully wrapped and handled more tenderly than his carbine. When Bob talked, words fit smoothly into words, building nets of step-by-step assertions that could snare a man in his own fumbling until he found himself running down into foolish silence while Bob just stood there and gibed at him with his eyes, cutting him with the slash of his grin.

"In the first place . . ." he began, forcing the words out against the barrier of Bob's obvious patient waiting until he left an opening to be attacked through, "Ted's brains are what gives him the right to sit in on meetings. He belongs there a hell of a lot more than I do, let me tell you! In the second place, Ted did *not* butcher his way through the West Side—he helped to take care of one small part of it. And I know damn well he didn't enjoy himself, because I was with him—which you weren't, sonny. And if he gets an idea that's going to make life safer for all of us, we're damn well going to follow it. Dad's getting old and we might as well face it. *He* listens to Ted, and so does Jack Holland. Personally, if Ted wants to push north—"

He stopped and stared helplessly at Bob, whose eyes had widened and who was half-laughing at him for giving himself away.

"All right, so he *does* intend to lead a force toward

144

Boston. So what? His reasons are damn good ones!" Jim blurted, trying to bolster his position.

"I'll bet they are," Bob said, and turned away as though he had won the argument conclusively, leaving Jim standing there fighting off the unfounded conviction that he really had.

"James Garvin, I'll thank you to stop cursing at your brother," his mother said angrily from the doorway.

"I was not . . ." Jim began, and then blew the breath out of his throat and shrugged hopelessly. "All right, Mom," he said, and went past her into the apartment with an apologetic look that was strongly tinged with frustration. He hung up his rifle and went to his room, where he sat down on the bed and stared angrily at the wall until dinner time.

Ted and Mary were eating with them that night, and through the first part of the meal, Jim sat uncomfortably between his father and Bob, hoping the present silence would continue but knowing that this was extremely unlikely with Bob in the mood he was. Ted was eating quietly, and Mary, sitting beside him, was her usual controlled self.

Jim bit off a piece of cornbread viciously, drawing an amused side-glance from Bob, who, as usual, missed nothing going on around him and who was probably enjoying the situation considerably.

Finally his father pushed his plate awkwardly away and looked up. "Jim, I suppose you've told your mother and Bob about what we decided at the meeting today?"

Jim grimaced. "I didn't get a chance to tell Mom.

Bob's got it all figured out for himself, of course."

His father shot him a quick, surprised, yet understanding look which was gone immediately as he turned to look inquiringly at Bob. Jim noticed that Ted was still eating with even, wasteless motions, finishing the last of his supper, and not looking up.

"Well, what do you think, Bob?" Matt asked.

Bob raised an eyebrow and twitched his eyes to Ted before he looked back at his father. "Are you sure it's all right for me to think while Big Chief's here to do it for me?"

Oh, no! Jim thought, wishing a thunderclap would come to erase the entire scene. Even his mother looked at Bob with complete astonishment. Jim didn't dare look at his father.

Ted looked up without seeming to be surprised at all. "Sounds like that's been building up a long time, Bob," he said quietly. "Want to tell me about it?"

Jim sighed as quietly as he could, feeling the shocked tension drain out of his father's body beside him. His mother, too, relaxed, and Mary, who had put down her fork and looked evenly at Bob, started eating again.

He took over, Jim thought. Ted had absorbed the force of Bob's explosion and removed its impact from them all, and now it was his responsibility, and his alone. And while Matt Garvin held his eyes riveted on his younger son, and no matter what he might feel, he did not speak.

Bob held his eyes level with Ted's, but Jim could see it was an effort. Finally, he said, "Yes, it has." His voice was low, but taut and desperate, and for one brief moment Jim caught a flash of what he must be feeling. He had thrown a stone into a pond, made an unexpectedly insignificant splash, and was now somehow in over his head. Jim wanted to smile grimly, but realized that this was no time for it.

"Yes, it has," Bob repeated, his voice rising. "I've been sitting here watching you take over in all directions, and I think it stinks!" His breathing was harsh, his face scarlet. He had put himself in an impossible position, and there was no direction in which to go but forward.

Ted nodded slowly. "I think you're right."

And, once again, Bob was helpless.

"I think you're right because I don't think anybody should be in my position," Ted continued, still without changing the quiet level of his voice. "Unfortunately, I seem to have grown into it."

"*With* a lot of force-feeding!" Bob shot back, recovering.

Ted shrugged, letting an uncharacteristic sigh seep out between his closed lips. "That's the nature of the times, Bob. If you're implying that I'm exercising some sort of pressure, I'd like to ask you where you think I got the authority to back it with. Rather than accept that premise, I'd say that the times are such that they produce the pressure which forces one man to make more decisions than another man. There's a certain step-by-step logic, inherent in human nature and the peculiarities of human psychology, which ensures that Man will always organize into the largest possible group. Civilization is inevitable, if you want a pat phrase. It so happens that, at this stage, we are in transition from a city-state to a national culture. Such a move always requires that the separate elements be welded into one by force. I'd like to remind you that Greece was nothing but a collection of enlightened but small, ineffectual, and squabbling city-states until the advent of Philip of Macedon."

Bob saw his opening. His mouth curved into its characteristic thin crook of a smile, and his voice gathered confidence again.

"Heil Berendtsen!"

Ted nodded. "If you want it that way, yes. Though I'd prefer—if that's the word—an analogy to Caesar. And if you think I enjoy the thought—" His voice hardened for the first time, and Jim paled as he saw something of the restless beast that prowled Ted's mind of nights, "—then, Bob, I'd suggest that you read your Gibbon more thoroughly."

"Very pretty," Bob answered. "Very pretty. Destiny has chosen a son, and all the stars point to Berendtsen! Thank you, I'll stick to Hitler."

"I'm afraid you're stuck with me," Ted said, and finished his peas.

"Why, you *egocentric*—"

"Robert, you'll go to your room and stay there!" his mother exclaimed, half-rising, her cheeks flushed. "Ted, I'm very sorry about all this. I don't know what to say."

Ted looked up. "I wasn't simply being polite when I said he was right, you know."

Margaret Garvin looked as bewildered as Bob had. "Well. Well," she fumbled, "I don't know. . . ."

"Suppose we just finish supper," Matt said, and for a moment Jim hoped he would be obeyed. But Bob pushed his chair farther back and stood up.

"I don't think I particularly care to eat here right now," he delivered, and strode out of the apartment.

"Forgot his carbine," Jim commented, glad of the opportunity to say something at last.

Ted looked at him, his lips twitching into a thin smile. "Wouldn't go too well with his attitude right now, would it?"

"Guess not," Jim admitted. He dropped his eyes to his plate, realizing that he had learned something about Ted Berendtsen today, but was still unable to see what it was that let him project the force of his calm authority as though it were a physical strength.

Jim looked up again, and saw Ted staring across the room at the blank wall, his eyes as old as Matt's, who was trying to reach across the length of the table and silently explain to Margaret with his expression alone.

"You ought to give him a district to run, pretty soon, Matt," Berendtsen said unexpectedly. He smiled at Matt's astonished look. "He uses his head."

Matt snorted—a somehow painful sound. The sound a man makes when he condemns something dear to him.

"It's still a republic," Ted reminded him. "I'd rather have him argue with me than have him sit there nodding dumbly. Right now, he's learning to think. Give him a little practice, and he'll be ready to learn how to think past his emotions. Don't forget, we're going to need administrators by the dozens."

Matt nodded slowly, some of his lost pride in his son returning. "I'll see."

"Do you suppose he was right?" Mary asked, looking gravely at her husband.

Jim turned his glance toward his sister. Her remark was completely characteristic. She sat quietly for hours, watching and listening, and what went on in her mind, perhaps Ted Berendtsen alone could guess. Perhaps not even he. And then finally, she said a few words much as she had now.

"Heil Berendtsen? I don't know," Ted admitted. "I don't think so—but then, a man can't tell when he's going paranoid, can he?"

And Jim caught another glimpse of the special hells that Berendtsen reserved for himself.

Boston was easy, by the time they came to it. They occupied the suburbs, isolating the city proper, and Matt sent a light naval force to control the harbor. The news of how Providence had fallen must have reached the city, for the opposition was light. It was not so much the overwhelming weight of Berendtsen's men that forced the surrender—it was the far more crushing power of the past year's bloody history. By the time they reached Boston, it was the dead, more than the army's living, who fought Berendtsen's battles.

An army they were, by now; The Army of Unification, no longer simply "the New York bunch." Men from Bridgeport and Kingston marched with them, beside others, now, from Lexington and Concord.

James Garvin, Sergeant-Rifleman, stood on a hilltop with his corporal, a lean-jawed, pipe-sucking man named Drumm, and watched the men forming up.

"The Army of Unification," Drumm said, his face reflective. "Another one of your brother-in-law's casually brilliant ideas. No regional tag, and a nice idealistic implication. No disgrace to be beaten by it, since it's an 'army,' and much easier to convince yourself into joining, since it has the built-in ideal of 'unification' to recommend it. You know, I'm more and more convinced that Berendtsen is one of your rare all-around geniuses."

Jim grunted and stuffed his own pipe full of the half-cured Connecticut tobacco he was gradually becoming accustomed to. He liked Drumm. He'd been a good man ever since he'd joined up, and he was somehow comfortable to talk to. "He does all right," Jim agreed.

Drumm smiled slightly. "He does a shade better than that." A reflective look crossed his face, and he turned his head to focus on the knot of officers clustered around Berendtsen's figure as he passed out orders. "I wonder, sometimes, what a man like that thinks of himself. Is he his own hero, or does he feel some gospel burning inside him? Does he perhaps think of himself as nothing more than a man doing a job? Does he shut out the signs that tell him some of his men hate him, and some love him? Does he understand that there are men, like us, who stand to one side and try to analyze every move he makes?"

"I don't know," Jim said. It was an old topic, and they found themselves bringing it up again and again. "My kid brother has a theory about him."

Drumm spat past his pipestem. "*Had* a theory—he's developed a dozen since, or he's false to type." He sighed. "Well, I suppose we have to have young intellectuals, if we're ever to survive to be middle-aged philosophers. But I wish some of them, at least, would realize that they themselves encourage the high mortality rate among them." He grinned wryly. "Particularly in these peculiar times. Well—" he nodded down at the men, "time to put it on the road again. Maine, here we come, ready or not."

Jim walked down the hill toward his platoon. Maine, here we come, he thought. And then back down the coast again, and home. And after that, out again, southward. The dirty, bitter, smoking frontier, and behind it, union. More and more, he could feel his own motives shifting from expediency to a faith in the abstract concept of a new nation, and civilization pushing itself upward again. But the dirt and the bitterness went first, and he and Harvey Drumm walked with it, following Ted Berendtsen.

They were deep in Connecticut on the backward swing, cleaning out a few pockets that had been missed, when Jack Holland, who was Jim's company commander now, came up to him.

Jack was still the same self-contained, controlled, fighting man he had been. His face, like Jim's, was burned a permanent brown, and he wore an old Army helmet, but he hadn't changed beyond that. His rifle was still slung from his shoulder at the same angle it had always held, and his eyes were steady. But his expression was set into a peculiar mask today, and Jim looked at him sharply.

"Ted wants to talk to you, Jim," he said, his voice unreadable. "You free?"

"Sure." Jim waved a hand to Drumm, and the corporal nodded.

"I'll keep their pants dry," he said, raising a chorus of derisive comments from the men.

"Okay, let's go," Jim said, and walked back beside Holland, who remained silent and gave him no opening to learn what had happened. They reached Berendtsen, who was standing alone without his usual group of officers waiting for instructions, and, once

152

again, Jim frowned as he saw that even Berendtsen's
mask was more firm than usual. There was something
frightening in that.

"Hello, Jim," Berendtsen said, holding out his hand.

"How's it going, Ted?" Jim said. The handshake was
firm, as friendly as it ever had been, and Jim wondered
if it had been his own attitude that made him think
they were far more apart than they once had been.

Berendtsen let a grim smile flicker around the corners of his mouth, but when it was gone his face was
sadder than Jim ever remembered seeing it.

"Bob just called me on the radio," he said gently.
"Matt died yesterday."

Jim felt the chill stretch the skin over his cheekbones, and he knew that Jack had put his hand on
his shoulder, but for those first few seconds, he could
not really feel anything. He could never clearly remember, through the rest of his life, exactly what that
moment had been like.

Finally he said, "How'd it happen?" because it was
the only thing he could think of to say that would
sound nearly normal and yet not snowball within
him into more emotion than he could hide.

"He died in bed," Berendtsen said, his voice even
softer. "Bob couldn't know what it really was. There
are so many things to go wrong with a man that
could be handled easily, if we had any trained doc-
tors. But all we have are some bright young men
who've read a lot of medical books and are too proud
to admit they're plumbers."

It was a sign of how much he'd thought of Matt,
that Ted should be openly bitter.

All the way back along the Hudson, Harvey Drumm

was the most important thing on Jim Garvin's mind.
Harvey Drumm, and something he'd said and done.

They had been bivouacked outside Albany. Jim
and Harvey had been leaning their backs against a
tree and smoking quietly in the darkness.

"Well," Drumm said at last, "you won't be seeing
me in the morning, I guess. That Sawtell boy in the
third squad'll make a good corporal. You can replace Miller with him, and move Miller up into my
spot. How's it sound?"

"Sounds fine for Miller and Sawtell," Jim answered.
"I'm not sure I like it. You going over the hill?"

Drumm sucked on his pipe. "Yes and no. You might
say I was going out to do missionary work."

That didn't make much sense. "You're crazy," Jim
said perfunctorily.

Drumm chuckled. "No. The only thing insane about
me is my curiosity. Trouble is, it keeps getting satisfied, and then I have to take it somewhere else. That,
and my mouth. My mouth wants to satisfy other
people's curiosity whether they want it or not. It's time
to take 'em both over the hill. Over the next range
of hills, maybe."

"Look, you know I'm your superior officer and I
could have you shot."

"Shoot me."

"Oh, God damn it! What do you want to get out
now, for? Ted's going to be taking the army lots of
new places. Don't you want to be along, if you're so
curious?"

"I know Ted's story from here on. I think maybe
he does, too." Drumm's voice no longer had anything
humorous in it. "I think maybe he read the same
books I did, after he realized what his job was. Not

that we go about it in the same way, but the source books *are* the same.

"See, you can learn a lot from books. They'll tell you simple, practical things. Things like what relationship a wrench has to a bolt, and what a bolt's function is. They won't tell you what the best way for *you* to hold a wrench might be, so *you* can do the best job. If you're any good, you can figure it out for yourself. And it's the same way with much more complicated things, too.

"You know, just before the plague, the United States was almost sure it was going to have a war with a country called the Union of Soviet Socialist Republics. At first they thought the principal weapons would be bombs. But after a while, the best opinion was that rather than wreck all the useful machinery, and poison the countryside for centuries, the weapons used would be bacteriological ones. Diseases. Short-term plant poisons. And crippling chemicals. To this day, nobody knows for sure whether the plague that hit us wasn't something designed to evade all the known antibiotics and bacteriophages—something that got away from somebody's stockpile, by accident. Everyone denied it, of course. I don't suppose that part of it matters.

"But just suppose somebody had written a book about what it would be like—*really* be like—for the people who lived through it. And suppose thousands of copies of that book had been lying around, out in the open in thousands of stores, for people to find after the plague.

"Think of the mistakes it might have saved them.

"That's what books are for. Books, and mouthy, curious people like me. We soak up a lot of stuff in our heads, while other people are too busy doing practical things. And then we go out, and give it to them as they need it.

"So I think I'm due to go off. There must be people out in the wide world who need somebody to tell 'em what a bolt does, and what a wrench does to a bolt."

"They'll shoot you as soon as you show up, most likely."

"So they'll shoot me. And then they'll never know. Their tough luck."

Jim Garvin sighed. "All right. Harv, have it your way."

"Almost always do."

"Where you headed?"

"South, I guess. Always hated the cold rain. South, and over the mountains. I don't figure Berendtsen'll have time to get to New Orleans. Shame. I hear it's a beautiful place."

"Well, if you're going, you're going," Jim said, passing over the Berendtsen part of what Harv had said. He'd be there himself to see about that. "I wish you weren't. For a mouthy guy, you make a good noncom."

"Sorry, Jim. I'd rather conquer the world."

They'd shaken hands in the darkness, and the last Jim Garvin ever saw of Harv Drumm, the long-legged man was walking away, whistling an old song Drumm used to sing around campfires, now and then. It was an old Australian Army marching song, he'd said: "Waltzing Matilda," it was called, and some of the words didn't make much sense.

* * *

156

"Well, what're you going to do?" Bob Garvin demanded, his mouth hooked to one side. The passage of a handful of years had not changed him.

Berendtsen looked at him coldly. "Take the army south. As soon as possible. Trenton's been taken over by the Philadelphia organization. You're more aware of that than I am. You got the original report."

Bob smiled thinly, and Jim, looking at him, winced. He tried to find some sort of comfort in his mother's expression, but she simply sat with her hands in her lap, her face troubled.

"Still a few worlds left to conquer, eh? Well, go and good riddance to you."

Mary looked up. "I don't think you should, Ted. You know as well as I do what he's up to. He got this man, Mackay, elected to Mayor. He's got half the minor administrative posts in his pocket. The reason he's so anxious to see you out of New York is because then he'll be able to take over completely."

Ted, like Mary, ignored Bob completely, and Jim smiled at his brother's annoyance.

"I'm sorry, Mary," Berendtsen said gently, "but this is a republic. Bob has every right to try and bring his group into a position of leadership. If the people decide they want him in, I have no right to block him with whatever prestige the Army might give me.

"And I *do* have to go out again. It's become increasingly clear to me that as much of the country has to be unified as possible. I do not especially like the techniques necessary to that unification, but the important thing—the one, basic, important thing—is the union. Everything else follows after. After that, it's up to the people to decide how that union's going to function internally. But first the unification must be made."

Mary shook her head in angry frustration, and, for the first time, Jim saw all the emotion she controlled beneath her placid surface.

"Aren't you sick of killing? Why do you hide behind these plans and purposes for tomorrow? Can't you, sometime, think in terms of *now*, of the people you are killing *now*?"

Ted sighed, and for one stark moment the mask fell away entirely, until even Bob Garvin turned pale.

"I'm sorry, darling. But I'm not building something for just *now*. And I can't think in terms of individual people—as you've said, I kill too many of them."

A silence that seemed to last for hours settled over them. Bob held the unsteady sneer on his face, but kept quiet. Jim looked at Berendtsen, who sat with his gaze reaching far beyond the open window.

Finally, Mary stood up awkwardly, her hands moving as though to grasp something that constantly turned and twisted just in front of her, there but unreachable.

"I—I don't know," she said unsteadily. "That's the kind of thing you can't answer." She looked at Ted, who turned his face up to her. "You're the same man I married," she went on. "Exactly the same man. I can't say, now, that I've changed my mind—that I'm backing out of it all. You're right. I've always thought you were right. But it's a kind of rightness that's terribly hard to bear. A man shouldn't—shouldn't *look* so far. He shouldn't work in terms of a hundred generations when he's only got his own to live. It's more than his own generation should be asked to bear."

"Would you like to call it off between us?" Ted asked gently.

Mary avoided his eyes, then bit her lip and faced him squarely. "I don't know, Ted." She shook her head. "I don't know myself as well as you do." She sat down, finally, indecisively, and looked at none of them.

"Well," Bob said. "What's *your* move, Jim?"

He'd been waiting for someone to get around to that, hoping illogically that the question would not be raised, knowing that it must. And he discovered that he was still afraid of his younger brother.

"What do you think, Mom?" he asked.

She looked helplessly at her two sons, her eyes uncertain. Her hands twisted in her lap.

"I wish I knew," she finally said. Her voice trembled. "When your father was alive," she burst out, "it was so easy to decide. He always knew what to do. I could understand him." She looked around helplessly again. "I don't understand any of you." She began to cry softly. "Do anything you like," she finished hopelessly, too bewildered to cope with the problem any longer.

So, in the end, the decision was given to him to face, without help from anyone. He braced his shoulders and met Bob's sardonic gaze. "I guess I'll follow Ted," he said.

The sun shone with a fierce, biting glare that stabbed from a thousand windows. Jim squinted up the column, the added reflection of the ranks of upraised rifles needling his eyes. He swung his head and looked up at the window where Mary and his mother were watching. Bob was somewhere in the crowd that stood on the sidewalks.

Through all the nights that he and Ted had spent in Berendtsen's old apartment, alone except for Ted's withdrawn, shadowlike mother, they had never talked. It had been as though one of the two of them had been a ghost, barely visible and never within reach.

Was it me, or was it Ted? he thought now. Or was it both of them, each locked in the secret prison of his body, each haunted in turn, each unable to share?

A whistle shrilled, and the truck engines raised their idling cough to a roar that seemed incredibly loud, here between the tall brick buildings.

"All right, move out!" Jim yelled to his men, and the first crash of massed footsteps came from the lines of men.

The army moved south.

SECTION THREE

PROLOGUE:

Custis had been asleep for about a half hour when somebody touched his shoulder. He turned over in one easy motion and caught the hand around the wrist. With his next move he was on his feet, and the girl's arm twisted back between her shoulder blades. "What's up, Honey?" he said quietly, putting just enough strain on her shoulder to turn her head toward him.

The girl was about eighteen or twenty, with a pale bony face and black hair hacked off around her shoulders. She was thin, and the top of her head came up to his collarbone. She was wearing a man's army shirt that bagged around her, and a skirt made by cutting off a pair of pants at the knees, opening the seams, and using the extra material to make gussets. The whole business was pretty crudely sewn, and came down to just above her dirty calves.

"I was bringing you something to eat, soldier," she said.

"O.K." He let go of her wrist, and she turned all the way around, putting the pail of stew down on the ground in front of him. There was a wooden spoon sticking up out of it. Custis sat down, folded his legs under him, and started to eat.

The girl sat down next to him. "Go easy," she said. "Half of that's mine."

Custis grunted. "The commander send you over here with this?" he asked, passing the spoon.

She shook her head. "He's busy. He always gets busy about this time of day, working on that bottle of his." She was eating as hungrily as Custis had, not looking up, and talking between mouthfuls.

Custis looked over toward the guard. The man was squatted down, with an empty dinner bucket beside him, scowling at Custis and the girl.

"That your man?" Custis asked her.

She looked up briefly. "You could say that. There's maybe six or seven of us that don't belong in anybody's hut. There's maybe fifty men without any families."

Custis nodded. He looked over toward the guard again, shrugged, and took the spoon from the girl. "The commander here—what's his name?"

"Eichler, Eisner—something like that. Anyhow, that's what he says. I was with the last bunch he took over up here, a couple of years ago. Never did get it straight. Who cares? Names come easy. He's the only commander we got."

So that didn't tell him anything. "What's your name?"

"Jody. You from Chicago, soldier?"

"Right now, yeah. Name's Joe Custis. You ever seen Chicago?"

She shook her head. "I was born up here. Never seen anything else. You going back to Chicago, Joe? Go ahead—finish that—I'm full."

Custis looked around at the cliffs and huts. "I figure I'll be getting out of here, maybe. Maybe Chicago's where I'll head for."

164

"Don't you know?"

"Don't much care. I live where my car is."

"Don't you like cities? I hear they've got all kinds of stores and things, and warehouses full of clothes and food."

"Where'd you hear that?"

"Some of the fellows here came out from Chicago, and Denver, and places like that. They tell me. But Chicago sounds like it's the best of all."

Custis grunted. "Ain't never been to Denver." He finished the stew. "Food's pretty good here. You cook it?"

She nodded. "You got a big car? Room for extra people to ride in?" She leaned back until her shoulder was touching his.

Cutis looked down at the stewpot. "You're a pretty good cook."

"I like it. I'm strong, too. I'm not afraid to work. And I shoot a rifle pretty good, when I have to."

Custis frowned. "You want me to take you to Chicago?"

The girl was quiet for a moment. "That's up to you." She was still leaning on his shoulder, looking straight out ahead of her.

"I'll think about it."

The guard had geen getting uglier and uglier in the face. Now he stood up. "All right, Jody, he's fed. Now get away from him."

Custis got slowly to his feet, using two fingers of his right hand to quietly push the girl's shoulder down and keep her where she was. He looked over toward the guard with a casual glance, and jumped him. He chopped out with his hands, and the rifle fell loose. Custis dropped the man, scooped up the rifle, and pulled out the clip. He worked the bolt and caught the extracted cartridge in mid-air. Then he handed the whole business back to the man.

"You tend to your job and I'll give you no trouble, son," he told him, and went back to where the girl was sitting. The guard was cursing, but by the time he'd reloaded the rifle he'd come to realize just how much Custis had done to him. If he didn't want the girl spreading his story all over the camp, his best move was to keep quiet from now on. He did it.

The girl looked sideward at Custis as he sat down again. "You always move that fast?"

"When it's gonna save me trouble, I do."

"You're a funny bird, you know? How come you've got that black smear around your eyes?"

"Rubber, off my goggles. Some of it's under the skin. Can't wash it off."

"You must of been wearing those goggles a long time."

"Ever since I was big enough to go along with my dad. He had a car of his own—full-track job. Found it, scroungin' around an old U.S. Army place called Fort Knox. That was back before everything got scrounged out. So he took the car and went out looking for people. What with one thing and another, he sort of got into working with people of one kind or another. I don't know where my mother is; couldn't be alive, I guess, if all I remember is being in the car with my dad.

"It wasn't a bad car. Too slow, though. On roads, I mean. We got caught that way in a town, once. This place was built around the only bridge standin' over the river, and we had to go through it. There was a couple of birds with a bazooka—anti-tank rocket launcher, is what that is—down at the far end of the town, behind some piled-up concrete. We opened up on them, but this car only had a 35-millimeter cannon. High velocity stuff, and that wears hell out of the riflin'. It was pretty far gone. We kept missing, and they kept trying to fire this bazooka thing. They must have had ten of the rockets that fit it, and one after another they was duds. One of them fired, all right, but when it hit us it didn't go off. Punched through the armor and got inside the car. The primer went off, but the charge was no good. The primer goin' off smoked up the inside of the car so bad we couldn't see. Dad was drivin', and I heard him trying to stay on the road. Then we hit something with one track—maybe they got us with another rocket—so we went around in a circle and flipped over sideways.

"Well, I crawled out and the car was between me and the birds with the bazooka. Then my dad crawled out. Both of us were busted up some, but our legs were okay. Meanwhile, these two birds were bangin' away with rifles. Dad and I, all we had was .45s. I figured the only thing to do was try and run for it, and I said so. Dad said the way to do it was to split up, or they'd get us both. And I couldn't see it, because if we got separated there was no tellin' when we'd get back together again. Well, Dad got this funny look on his face and gave me a shove away from him, and he started running. He yelled: 'Don't you waste me, hear?' and he was shooting at these guys. I got 'em both, later."

"Your dad must have been a funny kind of man."

Custis shrugged. He sat with the girl through the afternoon, making talk, until finally another rifleman came over to them from the line of huts.

167

He looked down at Custis and the girl, his eyes flicking back and forth once and letting it go at that. "This Henley fellow you brought wants to see you, soldier."

"What's his trouble?"

"I figured that's his business. He give me his wristwatch to come get you. I done that."

The man was a big, hairy type—bigger than Custis. But when Custis came smoothly to his feet, annoyance showing on his face, the rifleman took a step back. Custis looked at him curiously. The damnedest people were always doing that with him, and he had a hard time understanding it.

"I'll see you later," he said to the girl, and walked off.

Henley was pacing back and forth in his hut when Custis stopped in the dorway. He twitched his lips nervously. "It's time you got here. I watched you out there, lollygagging with that girl."

"Make your point, Henley. What'd you want to see me about?"

"What did I want to see you about! Why didn't you come here as soon as the commander released you? We have to make plans—we have to think this through. We have to decide what to do if our situation grows any worse. Hasn't it occurred to you that this man might be planning to do almost anything to us?"

Custis shrugged. "I didn't see any sense in getting all worked up about it. When he makes up his mind, we'll find out about it. No use making any plans of our own until we find out what his are."

Henley stared angrily at him. "Don't you care? Don't you care if you get killed?"

"Sure I do. But the time to worry about that was back on the plains."

"Yes, and you decided quite easily, didn't you?" Henley stared at Custis waspishly. "It wasn't very hard for you to risk all our lives." His eyes narrowed. "Unless— You *know* something, Custis. No man in his right mind would have acted the way you've acted unless you knew you weren't in any danger."

"That's a bad direction for you to think in."

"Is it? You drove up here like a man coming home. What do I know about you, after all? A freebooting car commander, off the same part of the plains where the outlaws run. Yes, I know you've worked for Chicago before, but what does that mean?" Custis could smell the hysteria soaking the officer's clothes. "You've sold us out, Custis! I can't understand how Chicago could ever have trusted you!"

"They must have, or I wouldn't of been hired for this job."

Henley gnawed his lip. "I don't know." He stopped and muttered down at the ground. "There are people who want my place for themselves. They might have planned all this to get rid of me."

"You're a damned fool, Henley."

Custis was thinking that, as late as a few years ago, he would have felt sorry for Henley. But since then he'd seen a lot of men go to pieces when they thought they might get killed. More of them died than would have if they'd kept thinking. It seemed to be something built into them. Custis had never felt it, and he wondered if there might not be something wrong with him. But, anyhow, Custis had learned it wasn't anything to feel one way or the other about. It was something some people did, and when you saw it you allowed for it.

Henley suddenly said: "Custis—if we get out of here, don't take me back to Chicago."

"What?"

"No, listen—they'll kill us if we go back without Berendtsen. Or maybe with him. Let's go somewhere else. Or let's stay on the plains. We can live off the country. We can raid farms. Put me in your crew. I don't care—I'll learn to shoot a machinegun, or whatever you want me to do. But we can't go back to Chicago."

"I wouldn't have you in my crew if I had to drive and fire the guns all by myself."

"Is that your final answer?" Henley's lips were quivering.

"Damned right!"

"You think you know all the answers!"

Custis growled: "Get a hold on yourself."

And Henley did it. He waited a moment, but then he stopped his pacing, and flicked one hand up to brush his perspired hair back into place. "I'll get out of this. You watch me—I'll get out and see you executed."

Custis said slowly, shaking his head: "Look, I want to get out of here just as much as you do. I think maybe I can. If I do, I'll try and take you along, because I got you into this. But if you can't stand the gaff, you shouldn't of come out here in the first place."

"Never mind the speeches, Custis. From now on,

I'll look after myself. Don't expect any help from me."

"Hey, you two," the rifleman said from the doorway, "commander wants you."

The sun was going down behind the mountains. It was still broad daylight farther up on the westward faces of the peaks, but the valley was filling with shadows. Custis followed Henley along the line of huts, feeling a little edgy in the thick gloom here at the base of the cliff, and wondering how all this was going to work out.

He watched Henley. The officer was walking in short, choppy strides, and Custis could see him working his self-control up to a high pitch. His face lost its desperate set, and the look of confidence came back to him. It was only if you knew what to look for that you could still see the panic in him, driving him like a fuel.

They reached the commander's hut.

"Come in," the commander said from his table, and Custis couldn't decide whether he was drunk on his home brew or not. The inside of the hut was so dark that all he could see of the old man was a shadow without a face. It might have been almost anyone sitting there.

Custis felt his belly tightening up. Henley stopped in front of the table, and Custis took a stand beside him.

"I'm glad to see you're still here, Custis," the old man said. "I was afraid you might be killed trying a break."

"I'm not crazy."

"I didn't think you were."

171

Henley interrupted. "Have you decided what you're going to do?"

The commander sighed. "Just why would you want Berendtsen back, Major?"

"Then, he's available?"

"Just answer the question, please. We'll do this my way."

Henley licked his lips. Custis could hear the sound plainly. "Well," the political officer finally said in a persuasive voice, "there's been no hope of stability anywhere since he was deposed. Governments come and go overnight. A constitution isn't worth the paper it's written on. We've never been under Berendtsen's rule, but his law stood up better than most. We need something like that in Chicago—the whole upper Middlewest needs it." Now that he'd gotten started, he was talking much more easily. "Paper money's so much mouse-stuffing, credit's nonexistent, and half the time your life's at the mercy of the next man's good will. We don't have a society—we have a poorly organized rabble. If Berendtsen's still alive, we need him. He's the only man anyone'll follow with any enthusiasm."

"Follow a corpse?"

"Follow a name—a legend. A legend of a time when there was civilization in the world."

"Do you really believe that, Henley?"

"Of course!"

"Oh, you believe that it'll *work*—you can see how a crowd would fall into line, believing it. But you realize, don't you, that if Berendtsen were to take over Chicago, the first thing he would do is order you and your gang hung."

Henley gave it one more try. "Would he? If we

172

were the ones who gave him the opportunity to come back and finish what he'd begun?"

"I don't think Ted Berendtsen would have shown that kind of suicidal gratitude. No."

"Then you won't do it?"

"I'm not Berendtsen."

"Then, who is? Do you know where he is?"

"Berendtsen's been dead thirty years," the old man said. "What in heaven's name did you expect? If he was alive—and he's not—he'd be sixty years old now. A man that age, in this world—your whole scheme's fantastic, Major, and rational men would know it. But you can't let yourselves think rationally about it. You need your Berendtsens too badly."

"Then that's your final word?"

"I want to ask Custis something, first. You stay and listen. It'll interest you."

Custis frowned.

"Custis?"

"Yes, sir?"

"Do you think I'm Berendtsen?"

"You asked me that. No."

"You don't. Well, do you think Berendtsen's alive?"

"No."

"I see. You don't think I'm Berendtsen, and you don't think Berendtsen's alive—then, what're you doing up here in these mountains? What were you hoping to find?"

Custis felt himself getting angry. He felt he was being chivvied into a corner. "Nothing, maybe. Maybe I'm just a guy doing a job, because he has to. Not looking for anything or anybody—just doing a job."

The commander laughed mirthlessly. The sound stabbed at Custis out of the growing darkness in the cabin. "It's time we stopped lying to each other, Joe. You put your car—your entire life—in a position where you might lose them instantly. You know it and I know it, and let's not argue the merits of dust grenades against napalm shells. Why did you take that kind of gamble? Why were you dangling that bait? Who were you hoping might snap at it?"

"It was a quick way of finding out what Henley wanted to know."

"And how did you propose to get out, once you'd gotten yourself in? You don't give two cents paper for Henley. You're an independent armored-car commander on a simple contract job; why all the extra effort? You must have known damned well this mission wasn't in the interests of the Seventh Republic. You're a child of the age. If you'd let yourself stop and think, you would have realized what was going on. But you don't care anything about the Eighth Republic, either. A man doesn't pledge allegiance to one of a meaningless string of numbers. No. What you wanted to do was to pledge allegiance to a man who's thirty years dead. Now deny it."

Custis didn't have an answer. It was dark outside. He'd played out his string, with the commander and with himself.

"You want me to tell you I'm Berendtsen, don't you?"

"Maybe," Custis said grudgingly.

The commander laughed again—a harsh, bitter croak of sound that made the hackles stand on Custis's neck. Henley was breathing heavily in the darkness.

"You and Henley—both damned fools. What would you do with your Berendtsen, Joe? Starve with him, up here in these mountains with an old man? If you found him, did you expect him to go and remake the world for you? He tried that, once. And maybe he succeeded, if men can still hope because he lived.

"But what could he do now, an old man? His sort of life is a young man's game—if it's anyone's.

"You, Joe—you're a different breed from this jackal beside you. What do you think Berendtsen started with? What's the matter with you, Custis? You've got a car, and a crew that'll follow you anywhere. What do you need some ready-made hero for?"

Custis had no answer at all.

"Don't worry, Joe—Henley's getting an earful. I can hear the gears turning in his head. Right now, he's planning how to use you. He can see it already. The Chicago machine swinging in behind you. The carefully built-up legend they'll manufacture around you. The indomitable strong American from the plains. All you'll have to do is stand up on a platform and shout, and his gang will take care of the rest. That's what he's thinking. But you don't have to worry about him. You can take care of him. It'll be a long time before anyone like you has to worry about anyone like Henley —years. And I can sit here and tell you this, and the likes of Henley'll still not worry, because they think they can always run things. Of course, in order to safeguard the legend of Joe Custis, he has to make sure, once and for all, that Berendtsen won't return—"

Custis heard the sound of steel snaking out of Henley's boot-top. He jumped for where the man had been, but Henley'd had minutes to get ready. Custis heard him bump into the desk, and the thin scream of his blade through the air.

The old man'll have moved, Custis thought. He'd had time.

175

He heard the ripe sound of Henley's dagger, and then the dull *chunk!* as its hilt stopped against flesh. He heard the old commander sigh.

He stood still, breathing open-mouthed, until he heard Henley move. He went in low, under where the blade might be. As Custis hit him, Henley whispered: "Don't be a fool! Don't make any noise! With any luck, we can walk out of here!"

He broke Henley apart with his hands, making no noise and permitting none from Henley. He let the officer slip to the floor and went silently around the table, to where he felt the old man folded over. He touched his shoulder. "Commander—"

"It's all right," the old man sighed. "I've been waiting for it." He stirred. "I've left things in a terrible mess. He was quicker to make up his mind than I had expected." He hunched himself up, his cracked fingernails scraping at his shirt. "I don't know now . . . you'll have to get out without me, somehow. I can't help you. Why am I so old?"

"It's O.K., Commander. I've had somethin' figured out. I'll make it."

"You'll need a weapon." The commander raised his head and pulled his shoulders back. "Here." He tugged at his chest and fumbled the wet knife into Custis's hand.

CHAPTER SIX:

Here is New York City, quite a few years earlier, and this is what happened:

I

Bob Garvin watched the Army go, his hands in his pockets, an odd light burning in his eyes. He waited until the last truck had swung off Fourteenth Street and turned toward the Lincoln Tunnel, until the last man had marched out of sight, until the flashes of sun on gun barrels had winked out. Then he stepped back, apologized to a citizen he bumped, and walked over to the group clustered around Brent Mackay.

"Morning, Mayor," he said.

"Ah, good morning, counselor! Out here like all the rest of us, I see." Mackay was an oddity. He looked as lean and hard as any man, but he was soft at the core—like a bag so full of wind that the cloth stretched drum-tight and strong; but, nevertheless, only full of wind.

"Have to wave bye-bye to the brave soldier boys, you know," Bob said.

One of the Mayor's retinue—a steely-eyed man named Mert Hollis—laughed metallically. A wave of sly chuckles swept over the group.

"Well," Bob Garvin said, "let's get back to work. There's still a government in this city, even if the Crown Prince has gone a-hunting again."

Mackay nodded hastily. "Of course! You're quite right, counselor." He turned to the rest of the members of the City Council and their assistants. "Let's go, boys! Back to the salt mines. Got to get that sewer project in the works."

"Ah—Mayor . . ." Garvin interceded softly.

"Yes, counselor?"

"I'd think that could wait a little. Rome wasn't built in a day, you know. I'd like to get that question of voter eligibility straightened out this morning."

"Why, *certainly*, counselor!" Mackay chuckled easily. "You know, that had slipped my mind. Thanks for reminding me."

"You're welcome, I'm sure."

The Army of Unification took Trenton easily. It ran into a very strong defense in Philadelphia, and, for a moment, Berendtsen debated whether it might not have been a better idea to enter southern New Jersey, instead of by-passing it. But a flanking column finally battered its way up from Chester, and the city fell. Camden then fell with it, and the strategy of quick gain was justified. With a strong garrison in the Camden-Philadelphia district, southern New Jersey was bound to be gradually assimilated, with a far lower ratio of losses, and meanwhile weeks of time were gained.

The Army pushed south.

* * *

Eating slowly, Bob Garvin savored his mother's cooking. He smiled at her fondly as she spooned another portion of potatoes on his plate. "Thanks, Mom, but I'm just about full.

"Don't you like them?" his mother asked anxiously.

"No, no, they're fine, Mom!" he protested. "But there's only so much room, and I'll want some of that pumpkin pie."

Mary looked at him acidly. "Home life of the public figure," she said. "Popular candidate for Councilman from the Sixth District enjoys home cooking. Goes home for one of Mom's pies on night before municipal elections."

"Mary!" Margaret Garvin looked at her daughter reproachfully.

Mary looked down at her plate. "Sorry, Mother."

"I can't understand what's come over you lately," Margaret Garvin was saying, her face troubled. "You never used to be this way."

Mary shrugged. "Nobody's the way they used to be." She toyed with her knife. "But I'm sorry. I won't do it again."

Margaret Garvin looked anxiously at her son. Bob was smiling slightly, as he often seemed to be. Apparently, he was impervious to anything his sister might say.

"Well . . ." Margaret Garvin began irresolutely. She frowned as she realized she had no idea of what she was going to say next. She'd been this way more and more often, since Matt . . .

Matt was gone. There was no sense in hurting herself by thinking about it. He was gone, and she was here. And if she seemed to miss his strength more and more every day—well, everyone grew old, some time or the other.

"I'm going over to see Carol Berendtsen," she said at last. "You children can manage your own dessert without any trouble. The poor woman's worn down to a shadow."

She missed Ted. Her boy had been her life, since Gus . . .

She *would not* think of death!

. . . Since Carol didn't have Gus anymore. And no one knew where Ted was, beyond an occasional radio report about this city besieged, that town captured. And more than that. More than that—and the same thing that put the pain in Mary's eyes. Wife and mother, both wondering what was happening inside the man one had borne and the other married, but neither understood.

Margaret Garvin stood up. Her own oldest boy, Jim, was with Ted. Perhaps she, too, should be worried. But she never worried about Jim. Jim was like seasoned timber, holding up a building. Nothing could hurt him, nothing could move him. Jim could take care of himself. Never worried? Well, no, not that. She knew that Jim was as weak as any man whom a bullet might strike down. But Jim was not the complex, delicate organism that Ted was, or that Bob was. It was impossible to believe of him, as one could easily believe of the other two, that one slight shock could jar the entire mechanism.

"Will you be here when I come back, Bob?" she asked.

Bob shook his head regretfully. "Afraid not, Mom.

I need a good night's sleep before tomorrow. Vote early and often, you know." He chuckled easily.

She went over to him and kissed him good night. "Take care of yourself, Bob," she said gently.

"Always do, Mom."

Bob shot a glance at Mary after his mother had left. Mary Berendtsen was staring distantly at her teacup, her eyes lost.

"Worried about Ted?" Bob asked softly.

Mary did not look at him. Her mouth twitched into a thin line.

"I have no quarrel with you," he said sincerely.

"You've got one with my husband."

Bob shook his head violently. "Not with him. With his ideals. His social theories, if you will."

Mary looked up, smiling thinly. "*You* tell *me* where the one leaves off and the other begins."

Bob shrugged. "That's what makes it look like I hate him personally. But I don't! You know that."

"You'd have him killed if you could get away with it. If you could have gotten him killed, you'd have done it two years ago, when he came back from the north."

Bob nodded. "I'll admit that. But not because I hate him—or don't admire him, for that matter. Because he stands for the reigning social theory. A theory that's going to drive us back to the caves and snipers if it keeps on."

"Don't campaign around me!" Mary snapped. "Don't fog your pretty speeches at me! What it boils down to is that, despite Mackay, despite Chief of Police Merton Hollis, despite the City Council in your pocket, you know damned well that if Ted comes

181

back to stay you'll be on the outside in two bounces! And then all the pretty plans and fat jobs won't be worth this!" She snapped her fingers.

Bob shook his head. "No, Mary," he said gently. "You're mad at me, but you know that's not true. Mackay's a tool, true, and not a clean one, either. Neither are the things I'm forced to do. But you know why I want to control the government. And it's not the fat jobs."

Her anger spent, Mary nodded grudgingly. "I know," she sighed. "You're sincere enough." She laughed shortly. "Heaven protect the human race from the sincere idealist!"

"And what's Ted?"

Mary winced. "Touché."

Bob shook his head. "No, not touché. It's not a new point. What makes it hurt is that you've been driving yourself insane with it all along."

This time, Mary's face went white, and a mask slipped tightly down over her features as she fled into the shelter of herself.

"Look, Mims, you know what I believe—what I've believed ever since I can remember. We were born equal. We were born with a heritage of personal weapons to enforce our equality, and it is the personal weapons, in the hands of free men, which should ensure that each man will not be trespassed against—that no one, ever, will be able to regiment, to demand, to tithe, to take from another man what is rightfully his. If we are each equally armed, what man is better than his neighbors? If we are all armed, who dares to be a thief, whether he steals liberty or possessions?

"And what is Ted Berendtsen's belief? That men

should band together in a group for the purpose of forcing other men to serve that group. How can I compromise to such a man? How can I sit still and let him enforce his tyranny upon us? How can I let him, or his beliefs, live in the same world with myself and my beliefs?"

For once, Bob's cynical self-possession had deserted him. He found himself on his feet, his palms resting on the edge of the table, staring fiercely down at Ted Berendtsen's wife.

Mary raised her head, her face blanched completely white.

"Have you been campaigning on *that* platform?" she demanded.

Bob Garvin shook his head. "No. Not yet."

The Army of Unification took Richmond, Atlanta, and Jacksonville. Berendtsen's men moved south.

Someone threw a rotten cabbage at Mary Berendtsen in the street.

Newly-elected City Councilman Robert Garvin sat at one end of the long desk—at the head. Brent Mackay, Mayor of the City of New York, sat at the other end, at the foot.

Merton Hollis, the police chief, sat next to Bob Garvin.

"All right, then, boys," Garvin was saying, "in this matter of the upcoming national elections, it breaks down like this. Under the Voters' Eligibility Statute, any one specific member of the family can cast the vote of an absentee member of the Army of Unification, in addition to his own. Right?"

The City Council nodded.

"Okay. Now, technically speaking, that extra vote is to be cast in accordance with the expressed wishes of the absentee."

He spreads his hands in a helpless gesture. "But with the Army on the move like it is, with no one knowing for sure exactly what it's doing . . . Why, without casualty lists, no one even knows who's dead and who isn't."

"But Robert, we do know—" Mackay began.

Garvin stopped him with a patient smile. "*Please,* Mr. Mayor. We've got radio reports, true. But they're vague, and they're garbled, and who's to say Berendtsen isn't concealing setbacks by ordering his operators to give false locations?"

He shook his head. "No, we can't go by hearsay. We'll simply have to accept those votes as if they'd been directed by the absentees. After all, we can't prove they aren't."

There was a low chorus of suppressed chuckles of appreciation from the members of the City Council.

"But suppose those votes aren't cast?" Mackay protested. "After all, the families *know* they haven't been in touch with the men. How can they cast those votes, in all conscience?"

Garvin looked at him in cold amusement. "Mr. Mayor—have you ever heard of anyone, once he's ready to vote at all, who wouldn't vote as hard as he could?"

This time the chuckles were louder.

"What's more," Garvin said softly, "while the voters will not be able to get individual directions, I'm sure they can be made to know how the Army as a whole feels about Berendtsen, and his theories."

Several heads along the table snapped to sudden attention.

"As you know," Robert Garvin went on, still softly, "the garrison commander at Philadelphia, Commander Willets, is a staunch follower of Theodore Berendtsen's. He has distinguished himself in following Berendtsen's methods and policies exactly. His administration of the garrison, too, has been identical with the pattern laid down by his chief. In short, we have, in Philadelphia, a miniature Berendtsen, with a miniature Army of Unification, administering a miniature Republic. It follows that the reaction of the garrison, and of the people of Philadelphia, to Commander Willets, will be identical with the reaction of the Army as a whole to Theodore Berendtsen. There will also be the close parallel between the condition of the Philadelphians and the condition the citizens of the Republic may expect for themselves should Berendtsen ever become head of the Republic."

Those members of the City Council who were closest to Garvin laughed aloud and looked at each other with triumphant grins on their faces.

Mackay looked down the length of the table in shock. "But—but that isn't an AU garrison any more!" he protested. "Hollis took a draft of City policemen down there last year, and rotated the original garrison home!"

Garvin nodded. "Quite so. And the original garrison is now on constabulary duty in Maine. We know that. What's your point, Mayor?"

Mackay licked his lips in confusion. "Well—" He shot a glance at Hollis, hesitated, but then pressed on. "You know what kind of men we sent down there. And you know we haven't given Willets any support from here, when he's demanded replacements and support. Good God, man, he's been a virtual prisoner down there! Even his communications with Berendtsen are monitored. He's no more responsible for what's been going on down in Philadelphia than—than—"

He stopped, at a loss for a comparison.

"—Than Berendtsen is, Mr. Mayor?" Garvin smiled. "Of course. But who knows that, outside of ourselves?"

"Nobody. But it isn't right! You *can't* just rig something as cold-bloodedly as this!"

"And what did you think we were doing in Philadelphia, Mr. Mayor? Conducting an interesting social experiment?"

"No, no, of course not! But this—"

Garvin sighed and ignored him from that point on. He turned to the other members of the city's government—and thereby, the Republic's.

"Commander Willets will be recalled home to answer charges of oppression, misadministration, and treason. His trial will take place a week before elections. Our slate of candidates is as follows: for Commander-In-Chief, Merton Hollis." There was a light spatter of applause from the Council, and Garvin shook the steely-eyed man's hand vigorously. Then he continued:

"For First Citizen—a new office, as you know, in place of the old designation of 'President': Robert Garvin."

The applause was violent this time, and Hollis solemnly shook Garvin's hand.

"And, for Mayor of the City of New York—" Garvin

looked down the table at a smiling Councilman, "William Hammersby."

Garvin's look shifted, and Mackay found himself staring helplessly into the eyes of the end.

The man in the vaguely army-ish clothes clambered to the top of the wall in Union Square, gripping a lamp post for support. He waved the Army of Unification's blue-and-silver pennant wildly over his head.

"Listen!" he shouted. "Listen, citizens! I was in Philadelphia. I was with Berendtsen for over three years! And I say to hell with the madman, and to hell with his flag!" He ripped away the silver stripe. "I've had enough of the color of bayonets!" He threw the tattered pennant away and waved another one over his head, this one colored blue and red. "This is the flag for me! Blue for honor, and red to remember the blood that Berendtsen has drunk!"

"But no white for purity," Mary Berendtsen murmured to herself from the edge of the crowd. No one in that milling, election-eve crowd heard her. Luckily for her, no one recognized her, either.

Garvin smiled pleasantly down at the new communications officer. "I'm sure you understand your duties, Colonel. Now, here's the text of your nightly report to Berendtsen."

And Brent Mackay's body drifted slowly down the Hudson, out to the broad and waiting ocean.

II

Jim Garvin stood with his hands deep in his pockets, listening to the wind flapping in the sides of tents as it swept gloomily across the bivouac area. The wind was very cold, condensing his breath into an unpleasant brittle wetness on the thick pile of his collar. He shivered violently as a gust needled his tender right leg, still sensitive from the scattering of buckshot that had chipped its bones two years ago, during the occupation of Jacksonville. A thin light seeped from behind the stringy pines to the east. It was going to be a cold and miserable day.

He looked at his wristwatch and walked toward the nearest tent, glad to be moving. He unsnapped the flap, tightly sealed and stubborn to his numb fingers, and shook the head of the nearer of the two men who slept inside. "All right, Miller, let's go!"

Miller grunted incoherently and then came awake, rolling over in his wadding of blankets. He found his helmet with a blind movement of his arm, jammed his head into it, and crawled out, nudging his tentmate with a boot as he came. Still bundled, he zipped up his jacket under the blankets before he pulled them off his shoulders, and threw them back into the

188

tent. Begley, the tentmate, crawled out after him, mumbling a string of curses while he handed Miller the canvas flagbag.

"It's a sonofabitch cold day," Begley said spitefully as he picked up his bugle.

"Stinkin' South sucked all the goddam blood out of us," Miller agreed.

Garvin grunted. Whenever he'd bothered to think about it at all, he'd somehow assumed that the last days of this campaign would be the same as they had been when the still young Army of Unification had swung back down the Jersey palisades into New York —crisp, clear weather with a promise of winter. Instead, the winter was almost over now, and the ground was soaking with rain and molten frost. The raw wind clawed at a man's insides. It would be a good month before the weather was fit for anything.

But, considering what the last homecoming had been like, it was probably as good a thing for this one to be different as not. So, he merely grunted.

They walked across the bivouac area to Berendtsen's trailer without further words. When they reached it, Miller snapped the AU pennant to the jackstaff shrouds while Begley twisted a mouthpiece into his bugle. Garvin stood motionless beside the trailer, his head stiff and erect under its gray helmet, the Senior Sergeant's green swath dull under a coat of frost. His shoulders were taut, his boots at a forty-five-degree angle.

He looked at his watch again.

"Flag . . ." He counted to three. "Up!"

Miller sent the blue-and-silver pennant whipping up into the wind, and Garvin's jacket stretched over his stiff back as Begley blew Assembly. He held to attention while the men kicked their way out of their tents and lined up for roll call.

"This is an army, now," Berendtsen had said. "It represents a nation. And a nation must have a continuing army. The answer is a tradition of always having an army. Jim, I want you to see that it looks a little like an army."

If Berendtsen wanted him to set examples of discipline, it was no skin off his nose one way or the other. The men had gradually gotten used to the idea, once they'd realized it made them a more efficient organization when held within reasonable limits. And this was only one of many changes that had come about while the AU was beating its way down the eastern seaboard.

The AU had come a long way, in distance and in time, from the rabble of men who couldn't have stood before one platoon of this regiment which now made up Berendtsen's army. Even the bloodied and organized force that had marched back to New York from the Northern Campagin would have been broken by one of the now existing specialist groups—Eisner's armored cars, probably, that had prowled through the torrential rain of the siege of Tampa like fire-clawed hounds—and left to be mopped up by infantry. The AU had learned a lot by the time the blue-and-silver pennant flew over Key West. Learned a lot, enlisted many, looted much. It had learned still more as it returned northwards, cleaning out pockets and dropping garrisons in the familiar strategy that Berendtsen had developed during the Northern Campaign.

So, everything east of the Alleghenies was Berendtsen's now. Garvin's gaze swung as he looked bleakly at the lines of silent men, waiting at attention.

The men were lean and hard in their uniforms—old Marine uniforms with helmets and belt buckles finished in crackle-gray paint from a business-machines factory. Most of them would probably have been a match for any soldier that ever walked the Earth, winnowed and weeded as they had been. As to why they fought . . . Three meals a day and a purpose in life were as good a reason as any. A soldier got his pick of loot—such loot as watches and cigarette lighters, less luxury than convenience—his choice of land to work after his discharge, and a chance to find himself a woman.

Garvin took the roll call report without taking his eyes off the men.

Only a few of them were personally loyal to Berendtsen, but all of them followed him. Garvin wondered how they'd feel when they were pushed across the Appalachians to the west. He wondered, too, how he'd feel personally—and discovered that his mind had been avoiding the subject.

He heard Berendtsen's hand on the inside latch of the trailer's door. "Tenn—*hut*," he barked, and the men, already stiff, turned their waiting eyes on the door. In their tents, some of them swore they'd keep their eyes oblique the next morning when the trailer door opened. None of them did.

The door opened, and Garvin stepped aside and held it, then swung it back as Berendtsen took three steps forward into the bivouac area.

He was wearing a belted coverall that had been dyed black, and only Garvin, standing slightly behind and a few feet to one side, was in a position to

191

notice that his stomach was heavier than it had been. He surveyed the regiment with his usual unrevealing expression, and today, for the first time and for no obvious reason, Garvin saw that the youthfulness of his face was no more than a mask. His facial skin was waxy, as though someone had taken a cast of young Ted Berendtsen's features and put it against this older skull under the boyishly-combed but darkening hair, and let his weary eyes look through. His neck was girdled by deep creases.

"All men present, sir," Garvin said.

Berendtsen nodded curtly. "Good morning, Jim." His eyes did not change their impersonal and yet intense expression. His face did not lose whatever singleness of purpose it was that gave it its unvarying mold.

And now Garvin realized, in the wake of his sudden glimpse of a Berendtsen stripped of all youth, that Berendtsen had years ago closed the last door that opened from himself to the world, and that now the sound of it had finally reached Garvin's ears.

"Dismiss the men, Sergeant. All companies messed down and ready to move out in an hour. I want you and Commanders Eisner and Holland in my quarters in five minutes."

"Yes, sir." Garvin saluted, issued the orders, and dismissed the men. He walked across the area to where the company commanders were standing in the dawn gloom, leaving the old-young stranger behind.

"We are here." Berendtsen touched his finger to the contour map of Bucks County and then, characteristically, added a belated "As you know." Garvin noted that Holland twitched his thin lips opposite him at the map table. Eisner, whose hands were permanently blackened by grease and gear-box dust, and who was completely withdrawn when away from his cars, kept his face expressionless.

"We will be in New York on the day after tomorrow," Berendtsen went on. "That is—the main body will." He removed the map and substituted another covering the lower part of New Jersey.

"Now. Our main line of communication between New York and the Philadelphia area, as well as our route to the south in general, cuts across northern New Jersey and across the Delaware at Trenton. Up to now, there has been no reason to enter southern New Jersey at all, with the Camden garrison there to guard our flank, because of the area's peninsular nature. Which, I am sure, is obvious to all of us.

"Accordingly, A Company, under Commander Holland, will now detach itself from the main body, cross the river at any practicable point, and proceed to occupy southern New Jersey. Garvin, you will take over the First Platoon of A Company, and act as Commander Holland's Aide-in-the-Field. You will be accompanied by as many armored cars, under the subsidiary command of whatever junior officer Commander Eisner appoints, as the commander feels such a detachment will require. You will draw supplies and support weapons within Commander Holland's discretion, and will provision from the land, carrying a basic ration for emergencies. Is that clear?"

Holland and Eisner nodded. Garvin, as an NCO, said, "Yes, sir." He kept his face blank. Berendtsen's orders made him, in effect, superior in command to whoever the Armored officer would be. They also gave him the duties of a full Lieutenant. He had known, of course, that Berendtsen would someday make him an officer in spite of his many refusals to accept the rank. But now he wondered. Why had Berendtsen waited until now to exercise this elementary circumvention? Up to now, this had looked like a standard mop-up. Now a new factor had entered the circumstances, and Garvin wondered what it really was.

Berendtsen resumed. "Very well. You will send patrols into every town of significant size, and establish communications posts. Liaison is to be maintained by radio with the Camden-Philadelphia Garrison Office, for the purpose of transmitting regular reports. You will set up new garrisons at Atlantic City, Bridgeton, and in the former naval installations at Cape May."

Berendtsen looked up from the map. "Those are your objectives. You will, of course, pursue our standard occupation and recruitment policies. As usual, hereditary officers in communities surviving around former military installations are to be handled carefully."

He stopped, and something crossed his face briefly, too rapidly for Garvin to read.

"The Philadelphia garrison commander has reported that the area is only sparsely populated, no penetration having been made by any civilian groups since the dislocation of the old Philadelphia organization six years ago. I am told that there was never an opportunity for Philadelphia to conduct large-scale resettlements in the area.

"For this reason, I am sending only one company. However, the Philadelphia garrison had probed the area only lightly, in spite of whatever generalized conclusions the commander may have drawn. The commander, as you have no way of knowing, is a man sent out from New York to replace Commander Willets." He smiled dryly. "For that reason, I am augmenting the company with the armored detachment, and staffing it with my best men. Commander Eisner, I'll ask you to bear these remarks in mind when you detail your own officer.

"A few final orders, which I'll confirm in writing as soon as my clerk has them typed. Be sure you have them before you leave, Commander Holland. As follows: You will maintain radio contact with Philadelphia and New York, but you are an entirely independent command until the area has been completely occupied and assimilated into the Republic. Once this has been accomplished, the Southern New Jersey Command will be subordinated to the Philadelphia Military District, and will be subject to orders from the Philadelphia garrison commander. Until such time, you are on record as a detached unit of the Army of Unification in the field, and are subject only to the orders of the Commander-in-Chief."

Garvin tried to find something readable in either Berendtsen's or Holland's faces, but failed.

Berendtsen didn't trust his Philadelphia commander, that was sure. And his third-person reference to himself as Commander-in-Chief seemed unnecessarily oblique.

More and more, Garvin began to suspect that there was something wrong. Perhaps the AU had grown to proportions which kept Berendtsen from personally supervising the entire organization, but the Philadelphia garrison was an important one, and it seemed inconceivable that an undependable man had gotten the post.

"Any questions?"

Garvin kept silent, as did the two commanders.

"Suggestions?"

"I'd like to take that detachment in myself, sir," Eisner said. Life in New York, uneventful as it must inevitably be, held no attraction for him. The New Jersey operation offered an extra month's action.

Berendtsen shook his head. "I'd considered sending you," he said, "but I want you in New York too much."

Eisner's brows twitched, and the man's face, unaccustomed to masking his thoughts, showed his plain doubt.

"I'm sorry," Berendtsen said flatly.

"Yes, sir," Eisner answered.

"All right, then," Berendtsen concluded, "You're dismissed—and good luck."

Garvin followed the two commanders out of the trailer, while the clerk's typewriter hammered an accompaniment from their orders—their disquieting official orders that plugged all possible loopholes . . . against what?

And the wind that keened between the tents seemed stronger now, and more piercing than it had been at reveille.

Berendtsen watched the company roll out, missing them already. He could feel the gap in the Army almost as surely as if a chunk had been cut out of his side. But there was no help for it.

Perhaps he should have gone in with the whole Army. He'd been tempted to. But the men were close to home—the New York ones, anyway—and they wanted to get back. The rest of them were looking forward to a spree in the city. For some of them it was the first real let-up in six years.

And he had no good reason, really, to be as much nagged as he was. Whatever was going on in Philadelphia was probably local political maneuvering. Holland's company could handle anything New Jersey might have to put up. Especially with the cars along. And if they got into a serious jam, they could call on Philadelphia. No matter what was going on there, they'd *have* to turn out garrison on call, whatever they thought of it.

Perhaps he should have taken the Army into Philadelphia.

What for? Just because Willets had suddenly turned noncommunicative and finally gone back to New York? Willets was an old man by now. Old men developed odd quirks.

He wanted no part of politics. He'd decided that a long time ago, and he couldn't change now. Under no circumstances could he begin dabbling with the internal affairs of the Republic. He had no desire to become a military dictator.

Why should there be any reason for him to be a military dictator?

What was going on in the back of his mind?

He turned away and went back into his trailer, throwing himself on his bunk and staring up at the ceiling.

He'd cut Holland loose. Given him a completely independent command. Why? What had made him decide he might not be in control of the Army much longer?

Was this it? Was this the end he had always somehow felt, waiting in the future, waiting for him to live as he had to, do what he had to, until he finally caught up to it?

Why had he kept Eisner with him?

Why was he Theodore Berendtsen?

The Delaware had picked up heat at its headwaters, and the warmth was running southward with the river. The last cold air mass of the year had spilled over the mountains in the west northwest to meet it, had been deflected slightly by the rising warmth to the north, and was now rolling into Delaware Bay like a downhill tide, picking up speed in its southwesterly mean direction while spinning slowly. Like a scooping hand, it gathered up condensed moisture from the warmer air above the bay, and hurled patches of fog and gusts of cold into the face of the marching column.

Akin to all the troop movements of the Earth's long military history, the column moved forward at the pace of its slowest element—the 100 thirty-inch strides per minute of the rifle platoons. Garvin sat motionless atop one of the two armored cars spotted between the Second and Third Platoons, his boots braced against a cleat, watching the column's forward half-snaking into the cold and fog, while his body vibrated gently to the labor of the car's throttled-back motors. His hands and face were coldly slick, but he stayed where he was rather than drop into the car's warm interior, where he would not be able to survey the entire column. Occasionally, he broke into short frenzies of shivering. But he did not climb down off his perch.

He looked back over his shoulder, and saw Carmody's jeep coming up from the column's rear, where four more of the total of ten cars were posted. He frowned slightly, turning his head to peer forward once more. Holland had kept the column clear of Philadelphia, pointing for the Tacony-Palmyra Bridge. Probably, they were about to make contact with the Philadelphian command post set up there.

Garvin bared his teeth in an uneasy grimace, and rose to an abrupt crouch. He waved to the jeep's driver as the vehicle whined up close to the armored car, and scrambled over the turret. He clung momentarily to the rung of a step, then dropped off into the road, easily matching the car's speed without a stumble. He caught a handhold on the jeep and swung himself into the back seat, behind Carmody, the Armored Lieutenant, a balding man descended from the remains of the old Marine colony at Quantico.

"Got a contact," he said. "My lead car just radioed back—in Tampa code. There's some sort of half-arsed CP at the bridge, all right, but my boy's upset about something and Dunc doesn't upset very easy."

Garvin frowned. Tampa had been intercepting their communications, and they'd had to improve a code during the siege. Now Carmody's man in the scouting armored car was using it again—which could only mean that he didn't want Philadelphia to intercept his observations on the Philadelphian post.

"Think he expects them to give us any trouble?" he asked.

"Be a crazy thing to do, with our armor."

"Might blow the bridge," Garvin pointed out.

Now, what's making me think they'd do a thing

199

like that? he wondered with a stab of illogical panic.

"You think they'd feel that way?" Carmody asked, not quite incredulous enough for Garvin's peace of mind.

"I don't know," Garvin said slowly, abruptly realizing that here, deep in the Republic's territory, it was still as though they were moving into the silent lands to which they were accustomed, waiting for the crash and flame of hidden and unexpected dangers. It was as though they were on the verge of combat.

"But let's get up there in a hurry," he told Carmody.

The Command Post was a badly armored shack set beside the bridge approaches. An aerial projected from its roof, and there was a jeep with scabrous paint parked beside it. Someone had daubed a red-and-blue V of converging swaths on its hood.

"What the hell kind of army are you in?" Garvin barked at the man they had found there.

The man spat over his shoulder and stared grubbily up at Holland in the armored car's forward hatch. "He ain't Berendtsen, is he?"

"I asked you a question, mister!"

"I'm in the same goddamn army you are, I guess," the man said irritably. "He *ain't* Berendtsen, is he?"

"I'm Commander Holland, commanding A Company, Army of Unification," Holland said impatiently. "Where's the rest of your detail?"

"Ain't none," the man answered.

"What's your rank, Bud?" Garvin asked, looking at the man's grimy jumper.

"Sergeant, Philadelphia Military District," the man answered, spitting again.

"Okay, Sarge," Garvin said. "We're going to cross your little bridge." He could feel the veins pounding on the backs of his hands, and he could see mounded white crests bulging out the corners of Holland's jaws.

"Not without a pass from Commander Horton, you're not."

"Who the hell's he?"

"You kidding? He's Philadelphia Command, and nothing goes over this bridge east without his pass."

"*You* kidding?" Carmody said softly, and tracked his jeep's machinegun around to bear on the man.

The man turned pale, but he cursed Carmody at the same time. "You *still* ain't going over that bridge."

"That settles it," Garvin said to Holland. "They've got the bridge wired. Miller! Find anything like a detonator in that shack?"

"No soap, Jim," the corporal called back from the CP's door.

"Okay, sonny boy, let's you and me go for a ride," Jim said. He drew his Colt and aimed it at the man's belly. "Up on the hood with you," he said, motioning toward the CP's jeep. The man climbed on sullenly. Jim climbed behind the wheel and kicked the starter. The motor turned over balkily, and he had to nurse it for minutes before it was running well enough to move. Then he pulled out into the highway and pointed the jeep over the bridge.

The man on the hood turned around, his eyes staring. "Hey!" he yelled back, "You wanna get killed?"

Garvin cut his speed. "Where's she wired?"

The man licked his lips, but said nothing. Garvin gunned his motor.

"Okay, *okay!* There's trips buried in the asphalt

up ahead." He was breathing heavily, scared to death. Not of the mine trips, though, Jim decided, but of what would happen to him now he'd given away their location. He wondered what sort of methods Commander Horton used to enforce orders.

They blew the CP to scrap and shot the jeep's engine into uselessness. As they crossed the bridge, Garvin looked back and saw the black speck of the guard, half-running up the riverbank, away from Philadelphia. He looked at Jack Holland, and didn't like what he saw in the commander's eyes, because he knew the same expression was in his own. There was something wrong—something so wrong that it made him debate disregarding orders and recommending that the column turn toward New York at the fastest pace the men could march.

Holland looked at him and shook his head. "Berendtsen knew what he was doing when he sent us down here," he said. "Let's get to finding out what it was."

The Army marched into a New York City turned sullen. Berendtsen, feeling the hate like a clammy fog, sucked in his breath.

A crooked smile edged the corners of his mouth. He was almost always right. It was a feeling that prickled the back of his neck, each time he made a decision, apparently on the basis of no more than a feeling, and found that he had acted with almost prescient exactness.

Second sight? Or just a subconscious that worked immeasurably well?

There was no way of telling.

There were barricades up in the streets, and the people stayed behind them, kept there by squads of soldiery. There were armed men up on the housetops, and heavy weapons concentrated at strong points. And there was a flight of helicopters overhead, tagging them like whirling crows against the sky.

He could feel the Army growing apprehensive behind him. They had marched into enemy cities before.

He halted the first column in the familiar square in front of Stuyvesant Town, noticing, with a part of his mind, that the bare and rough-hewn outlines he had left were gone, furbished over, so that there was no sign that a block of buildings had once stood there.

The rest of the Army marched into the square and halted at attention, the sergeants' commands echoing sharply and yet alone in the silence.

And still the people looked out of the windows.

What were they expecting? What were they waiting for, from him? Were they waiting for him to suddenly sweep the buildings with fire? Did they think he'd conquer this city as he'd defeated the others? Did they think somehow, that he had done all this, fought all those battles, killed all those good men, for any sake but theirs?

He turned toward his Army, seeing their white faces turn up to him, noting the men who stole glances at the building, seeing the fingers curled around the rifles, the bodies ready to twist and crouch, firing. Most of these men were not New Yorkers. And all of them were his. All he had to do was issue a command.

He felt a breeze, coming down the street from one of the rivers, touching the skin of his face.

"Dismissed!" he ordered.

Company A maintained routine contact with Philadelphia and Camden, learning nothing. Horton's communications operators relayed their reports back into silence, and they heard nothing from Horton himself. Nor from Berendtsen. The fog that had hung over the Delaware seemed to have suddenly taken on far tougher substance, cutting them off from their commander, from the rest of the Republic, from the rest of the world. They learned nothing, heard nothing, knew nothing. The company marched into nothing, and Jim and Holland found it difficult to look into each other's eyes.

And yet, there had still been nothing to really disquiet them. The land at the other side of the bridge was bare, and they saw nothing. Philadelphia never mentioned the incident at the bridge, or even asked if they had seen the CP's sergeant. It was as though none of that had happened.

But it had.

They swept out in a broad arc as they moved into the central part of the peninsula, maintaining a light skirmish line backed up by the cars, which quartered back and forth.

But the infection of disquiet had spread to the men. Garvin, riding with Carmody as they worked into position for a standard two-pronged envelopment of the first fair-sized town they had come to, slapped his hand irritably on the hatch coaming.

"Goddamn it, Bill, *look* at those riflemen! They're all over the bloody terrain, exposed seven ways from breakfast, none of their heads down, nothing! They act like they're on a walking tour.

"A vacuum. We're slogging around in this freakin' mental vacuum, and it's turning a bunch of professional soldiers into milk maids!"

"Easy, Jim," Carmody said, his own voice ragged. "That goes for officers, too, if we're not careful!"

"You're damn right it does! I almost wish something would happen to put the edge back on us."

A sheet of corrugated iron, snapped out like a crumb-laden tablecloth, would have made the same sudden noise.

He caught a glimpse of soldiers tumbling while the harsh roar of controlled, heavy machinegun fire swept down upon them.

"Holy Jesus!" Carmody said. "You whistled one up that time!" and then the bazooka rocket crashed into the car and exploded.

Garvin crawled down the side of the flaming car somehow, dragging his legs, and tumbled into a ditch. He lay there, sobbing curses, while pain ate him.

It took three days to level the town, going systematically from house to stubborn house after losing a platoon of men to the machinegun emplacements. They found themselves fighting women and children as well as men, and when it was all over, they reformed into a scratch company of three understrength platoons and eight cars.

Jack Holland came to see Jim before they pulled out to continue the operation. He walked into the

flimsy barn which had been virtually the only undefended structure in the town, picking his way among
the other wounded men.

"How's it going, Jim?" he asked first.

Garvin shrugged. "Wish I could shake it off as fast
as it happened." He grimaced. "What the hell, I had
it coming to me after all these years. I don't have
a real kick." He looked up quickly.

"Hear anything from Ted?"

Holland shook his head, and the creases bunched
up tightly on his forehead. "No. Not from him, or
anybody else. I sent in a report on this little place,
with a special tagline for Horton, telling him what
a crumby job of scouting he'd done. Hoped to get a
rise out of him." He squatted down beside Garvin's
cot and lowered his voice.

"Didn't get one. I know why, too. Jim, this isn't
any no-man's land down here. Horton's men were all
through here. They weren't doing any fighting, though.
They've spent three years telling these farmers what
a bastard Ted is. They handed out a line of crap
that'd make your blood run cold. Why do you think
these boys were all set up for us? Why do you think
they fought like they did? And where do you think
they got their weapons?"

Jim whistled softly between his clenched teeth.
"What the hell's going on around here?"

Holland shook his head bleakly. "I don't know
for sure, yet. Listen, I asked for nursing volunteers
from the survivors. There'll be about eight or ten
girls coming up here. Maybe they're grateful for us
not fulfilling some of the picturesque promises that
were made for us. Maybe they're not. I'm damned
well sure there's a grapevine in this territory that

leads straight back to Horton, and the smart move would be for them to be on it. Well, maybe it can work in both directions. Anyway, take a crack at finding out what you can."

Jim nodded. "Will do." He looked up at Holland, who had gotten to his feet again. "What're we messed up in, Jack? How did all this happen? What made Horton think he could get away with this?"

But there was no answer, of course. Not yet. Perhaps never, and if, perhaps, they did somehow find it out, it might be too late.

Holland's look said the same. He gestured awkwardly. "Well, I'm about due to shove off."

"Good luck. I'll see you in about two weeks, huh?" Holland's mouth twitched. "I hope so."

"Well, so long," Jim said, and watched Holland walking out between the rows of wounded men, saying goodbye to each of them.

His nurse was a girl of about eighteen, a pale, dark-haired shape in the barn's gloom. Her name was Edith, and her voice was pitched so low that he sometimes had to strain to hear it.

"Hurt?" she asked as she shifted his blankets.

He grunted. "About as much as it should. But don't worry about it, hon—it's my department."

He lay on his back, looking up at her as she filled a glass with water. She'd been coming to tend him regularly for the past five days, leaving the other men to the girls who came with her, concentrating on him alone.

He'd asked her about that. "Shouldn't you be spending less time on me? I'm not that bad off."

"But you're an officer," she'd answered.

He wondered where she'd picked up that philosophy,

and thought of Horton's men. It made interesting thinking.

"Is that why all you girls are up here? Because it's your natural duty to tend wounded soldiers?"

"Well ... Well, no, it's just a—a thing you do, that's all."

He hadn't liked that answer. It explained nothing. It was lame with vagueness. Now he looked up at her, and wondered if Holland had been right about the grapevine.

"You always live around here, Eadie?"

She shook her head and handed him the glass, helping him raise his shoulders so he could drink. "Oh, no. I came here from Pennsylvania with my folks. All of us did. There wasn't anybody living here then."

He digested that, and wondered how far Horton's treason had gone.

"Sorry you came, now?"

"Oh, *no!* If we'd stayed where we were, Berendtsen would have gotten us."

"But we're Berendtsen's men."

"I know," she said. "But you're not *anything* like him."

She sounded so gravely positive that he almost laughed, stopping himself just in time.

"Did you know he was married to my sister?"

"Your *sister!*" He seemed to have shocked her profoundly. "Is she—is she a *good* woman?"

This time he did laugh, while she buried her face in her hands.

"Oh, I'm sorry. I don't know *why* I said that!"

He reached out and stroked her hair. "It's all right. And yes, she's a good woman."

But he was beginning to understand what Holland had meant about propaganda. Somebody had been giving these people a near lethal dose.

Someone knocked on the apartment door. Mary look at Ted.

"Now?"

Berendtsen nodded. "It's the best time. The Army's dispersed, but the men haven't really had a chance to start talking yet. It'll be days before the general public has more than a faint notion that there's been something odd going on."

"You shouldn't have sent Eisner away," Mary declared with sudden fierceness. "You convinced everybody that you were guilty. They were positive Eisner just didn't want to face the consequences of what he'd been doing under your orders. So what will they think of the man who gave those orders?"

Berendtsen shrugged. "Does it make any difference what they think? Does it make any difference whether I'm the bloody butcher they think I am or not? Eisner and his men are free, and heading west."

He smiled suddenly. "I just ordered him out. He turned west of his own accord."

Mary jumped up. "And does that satisfy you? Does it make you happy to know that the great Master Plan is being carried out, that Berendtsen's dream of unification goes marching on, even if only to that small extent?"

Berendtsen sighed as the knock fell on the door again. "I don't care whose plan it is, or what it's called. I do know that I gave Eisner an order I couldn't possibly enforce. He carried it out anyway."

He got up and went to the door, opening it. "How are you, Bob?" he said.

Robert Garvin looked at him silently for a moment. Then he exhaled loudly, as though sighing in relief at the long-delayed accomplishment of a complex and difficult task.

"You're being called upon to answer charges of treason," he said bluntly. "Your trial begins tomorrow."

It was three weeks, not two, when Jack Holland came back with A Company, and Jim, sitting outside the barn with his legs in crude casts, winced as he saw them. There were four armored cars now, with wounded riding on their decks, and the last car was being towed by the one ahead. He ran his eyes over the marchers, counting, and didn't believe the count until he saw Jack's face.

"We're done," Holland said bluntly, dropping down beside him. "We couldn't beat off an attack by archers, right now."

"What'd you run into?" Jim asked, not knowing what else to say.

"The gamut. Bazookas, mortars, fragmentation grenades, antipersonnel mines . . . Name it, and we got it. And we're not recruiting, Jim. We can beat 'em, but we can't recruit 'em. They just aren't interested. They're scared white at first, and then they find out we won't flay them alive for breathing in the wrong direction. Then some of them get sassy. But mostly they just sit and stare at us as if we were conquerors, or something. We gave them the offer every time before we moved in. We put up signs, we broadcast, we yelled. But they wouldn't trust us enough to listen.

Then we have to knock them over, and that makes us conquerors. The conquerors of South Jersey! I don't know, Jim. It's the creepiest goddamned feeling I've ever had. It's nothing like it used to be."

Jim nodded. "I've been getting my licks at it. They're so full of this Bogeyman Berendtsen stuff that nothing's going to penetrate. *We're* all right, catch? Even if we are the monster's men. But Berendtsen himself? Brr!"

"You know what kind of rifles they're using, Jim?"

"M-16s."

"The woods are full of them."

"Horton's been a busy boy around here, I see," Jim said sourly. "I've been thinking about that bridge. That was awfully easy getting across."

"Yeah," Holland agreed. "One lousy little man playing roadblock. If we hadn't found anybody, we'd have reported it to Ted. If we found too many, we'd have reported that. But we found just about what we expected to. We were suckered into this, all right."

"You figure Ted wasn't supposed to trust Philly?"

"Ahuh. Makes sense. He splits off a healthy piece of his army. He doesn't go with the whole army, though—he's not supposed to think it's *really* going to be rugged, and do that, because whoever's behind this knows damn well the AU can't be stopped by anything this side of hell. If Ted went down here and smelled a rat, he'd turn around and knock Philly on its ear all over again. And if he got mad enough, he might come roaring into New York, instead of feeling his way like he's doing now—or was doing, I guess."

"Sounds like the kind of thing somebody with real brains would dream up."

"A whole bunch of them, more than likely. I don't think there's any one man that can out-think Ted," Holland said.

"I wonder what Bob's doing these days," Jim said half to himself, his eyes narrowing. "Anyway, here we sit, dying on the vine."

"With the farmers hacking at the roots, yeah."

Jim wet his lips. He asked the unnecessary question. "You tried to get ahold of Ted?"

"Sure." Holland sighed. "I've been trying, for the last two weeks. All I get is some snotnose in New York. 'Relay all messages through me, please!'" he mimicked viciously.

Jim closed his eyes, letting his head sink. "Ted knew what he was doing, making us an independent command."

Even if we couldn't get up even a rousing football scrimmage, the shape we're in, he thought.

"He knew why he wanted Eisner in Manhattan with him, too," Holland said. "Boy, can't you just see those rolling roadblocks cleaning up Manhattan like nobody's business?"

Suddenly they stopped and looked at each other, realizing the scale on which they had been thinking. This was more than just Horton, playing out some game of his own. This was New York and Philadelphia working together. This was a whole nation, suddenly aligned against them.

And that night, there was the first message from New York.

To Officer Commanding, A Company and attached armored units, Army of Unification. From

Interim Commander-in-Chief. Orders follow:

You will proceed immediately to demobilize all units AU under your command, permitting each man to retain his personal equipment and weapons. Common supplies will be held under interim custody until arrival of civil governor, your former military district. Maintain volunteer militia force to keep order if necessary. Such militia units are not to display AU insignia of any nature. Keep frequency open for further orders. Do not initiate independent messaging.

Hollis,
Interim C.I.C.

Holland looked at Garvin, who had been moved into the communications center the men had knocked together. "You ever heard of anyone named Hollis?" he asked.

Jim looked up. "I guess there are a lot of people in New York nowadays that we never heard of." He stared hopelessly down at his immobilized legs. "I wonder what happened to Ted?" he asked, conscious of the lost note in his voice. But both of them knew that it no longer mattered. Somewhere in New York, the initiative of leadership had been taken up by other men, with other purposes. The AU was dead, and the purpose behind it had ended. Ted Berendtsen had kept some sort of appointment with history, and even if he lived, his time was over. And when the force that had been he and his work was ended, the arm that he had stretched out into this last territory was as powerless as all the rest.

They were finished. Cut off and finished.

"What do we do?" Jim asked.

"What can we do?" Holland answered. "We do what Boston and Tampa did. We're licked. There's nothing we have to say about it anymore. It's still one nation—one organization. We don't run it anymore, but we've still got to work in it, to keep it alive, just because it *is* an organization."

He grinned crookedly. "Ted was right—again."

But the messages had not ended. They listened to a general broadcast from New York, and, following orders, broadcast it over a public address system to the general population.

> This is Robert Garvin, President of the Constitutional Council for the Second Free American Republic.
>
> Once again, we are free. The power of the Army of Unification has been broken, and this nation, risen from the ash of dissolution and hopelessness, can once more grow, broad and prosperous, toward the sun. From Maine to Florida, we are one people, one union, inseparable and unyoked. We are a nation of free men armed, each equal to the other, each a brother to the other, each firm in his resolve that no one man shall again impose his twisted will on other men.
>
> The right to bear arms is inherent in each of us. The right to subjugate is not. No man may say to another "You will do thus and so because I decree it, because I have gathered up an army to pillage your home and rob you of your substance."

Soon, civil governors will be sent to you. They will establish an organization whereby a free election may be held. You will be asked to elect local officers to administer your territory under the general supervision of the governor.

People of the Second Free American Republic, we bring you liberty.

Holland spat. "We bring you civil governors, rather than an army," he said bitterly. "Please excuse the fact that these officers have been appointed by us. Didn't we do it in the name of liberty? And who the hell do they think *gave* them their precious union in the first place?"

Jim grinned sadly. "I guess Ted always knew that when the people chose a new government, it wouldn't be one that approved of Berendtsen."

"Did you notice something, though?" Holland pointed out. "No mention of Ted. Just a couple of passing references. They're not sure yet—not sure at all that it's safe to really go all-out and call him names. They're nervous."

"I wonder what's going on in New York?" Jim Garvin asked. What he felt about Bob, he kept to himself.

III

Robert Garvin sat easily in his chair, flanked by the other judges, looking down at the man who stood below their rostrum.

Garvin smiled thinly, and a little regretfully. He felt the weight of what he had done. But he had done it nevertheless, because in doing it he had fulfilled his greater duty to freedom, to liberty from oppression, to liberty from such as Berendtsen.

He leaned forward. "Theodore Berendtsen, you have been found guilty of treason against the human rights of the citizens of the Second Free American Republic. Have you anything to say before sentence is passed upon you?"

It did not matter what he said, now. Whatever words Berendtsen might have were weightless now. He had no Army. He had no weapons.

Garvin touched the carbine resting against his chair. Weapons were the mark of a man's freedom, and all free men carried them now. To be sure, some of them looked ludicrous, but, nevertheless, the symbol was there. Touch me not!

Berendtsen seemed to be hesitating, as though undecided whether to speak or not.

Berendtsen had no personal weapons.

He began to speak:

"I did not come here to defend myself," he said. "For I am indefensible. I have burned, killed, and looted, and my men have done worse, at times . . ."

Robert Garvin hardly heard the words. He sat patiently, not listening, but nevertheless watching the man. Berendtsen was standing with his hands hanging loosely at his sides, his head up. It was impossible to tell, from this angle, what he might be looking at.

Garvin felt a ripple of excitement sweep momentarily over the small audience, even reaching the judges' bench. He shrugged inwardly. Undoubtedly, his brother-in-law had scored some emotional point or other.

But emotional points were things you could score all day, and still not change the facts. Garvin had built his way to power on emotional points—what counted was the cold logical ideal behind them. You could sway a crowd with semantics. Make it do things for you. But this was not a crowd. These were Berendtsen's judges, their verdict already delivered, their sentence a foregone conclusion.

"Robert Garvin!"

Garvin's head snapped up, and his eyes re-focused on Berendtsen.

"You have given the people personal weapons," Berendtsen was saying. "You have told them that, from this day onward, they were free to bear arms; that they were equal, one and several, with all other men. That, henceforth, no man might tell him what was theirs and what was not. That each man was inviolable, and that no man is master."

Garvin nodded automatically, realizing only later that there was no need for him to do so.

"Well, then, Bob," Berendtsen said softly, as though they were once more across a dinner table from each other, "who gave you the right to confer the right?"

Something jumped behind Garvin's eyes.

"We bore arms, once. Each and every one of us. We had to. Gradually, we began to live so that we no longer had to. Despite the theories, some of us bore our arms uncomfortably, and were glad to lay them down when there were no longer snipers in the streets. Some of us were free to enter peaceful pursuits—such as politics."

Despite the time, and place, there was a ripple of laughter that grated at Robert Garvin's nerves before it died down.

Berendtsen smiled thinly up at Garvin. "You are where you are today because you did not bear arms—because there was an organization of free men, ready to return to the weapons if need be, but glad to have laid them down, who were cooperating in a civilization which had time to support an individual such as yourself. Those who bear arms are their own administrators. Those who do not, need others to administer to them.

"So you are here, an administrator elected by an organization, and you have given them their weapons back. You have practically forced those weapons on them, distributing them on streetcorners willy-nilly. But, once more, I'd like to know—who gave you the right?"

Berendtsen smiled wryly. "It would seem that I did. I built the organization that supports you. I built it without knowing what sort of society it would evolve. I never for a moment thought that any one man could be so wise, so foresighted as to impose his personal concept of the ideal society. I simply built a union, and left its structure to the people."

He looked squarely up at Garvin. "You have given the people rifles, and thought that you were giving them weapons. But people have a deadlier weapon than anything a gunsmith could design.

"People want to be safe, and comfortable. If safety and comfort are to be found in guns, then they will take up guns—of their own accord, in their own need. And when safety and comfort are found in libraries, then the guns rust."

The quiet, troubled and yet somehow untroubled eyes bored away at Garvin's foundations.

"You think that men like yourself direct the people. Undoubtedly, you grant me that status, as well. You are wrong. We exist—we find our way into the pages of those history books which are written from the wrong viewpoint—because, for however long or short a time it is, the people think there is safety and comfort in us."

He laughed shortly and finished. "They are often wrong. But they repair their errors."

Garvin felt every eye in the room on his face. Probably, he had turned a little pale. It was only natural, with the strain of what he had to do.

"Theodore Berendtsen, you have been convicted of treason, and the citizens of this Republic are aware of your crime. You are sentenced to go about whatever pursuits you choose, unarmed."

Berendtsen bowed his head. Garvin saw, for the first, startling time, that he was far older than he seemed—that his stomach bulged a little, and that his face was completely exhausted.

Then Berendtsen looked up for one last time, and

Robert Garvin saw the underlying expression of his face, always there, no matter what superficial mood might flicker across it. He understood what had been giving him the constant impression that Berendtsen was still the same calm, somehow unassailable man who had taken so many meals on the other side of the table.

A running series of directives came into the communications shack in New Jersey:

To all units, interim military command, SFAR: Be advised that the following former officers of the disbanded Army of Unification are enemies of the people:

> Samuel Ryder
> Randolph Willets
> John Eisner

All efforts are to be made to intercept these men, together with renegade units as they may command. These men have been proscribed. They are not in any way representatives of the SFAR or the Constitutional Council. You will attempt to capture these men and hold them for transportation back to New York, where they will be held for courts-martial. Any citizen, civilian or militia, attempting to aid or encourage these men, is summarily classified as an enemy of the people, and the above orders apply to such persons. Any person of undoubted civilian status, engaging in seditious discussion of these men is to be arrested immediately and held for the judgment of the civil governor. Any member of the militia engaging in similar talk is to be court-martialed immediately, the extreme sentence to be death by firing squad. Any militia officers refusing to carry out these orders will be arrested at the discretion of the highest ranking loyal officer, who will carry out the directives above and assume command.

Hollis,
Commander-in-Chief, SFAR

Jim looked incredulously at Holland. "What do you think's happened?"

Holland, his face grave, shook his head. "I'm not sure—but I think I know why Ted wanted Eisner with him. I'm pretty sure John's last orders were to point his cars west."

"You think Ted's with him?"

Holland's face held a queer expression for a moment. "Not in the flesh."

To all units, interim military command, SFAR: Be advised that the renegade military units under the command of former AU officers Eisner, Willets, and Ryder have fled out of the borders of the SFAR under determined pursuit by units of the New York Popular Militia. The rebels suffered heavy losses. Our units returned intact.

Holland and Garvin laughed savagely.

Be further advised that any evidences of Berendtsenism among the populace or in the ranks of military units are to be dealt with summarily.

Hollis,
C.I.C., SFAR

The operator who read the message had a nervous voice.

Holland raised an eyebrow. "Berendtsenism?"

For a moment, a savage light gleamed in his and Jim's eyes, washing out the dull resignation that had begun to settle there.

"Do you suppose Ted wasn't as dumb as New York thought he'd be?" Jim asked. "It sounds just a leetle bit like things are going to pieces up there. Suppose he realized that he might want somebody to break out, and hung on to Eisner for that purpose? And maybe he threw us in here to hole up until New York worked itself into the ground?"

Holland shook his head in bafflement. "I don't know. You could never tell with Ted. You could only wonder."

Robert Garvin spun around as Mayor Hammersby came through the door.

"Well?" he snapped.

Hammersby shrugged. "Not yet."

"What's the matter with them!"

Hammersby gave him a sidelong look. "Easy, Garvin. It'll happen."

Robert Garvin stared at him through a film of overpowering rage. It almost seemed as though even Hammersby were drawing a sort of insolence out of the impossible situation.

"We can't wait any longer. The old Army men have already delayed us with their talking. If we hold off much more, we'll have a revolution on our hands."

"Isn't that the theory?" Hammersby asked dryly. "Armed freemen, choosing their own leaders? Why should you object?"

The words dashed themselves against Robert Garvin like cold surf. Hammersby was right, of course. The people had a perfect right to choose for themselves, to kill or not to kill.

"Berendtsen's got to die!" he suddenly shouted. "Send out one of Hollis's patented mobs."

"The people will rule, eh? With an occasional nudge."

"*Damn it,* Hammersby!"

"Oh, I'll do it, all right. I'm just as worried about my neck as you are." The Mayor turned and left, with Garvin staring angrily at his back.

He couldn't shoot a man in the back, of course.

The last message from New York came metallically into the radio shack:

"To be re-broadcast to the general population at your discretion":

This is what Theodore Berendtsen said to his judges. It is the only public speech he ever made, and he made it surrounded by men who had been his friends. He did not look at anyone when he said this. His eyes were on something none of us, in that room with him, could see. But I am sure he saw it, as I am sure that, when someone reads these words, a hundred years from now, he will

know that a man living in our time was great
enough to plan beyond his own life.

The voice was a completely unknown one, and
trembled with feeling. It might be false, or it might
be real. Almost certainly, the man speaking was in
the grip of an overpowering emotion, and would grin
sheepishly at himself when he remembered it later.
But some obscure one of Berendtsen's judges had per-
formed that judgment better than had been expected
of him. Jim felt a cold chill run along his hackles as
he listened, and, when he touched a switch, heard the
speakers echoing mournfully outside.

He got to his feet and swung himself carefully over
to the window, leaning heavily on his crutches and
watching the faces of the people as they listened. And
then the tape-recorded voice cut in, and Garvin saw
the people gasp.

"I am not here to defend myself," Berendtsen
said. "For I am indefensible. I have burned,
killed, and looted, and my men have done worse,
at times.

"I killed because some men would rather destroy
than build—because their individual power was
sweeter to them than the mutual liberty of all
men. I killed, too, because I was born to a society,
and men would not accept that society. For that,
I am doubly guilty—but I could do nothing else.
Some issues are not clear-cut. Whatever the evils
of our society might be, I can only say that it was
my firm conviction that it would have been intolerable to us had some outside way of life sup-

planted it. In the last analysis, I made few judgments. I am not a superhuman hero. I am a man.

"I burned as a weapon of war—a war not against
individuals, but against what seemed to me to be
darkness. I looted because I needed the equipment
with which to kill and burn.

"I did these things in order to bring union to
what had been scattered tribes and uncoordinated
city-states. We stood on the bare brink of the
jungle we had newly emerged from, and, left
alone, it would have been centuries before the
scattered principalities fought out such a bloody
peace as would, at last, have given us civilization
again—after it was too late, after the books had
rotted and the machinery rusted.

"What binds an organization of people is unimportant. Political ideologies change. Purposes
change. The rule of one man comes to an end.
But the fact of organization continues, no matter
what changes occur within that organization.

"I have committed my last crime against today.
I leave you an organization to do with as you
will. I have set my hand on today, but I have not
presumed upon tomorrow."

There was a moment's crackling silence, and then
the New York broadcaster cut off, but the name he
signed to the message was completely devoid of title
or military rank, and there was no mention of Hollis
or the SFAR, or of Robert Garvin. Whatever had
brewed in New York was over, and this, not the blank,
deadly silence, was the proper end to Theodore Berendtsen's time.

* * *

"What the hell *is* that thing?" Jim said, squinting up into the sun.

"Helicopter, I guess. Looks like the picture," Holland answered. "You notice the cabin's got a blue-red stripe on it?"

Garvin nodded. "Yeah, I saw it." He leaned more heavily on his crutches.

There was a crowd of villagers around them, straining against the militiamen who were uncertain enough of their present authority to let the line bulge out raggedly.

"You notice that?" Holland said, pointing.

Jim looked at the ugly pockmarks of bullet scars on the cabin and nodded. Then the aircraft stormed over them, gargling its way downward until the landing skids touched the ground and the engine died. The cabin door opened.

"So that's what happened to Bob," Jim said softly. He smiled crookedly and began swinging toward the craft, Holland keeping pace with him. They were almost beside it when Holland suddenly touched Jim's arm.

Another man had gotten out with Bob, and now both of them were turning around to help the other passenger out. The breath caught in Jim's throat as he recognized his mother. Then he stopped and braced himself. When his mother looked at him, the shock of recognition in her eyes followed instantly by pain and indecision, he was ready.

"Hello, Mom," he said. "Nothing big—I'll be all right in a couple of weeks." She looked at him uncertainly, and finally put her arm through Bob's.

"Hello, Jimmy," she said. She had grown much

older than he remembered her, and needed Bob to support her after the long trip. Jim smiled and nodded reassuringly again.

"Hello, Holland," Bob said, licking his lips nervously. "This is Merton Hollis," he added, indicating the other man, who looked at the crowd uneasily, the arrogant lines of his face lost in the lax indecision of his face.

Holland raised his eyebrows.

"Can you—can you find us a place to stay here?" Bob asked.

Holland grinned crookedly. "Permanently, I take it? Exile is such a nasty word, isn't it?"

Garvin winced, but said nothing.

"Hello, Bob," Jim said.

"Hello, Jim," his brother answered without looking at him.

"I guess there's lots of room around here," Holland said. He grinned savagely. "Just one thing—I'm staying around. There's three sisters with a big farm and no man around. I kind of like one of them. One thing, like I said. Don't trespass." He patted the stock of his rifle.

"What happened to Mary, Mom?" Jim asked her.

Slow tears began to seep over Margaret Garvin's face. "She's dead, Jimmy. She and Ted. The—the people came and . . . and they . . ." She looked at Jim with complete bewilderment. "But now the people say they're sorry. Now they say they love them, and they keep telling me they're sorry . . . I don't understand, Jimmy."

Jim and Holland looked at Bob's face, and found corroboration in it. Jim laughed at his expression. Then he swung himself forward and looked into the helicopter's cabin. "Take a passenger back to New York, buddy?" he asked the pilot.

The man shrugged. "Makes me no never-mind. You'll have to wait a couple of minutes, though." He pulled a jackknife out of his pocket and jumped to the ground. He began to scrape out the blue-red stripe.

"Hey, don't be an idiot, Jim." Garvin cried. "They ask you what kind of a Garvin you are, nowadays."

Jim looked at him wearily. "When you find out, let me know, huh?"

He happened to glance at the crowd, and saw Edith, pressed forward by the villagers.

"Why is he taking out the stripe?" she was saying excitedly to a militiaman. "Why is he doing that? That's the freedom flag! He *can't* do that."

"Got a tip for you, Bob," Jim said, smiling thinly. "You've got one friend here, anyway." He wondered how that would work out.

He wondered, as the helicopter jounced northward, how a lot of things would work out. He wondered just exactly what legacy Ted Berendtsen had left the human race.

Had he died just in time, or too soon?

And Jim knew that no historian, probing back, could ever know, any more than he or Jack could know. Even now, even in the end, you had to trust Berendtsen's judgment.

CHAPTER SEVEN:

This happened in New Jersey a generation later, with Robert Garvin and Merton Hollis both dead in a duel with each other. Robert Garvin left a legacy, and this is what happened to it:

Cottrell Slade Garvin was twenty-six, and had been a sex criminal for three years, when his mother called him into her parlor and explained why she could not introduce him to the girl on whom he had been spying.

"Cottrell, darling," she said, laying her delicately veined hand on his sun-darkened own, "You understand that my opinion of Barbara is that she is a fine girl; one whom any young man of your class and station would ordinarily be honored to meet, and, in due course of time, betroth. But, surely, you must consider that her family,"—there was the faintest inhalation through the fragile nose—"particularly on the male side, is not one which could be accepted into our own." Her expression was genuinely regretful. "Quite frankly, her father's opinion on the proper conduct of a domicile . . ." The sniff was more audible. "His actions in accord with that opinion are such that our entire family would be embroiled in endless Affairs of Integrity, and you yourself would be forced to bear the brunt of most of these encounters. In addition, you would have the responsibility of defending the notoriously untenable properties which Mr. Holland pleases to designate as Barbara's dowry.

"No, Cottrell, I'm afraid that, much as such a match might appeal to you at first glance, you would find that the responsibilities more than offset the benefits." Her hand patted his as lightly as the touch of a falling autumn leaf. "I'm sorry, Cottrell." A tear sparkled at the corner of each eye, and it was obvious that the discussion had been a great strain to her, for she genuinely loved her son.

Cottrell sighed. "All right, mother," he said. There was nothing more he could do, at this time. "But, should circumstances change, you *will* reconsider, won't you?" he asked.

His mother smiled, and nodded as she said, "Of course, Cottrell." But the smile faded a bit. "However, that does seem rather unlikely, doesn't it? Are there no other young ladies?" At his expression, the smile returned, and her voice became reassuring. "But, we'll see. We'll see."

"Thank you, mother." At least, he had that much. He rose from his chair and kissed her cheek. "I have to be sure the cows have all been stalled." With a final smile exchanged between them, he left her, hurrying across the yard to the barn. The cows had all been attended to, of course, but he stayed in the barn for a few moments, driving his work-formed fist into a grain sack again and again, sweat breaking out on his forehead and running down his temples and along the sides of his face, while the breath grunted out of his nostrils and he half-articulated curses that were all the more terrible because he did not fully understand at whom or what they were directed.

Vaguely sick to his stomach, he gently closed the barn door behind him, and saw from the color of the sunset and the feel of the wind, that it would be a good night. The realization was one that filled him with equal parts of anticipation and guilt.

The air temperature was just right, and the dew had left a perfect leavening of dampness in the night. Cot let the false door close quietly behind him, and slipped noiselessly up and across the moist lawn at an angle that brought him out on the clay road precisely at the point where his property ended and Mr. Holland's began.

He walked through the darkness with gravel shifting silently under his moccasins, his bandolier bumping gently against his body, with the occasional feel of oily metal against his cheek as the carbine, slung from his shoulder, touched him with its curving magazine. It was a comforting sensation—his father had felt it before him, and his father's father. It had been the mark of free men for all of them.

When he had come as close to Mr. Holland's house as he could without disturbing the dog, he left the road and slid into the ditch that ran beside it, cradling his carbine in the crooks of his bent arms, and belly-crawled silently and rapidly until he was as near the house as the ditch would take him.

He raised his head behind a clump of weeds he had planted during a spring rainstorm, and, using this as cover, swept the front of the house with his vision.

For any of this to be possible without the dog's winding him, the breeze had to be just right. On such nights, it was.

The parlor window—perhaps the only surface-level parlor window in this area, he commented to himself—was lighted, and she was in the room. Cot checked the sharp sound of his breath and sank his teeth against his lower lip. He kept his hands carefully away from the metalwork of his carbine, for his palms were sweated.

He waited until, finally, she put the light out and went downstairs to bed, then dropped his head and rested it on his folded arms for a moment, his eyes closed and his breath uncontrollably uneven, before he twisted quietly and began to crawl back up the ditch. Tonight, so soon after what his mother had told him, he was shocked but not truly surprised to discover that his vision was badly blurred.

He reached the point where it was safe to leave the ditch and stood up quietly. He put one foot on the road and sprang up to the clay surface of the road with an easy contraction of his muscles. He had no warning of a darker shadow among the dappled splotches thrown by the roadside weeds and bushes. Mr. Holland said "Hi, boy," quietly.

Cot dropped his shoulder, ready to let the carbine he had just reslung slide down his arm and into his hand. He stood motionless, peering at Mr. Holland, who had stepped up to him.

"Mr. Holland!"

The old man chuckled. "Weren't expecting me, huh?"

Cot took a measure of relief from the man's obvious

lack of righteous anger. "Good—uh—good evening, sir," he mumbled. Apparently, he was not going to die immediately, but there was no telling what was going on in his neighbor's mind.

"Guess I was right about that patch of weeds springing up kind of sudden."

Cot felt the heat rush into his ears, but he said "Weeds, sir?"

"Pretty slick. You got the makings of a damn good combat man."

Cot was thankful for the darkness as one cause for his flush was replaced by another. The lack of light, however, did not keep his voice from betraying more than it should have. Mr. Holland's implication had been obvious. "My family, sir, prefers not to acknowledge those kin who had sunk below their proper station. You will understand that, under differing circumstances, I might thus consider your remark to be, in the least, not flattering."

Mr. Holland chuckled—a sound filled with the accumulated checks to hastiness acquired through a lifetime that was half over when Cot's began.

"No insults intended, son. There was a time when a guy like you wouldn't have stopped strutting for a week, after a pat on the back like that."

Cot could still feel the heat in his cheeks, and its cause overrode his sharp sense of incongruity at this midnight debate, a completely illogical development of circumstances under which any other two men would long ago have settled the question in a normal civilized manner.

"Fortunately, sir," he said, his voice now kept at its normal pitch with some effort, "we no longer live in such times."

"You don't maybe." Mr. Holand's voice was somewhat testy.

"I sincerely hope not, sir."

Mr. Holland made an impatient sound. "Boy, your Uncle Jim was the best goddamned rifleman that ever took out a patrol. Any family that gets snotty notions about being better than him—" He chopped the end of the sentence off with a raw and bitter curse.

Cot recoiled from the adjective. "Sir!"

"Excuse *me*," Mr. Holland said sarcastically. "I forgot you're living in refined times. Not too refined for a man to go crawling in ditches to sneak a look at a girl, though. A girl sitting and reading a book!" he added with something like shock.

Cot felt the adrenaline-propelled tingle sweep through his bloodstream and knot his muscles. At any moment, Mr. Holland was obviously going to call an Affair of Integrity. Even while he formulated the various points for and against a right to defend himself even if surprised in so palpably immoral an action, his reflexes let the carbine slip to the angle of his shoulder and hang precariously from the sling, which now, despite careful oiling, gave a perverse squeak. Cot set his teeth in annoyance.

"I haven't got a gun on you, boy," Mr. Holland said quietly. "There's better ways of protecting your integrity than shooting people."

Cot had long ago decided that his neighbor, like all the old people who had been born in the Wild Sixties and grown up through the Dirty Years was, to put it politely, unconventional. But the sheer lack of common sense in going unarmed into a situation

234

where one's Integrity might be molested was more than any unconventionality.

But that was neither here nor there. In such a case, the greater responsibiilty in carrying out the proprieties was obviously his to assume.

"Allow me to state the situation clearly, sir," he said, "In order that there might be no misunderstanding."

"No misunderstanding, son. Not about the situation, anyway. Hell, when I was your—"

"Nevertheless," Cot interposed, determined not to let Mr. Holland trap himself into a genuine social blunder, "The fact remains that I have trespassed on your property for a number of years—"

"For the purpose of peeping at Barbara," Mr. Holland finished for him. "Do me a favor, son?" Mr. Holland's voice was slightly touched by an amused annoyance.

"Certainly, sir."

"Can the—" Mr. Holland caught himself. "I mean, show a little less concern for the social amenities; ease up on this business of doing the right thing, come hell or high water, and just listen. Here. Sit down, and let's talk about a few things."

Cot's nerves had edged to the breaking point. He was neither hung nor pardoned. This final gaucherie was too much for him.

"I'm sorry, sir," he said, his voice, nerve-driven, harder and harsher than he intended, "but that's out of the question. I suggest that you either do your duty as the head of your family or else acknowledge your unwillingness to do so."

"Why?"

The question was not as surprising as it might have been, had it come at the beginning of this fantastic scene. But it served to crystallize one point. It was not meant as a defiant insult, Cot realized. It was a genuine and sincere inquiry. And the fact that Mr. Holland was incapable of appreciating the answer was proof that his mother's advice had been correct. Holland was not a gentleman.

Quite obviously, there was only one course now open to him, if he did not abandon all hope of Barbara's hand. Incredible as it might seem, it was to answer the question in all seriousness, in an attempt to force some understanding through the long-set and, bluntly, ossified, habits of Holland's thinking.

"I should think it would be hardly necessary to remind you that an individual's Integrity is his most prized moral possession. In this particular case, I have violated your daughter's Integrity, and, through blood connection, that of your family, as well." Cot shook his head in the darkness. Explain he might, but his voice was indication enough of his outrage.

"What's that?" Holland's own voice was wearing thin.

"I beg your pardon, sir?"

"Integrity, damn it! Give me a definition."

"Integrity, sir? Why, *everyone*—"

Holland cut him off with a frustrated curse. "I should have known better than to ask! You can't even verbalize it, but you'll cut each other down for it. All right, you go ahead, but don't expect me to help you make a damned fool of yourself." He sighed. "Go on home, son. Maybe, in about twenty years or so, you'll get up guts enough to come and knock on the door like a man, if you want to see Barbara."

Through the occlusion of his almost overwhelming rage, Cot realized that he could not, now, say anything further which might offend Holland. "I'm certain that if I were to do so, Miss Barbara would not receive me," he finally managed to say in an even voice, gratified at his ability to do so.

"No, she probably wouldn't," Holland said bitterly. "She's too goddamned well brought up, thanks to those bloody aunts of hers!"

Before Cot could react to this, Holland spat on the ground, and, turning his back like a coward, strode off down the road.

Cot stood alone in the night, his hands clutching his bandolier, grinding the looped cartridges together. Then he turned on his heel and loped home.

He left his carbine on the family arms-rack in the front parlor, and padded about the surface floor in his moccasins, resetting the alarms, occasionally interrupting himself to tense his arms or clamp his jaw as he thought of what had happened. The incredible complexity of the problem overwhelmed him, presenting no clear face which he could attack and rationalize logically.

Primarily, of course, the fault was his. He had committed a premeditated breach of Integrity. It was in its various ramifications that the question lost its clarity.

He had spied on Barbara Holland and done it repeatedly. Her father had become aware of the fact. Tonight, rather than issue a direct challenge, Holland had lain in wait for him. Then, having informed Cot that he was aware of his actions, Holland had not only not done the gentlemanly thing, but had actually ridiculed his expectation of it. The man had insulted

Cot and his family, and had derided his own daughter. He had referred to his sisters-in-law in a manner which, if made public, would have called for a bandolier-flogging at the hands of the male members of the female line.

But the fact nevertheless remained that whether Mr. Holland was a gentleman or Holland was not, Cot had been guilty of a serious offence. And, in Cot's mind as in that of every other human being, what had been a twinging secret shame was as disastrous and disgusting as a public horror.

And, since Holland had refused to solve the problem for him in the manner in which anyone else would unhesitatingly have done so, Cot was left with this to gnaw at his brain and send him into sudden short-lived bursts of anger intermingled with longer, quieter, and deadlier spells of remorseful shame.

Finally, when he had patrolled the entire surface floor, Cot walked noiselessly down to the living quarters, completely uncertain of the degree of his guilt, and, therefore, of his shame and disgrace, knowing that he would not sleep no matter how long he lay on his bed—and he fought down that part of his mind which recalled the image of Barbara Holland.

Fought—but lost. The remembered picture was as strong as the others beside which he placed it, beginning with the first one from five years ago, when, at the age of twenty-one, he had passed her window on his return from Graduate training. And, though he saw her almost every day at the post office or store, these special images were not obscured by the cold and proper aloofness with which she surrounded herself when she was not—he winced—alone.

Again, there was the entire problem of Barbara's

father. The man had been raised in the wild immorality and casual circumstances of the Dirty Years. Obviously, he could see nothing wrong with what Cot had been doing. He had sense enough not to tell anyone else about it, thank the good Lord—but, in some blundering attempt to "get you two kids together," or whatever he might call it, *what would he tell Barbara?*

Dawn came, and Cot welcomed the night's end.

As head of the family since his father's death in an affair of Integrity two years before—he had, of course, been the Party at Grievance—it was Cot's duty to plan each day's activities insofar as they were to vary from the normal farm routine. Today, with all the spring work done and summer chores still so light as to be insignificant, he was at a loss, but he was grateful for this opportunity to lose himself in a problem with which he had been trained to cope.

But after an hour of attempting to think, he was forced to fall back on what, in retrospect, must have been a device his father had put to similar use. If there was nothing else, there was always Drill.

Out of consideration for his grandmother's age, he waited until 7:58 before he touched the alarm stud, but not even the heavy slam of shutters being convulsively hurled into their places in the armor plate of the exterior walls, the sudden screech of the generators as the radar antennas came out of their half-sleep into madly whirling life, or the clatter as the household children fired test bursts from their machineguns were enough to quench the fire in his mind.

The drill ran until 10:00. By then, it was obvious that the household defenses were doing everything they had been designed to, and that the members of the household knew their parts perfectly. Even his grandmother's legendary skill with her rangefinder had not grown dull—though there was a distinct possibility that she had memorized the range of every likely target in the area. But that, if true, was not an evasion of her duties but, instead, a valuable accomplishment.

"Very good," he said over the household intercommunications system. "All members of the household are now free to return to their normal duties, with the exception of the children, who will report to me for their schooling."

His mother, whose battle station was at the radarscope a few feet away from his fire control board, smiled with approval as she returned the switches to AutoSurvey. She put her hand gently on his forearm as he rose from behind the board.

"I'm glad, Cottrell. Very glad," she said with her smile.

He did not understand what she meant, at first, and looked at her blankly.

"I was afraid you might neglect your duties, as so many of our neighbors are doing," she explained by continuing. "But I should not have doubted you, even to that degree." Her low voice was strongly underlaid with her pride in him. "Your fiber is stronger than that. Why, I was even afraid that your disappointment after our little talk yesterday might distract you. But I was wrong, and you'll never know how thrilled I am to see it."

He bent to kiss her quickly, so that she would not see his eyes, and hurried up to the parlor, where the children had already assembled and taken their weapons out of the arms-rack.

By mid-afternoon, the younger children had been excused, and only his two oldest brothers were out on the practice terrain with him.

"Stay down!" Cot shouted at Alister. "You'll never live to Graduate if you won't learn to flatten out at the crest of a rise!" He flung his carbine up to his cheek and snapped a branch beside his brother's rump to prove the point.

"Now, *you*," he whirled on Geoffrey. "How'd I estimate my windage? Quick!"

"Grass," Geoffrey said laconically.

"Wrong! You haven't been over that ground in two weeks. You've no accurate idea of how much wind will disturb that grass into its present pattern."

"Asked me how *you* did it," Geoffrey pointed out.

"All right," Cot snapped. "Score one for you. Now, how *would* you do it?"

"Feel. Watch me." Geoffrey's lighter weapon cracked with a noise uncannily like that of the branch, which now split at a point two inches below where Cot's heavy slug had broken it off.

"Have an instinct for it, do you?" Cot was perversely glad to find an outlet for his annoyance. "Do it again."

Geoffrey shrugged. He fired twice. The branch splintered, and there was a shout from Alister. Cot spun and glared at Geoffrey.

"Put it next to his hand," Geoffrey explained. "Guess he got some dirt in his face, too."

Cot looked at the point where the grass was undulating wildly as Alister tried to roll away under its cover. He found time to note his brother's clumsiness before he said, "You couldn't have seen his hand—or anything except the top of his rump, for that matter."

Geoffrey's seventeen-year-old face was secretly amused. "I just figured, if I was Alice, where would I keep my hands? Simple."

Cot could feel the challenge to his pre-eminence as the family's fighting man gathering thickly about him.

"Very good," he said bitingly. "You have an instinct for combat. Now, suppose that had been a defective cartridge—bad enough to tumble the bullet to the right and kill your brother. What then?"

"I hand-loaded those cases myself. Think I'm fool enough to trust that ham-handed would-be gunsmith at the store?" Geoffrey was impregnable. Cot felt his temper beginning to escape the clutch of his strained will.

"If you're so good, why don't you go off and join the Militia?"

Geoffrey took the insult without an expression on his face. "Think I'll stick around," he said calmly. "You're going to need help—if old man Holland ever catches you on those moonlight strolls of yours."

Cot could feel the sudden rush of blood pushing at the backs of his eyes. *What did you say?* The words drove out of his throat with low deadliness.

"You heard me." Geoffrey turned away, put a bullet to either side of the thrashing Alister, and one above and below. Alister's training broke completely, and he sprang out of the grass and began to run, shouts choking his throat. "A rabbit," Geoffrey spat contemptuously. "Just pure rabbit. Me, I've got Uncle

242

Jim's blood, but that Alice, he's strictly Mother." He fired again and snapped the heel off Alister's shoe. As Alister stumbled to the ground, Cot's open palm smashed against the side of Geoffrey's face.

Geoffrey took two sideward steps and stopped, his eyes wide with shock. The rifle hung limply from his hands. He had several years to grow before he would raise it instinctively.

"You'll never mention that relative's name again!" Cot said thickly. "Not to me, and not to anyone else. What's more, you'll consider it a breach of Integrity if anyone speaks of him in your presence. Is that understood? And as for your fantasies about myself and and Mr. Holland, if you mention *that* again, you'll learn that there is such a thing as a breach of Integrity between brothers!" But he knew that anything he might say now was as much of an admission as a shouted confession. He could feel the night's sickness seeping through his system again, turning his muscles into limp rags and sending the blood pounding through his ears.

Geoffrey narrowed his eyes, and his lip curled into a half-sneer.

"For a guy that hates armies and soldiers, you sure think you can act like a Senior Sergeant," he said bitterly. He turned around and began to stride away, then stopped and looked back. "And I'd drop you before you got the lead out of your pants," he added.

Geoffrey knows, echoed through his mind. *Geoffrey knows, and Mr. Holland found me out. How many others?* Like a sickening refrain, the thoughts tumbled over and over in his skull as he swung down the road with rapid and clumsy strides. The usual coordination

243

of all the muscles in his lithe body had been destroyed by the added shock of what he had learned on the practice terrain.

He pictured Geoffrey, watching from a window and snickering as he crawled down the ditch. He seemed to hear Mr. Holland's dry chuckle. Over the last three years, how many others of his neighbors had seen him? As he thought of it, it seemed incredible that pure chance had not ensured that the entire countryside was aware of his disgraceful actions.

But he could not run from it. It was not the way a man faced situations. The thing to do was to go to the club and watch the faces of the men as they looked at him. As they greeted him, there would be a little hidden demon of scorn in their eyes to be looked for.

The carbine's butt slapped his thigh as he climbed the club steps.

He could not be sure he had found it. As he looked down at the newly refilled mug of rum, he understood this with considerable clarity. He could not deny that a strange sort of perverse desire to see what was not really there might have put an imagined edge on the twinkle in Winter's eyes, the undercurrent of mirth that always accented Olsen's voice. If Lundy Hollis sneered a bit more than usual, it probably meant nothing more than that the man had discovered some new quality in himself that made him better than his fellows. But probably, probably, and nothing certain. Neither affirmation nor denial.

Cot's hand closed around the mug, and he scalded his throat with the drink. The remembered visions of Barbara were attaining a greater precision with every swallow.

"Hello, boy."

Oh, my God! he thought. He'd forgotten that Holland was a member of the club. But, of course, he was, though Cot couldn't understand how the old man managed to be kept in. He watched Mr. Holland slip into the seat opposite his, and wondered how many chuckles had accompanied the man's retelling of last night's events.

"How do you do, sir," he managed to say, remembering to maintain the necessary civilities.

"Don't mind if I work on my liquor at the same table with you, do you?"

Cot shook his head. "It's my pleasure, sir."

The chuckle came that Cot had been waiting for. "Say, boy, even with a few slugs in you, you don't forget to tack on those fancy parts of speech, do you?" Mr. Holland chuckled again.

"Guess I got a little mad at you last night," he went on. "Sorry about that. Everybody's got a right to live the way they want to."

Cot stared silently into his mug. The clarity that had begun to emerge from the rum was unaccountably gone, as though the very touch of Holland's presence was enough to plunge him headlong back into the mental chaos that had strangled his thinking through the night and most of the day. He was no longer sure that Mr. Holland had not kept the story to himself; he was no longer sure that Geoffrey had done more than make a shrewd guess . . . He was no longer sure.

"Look, boy . . ."

And the realization came that, for the first time since he had known him, Mr. Holland was as much unsure of his ground as he. He looked up, and saw the slow light of uncertainty in the man's glance.

"Yes, sir?"

"Boy—I don't know. I tried to talk to you last night, but I guess we were both kind of steamed up. Think you'll feel more like listening tonight? Particularly if I'm careful about picking my words?"

"Certainly, sir." That, at least, was common courtesy.

"Well, look—I was a friend of your Uncle Jim's."

Cot bristled. "Sir, I—" He stopped. In a sense, he was obligated to Mr. Holland. If he didn't say it now, it would have to be said later. "Sorry, sir. Please go on."

Mr. Holland nodded. "We campaigned with Berendtsen together, sure. That doesn't sit too well with some people around here. But it's true, and there's lots of people who remember it, so there's nothing wrong with my saying it."

Something that was half-reflex twisted Cot's mouth at the mention of the AU, but he kept silent.

"How else was Ted going to get a central government started among a bunch of forted-up farmers and lone-wolf nomads? Beat 'em individually at checkers? We needed a government—and fast, before we ran out of cartridges for the guns and went back to spears and arrows."

"They didn't have to do it the way they did it," Cot said bitterly.

Mr. Holland sighed. "Devil they didn't. And, besides, how do you know exactly how it was done? Were you there?"

"My mother and father were. My mother remembers very well," Cot shot back.

"Yeah," Mr. Holland said dryly. "Your father was there. And your mother was always good at remembering. Does she remember how your father came to be here in the first place?"

Cot frowned for a moment at the obscure reference to his father. "She remembers. She also remembers my uncle's leading the group that wiped out her family."

Holland smiled cryptically. "Funny, the way things change in people's memories," he murmured. He went on more loudly. "The way I heard it, her folks were from Pennsylvania. What were *they* doing, holding down Jersey land?" He leaned forward. "Look, son, it wasn't anybody's land. Her folks could have kept it, if they hadn't been too scared to believe us when we told them all we wanted was for them to join the Republic. And anyway, none of that kept her from marrying Bob."

Cot took a deep breath. "My father, sir, never fought under Berendtsen. His Integrity did not permit him to take other people's orders, or do their butchery."

"Ahuh," Mr. Holland said. "Your father got to be awful good with that carbine. He had to," he added in a lower voice. "And I guess he had to rationalize it somehow.

"Your father built up this household defense system," he said more clearly. "I guess he figured that an armored bunker was the thing to protect his property the same way his carbine protected him.

"Which wasn't a bad idea. Berendtsen unified this country, but he didn't exactly clean it up. That was more than they gave him time for."

Holland stopped and drained his mug. He put it down and wiped his mouth. "But, boy, don't you think those days are kind of over? Don't you think it's

247

time we came out of those hedgehog houses, and out of this hedgehog Integrity business?"

Mr. Holland put his palms on the table and held Cot's eyes with his own. "Don't you think it's time we finished the unifying job, and got us a community where a boy can walk up to his neighbor's house in broad daylight, knock on the door, and say hello to a girl if he wants to?"

Cot had been listening with his emotions so tangled that none of them could have been unraveled and classified. But now, Holland's last words reached him, and once again, the thought of what had happened the previous night was laid bare, and all his disgust for himself with it.

"I'm sorry, sir," he said stiffly. "But I'm afraid we have differing views on the subject. A man's home is his defense, and his Integrity and that of his family are what keep that defense strong and inviolate. Perhaps other parts of the Republic are not founded on that principle, as I've heard lately, but here the code by which we live is one which evolved for the fulfillment of those vital requisites to freedom. If we abandon them, we go back to the Dirty Years.

"And I am afraid, sir," he finished with a remembrance of the outrage he had felt the previous night, "that despite your questionable efforts, I shall still marry your daughter honorably, or not at all."

Holland shook his head and smiled to himself, and Cot realized how foolish that last sentence had sounded. Nevertheless, while he could not help his impulses, he was perfectly aware of the difference between right and wrong.

Holland stood up. "All right, boy. You stick to your

system. Only—it doesn't seem to work too well for you, does it?"

And, once again, Mr. Holland turned around and walked away, leaving Cot with nothing to say or do, and with no foundation for assurance. It was as though Cot grappled with a vague nightmare; a dark and terrible shape that presented no straightforward facet to be attacked, but which put out tentacles and pseudopods until he was completely enmeshed in it— only to fade away and leave him with his clawing arms hooked around nothing.

It was worse than any anger or insult could have been.

His footsteps were unsteady as he crossed the club floor. The rum he had drunk, combined with a sleepless night, had settled into a weight at the base of his skull. He was about to open the door when Charles Kittredge laid a hand on his arm.

Cot turned.

"How do you do, Cottrell," Kittredge said.

Cot nodded. Charles was his neighbor on the side away from Mr. Holland. "How do you do."

"You look a little tired," Charles remarked.

"I am, Charles." He grinned back in answer to his neighbor's smile.

"Shouldn't wonder—holding a drill at 0800."

Cot shrugged. "Have to keep the defenses in shape, you know."

Kittredge laughed. "Why, for God's sake? Or were you just rehearsing for the Fourth?"

Cot frowned. "Why—no, of course not. I've heard you holding Drill, often enough."

His neighbor nodded. "Sure—whenever one of the kids has a birthday. But you don't really mean you were holding a genuine dead-serious affair?"

Cot was having trouble maintaining his concentration. He squinted and shook his head slightly. "What's the matter with that?"

Kittredge's voice and manner became more serious. "Oh, now look, Cot, there's been nothing to defend against in fifteen years. Matter of fact, I'm thinking of dismounting my artillery and selling it to the Militia. They're offering a fair price."

Cot looked at him uncomprehendingly. "You can't be serious?"

Kittredge returned the look. "Sure."

"But you *can't*. They'd stay out of machinegun range and shell you to fragments with mortars and fieldpieces. They'd knock out your machinegun turrets, come in closer under rifle cover, and lob grenades into your living quarters."

Kittredge laughed. He slapped his thigh while his shoulders shook. "Who the devil is 'they,'" he gasped. "Berendtsen?"

Cot felt the first touch of anger as it penetrated the deadening blanket that had wrapped itself around his thoughts.

Kittredge gave one final chuckle. "Come off it, will you, Cot? As a matter of fact, while I wasn't going to mention it, all that banging going on at your place this morning practically ruined one of my cows. Ran head-on into a fence. It's not the first time it's happened, either. The only reason I've never said anything is because your own livestock probably has just as bad a time of it.

"Look, Cot, we can't afford to unnerve our livestock and poison our land. It was all right as long as it was the only way we could operate at all, but the most hostile thing that's been seen around here in years is a chicken hawk."

The touch of anger had become a genuine feeling. Cot could feel it settling into the pit of his stomach and vibrating at his fingertips.

"So, you're asking me to stop holding Drill, is that it?"

Kittredge heard the faint beginning of a rasp in Cot's voice, and frowned. "Not *altogether,* Cot. Not if you don't want to. But I wish you'd save it for celebrations."

"The weapons of my household aren't firecrackers." The words were carried as though at the flicking end of a whip.

"Oh, come *on,* Cot!"

For almost twenty-four hours, Cot had been encountering situations for which his experience held no solutions. He was baffled, frustrated, and angry. The carbine was off his shoulder and in his hands with the speed and smoothness of motion that his father had drilled into him until it was beyond impedance by exhaustion or alcohol. With the gun in his hands, he suddenly realized just how angry he was.

"Charles Kittredge, I charge you with attempt to breach the Integrity of my household. Load and fire."

The formula, too, was as ingrained in Cot as was his whole way of life. Chuck Kittredge knew it as well as he did. He blanched.

"You gone crazy?" It was a new voice, from slightly

251

beyond and beside Charles. Cot's surprised glance flickered over and saw Kittredge's younger brother, Michael.

"Do you stand with him?" Cot rapped out.

"Aw, now, look, Cot . . ." Charles Kittredge began. "You're not serious about this?"

"Stand or turn your back."

"*Cot!* All I said was—"

"Am I to understand that you are attempting to *explain* yourself?"

Michael Kittredge moved forward. "What's the matter with you, Garvin? You living in the Dirty Years or something?"

The knot of fury twisted itself tighter in Cot's stomach. "That will be far enough. I asked you once: Do you stand with him?"

"No, he doesn't!" Charles Kittredge said violently. "And I don't stand either. What kind of a fool thing's going on in your head, anyway? People just don't pull challenges like that at the drop of a hat anymore!"

"That's for each man to decide for himself," Cot answered. "Do you turn your back, then?"

An ugly red flush flamed at Kittredge's cheekbones. "Damned if I will." His mouth clamped into an etched white line. "All right, then, Cot, what goes through that door first, you or me?"

"Nobody will go anywhere. You'll stand or turn where you are."

"Right here *in the club?* You *are* crazy!"

"You chose the place, not I. Load and fire."

Kittredge put his hand on his rifle sling. "On the count, then," he said hopelessly.

Cot re-slung his carbine. "One," he said.

"Two." He and Kittredge picked up the count together.

"Three," in unison.

"Four."

"Fi—" Cot had not bothered to count five aloud. The carbine fell into his hooked and waiting hands, and jumped once. Kittredge, interrupted in the middle of his last word, collapsed to the club floor.

Cot looked down at him, and then back to Michael, who was standing where he had been looking at Cot's face.

"Do you stand with him?" Cot repeated the formula once more.

Michael shook his head dumbly.

"Then turn."

Michatel nodded. "I'll turn. Sure, I'll be a coward." There was a peculiar quality to his voice. Cot had seen men turn before, but never as though by free choice. *Except for Holland, of course,* the thought came.

Cot looked at the width of Michael's back, and reslung his carbine. "All right, Michael. Take your dead home to your household." He stood where he was while Michael hoisted his bother's body over his shoulder. According to the formula, he should have publicly called the boy a coward. But he did not, and his next words betrayed his reason. "He was a good friend of mine, Michael. I'm sorry he forced me to do it."

As he walked home, past Mr. Holland's house, Cot did not turn his head to see if there were lights in any of the windows. He had kept his family's Integrity unbreached. He had forced another man to turn. But he did not himself know whether he hoped Barbara would understand that, in a sense, he had done it to redeem himself for her.

Two days later, at dinnertime Geoffrey and Alister came in five minutes late. Geoffrey's face was wide and numb with shock, and Alister's was glowing with a rampant inner joy. It was only when Geoffrey turned that Cot saw his left sleeve soaked in blood.

"Geoffrey!" Cot's mother pushed her chair back and ran to him. She pulled a medkit off its wall bracket and began cutting the sleeve away.

"What happened?" Cot asked.

"I got my man today," Geoffrey said, his voice as numb as his features. "He rightfully belongs to Al, here, though." A grin broke through the numbness, and a babble of words came out as the shock of the wound passed into hysteria.

"That crazy Michael Kittredge climbed a tree up at the edge of the practice terrain. Had a 'scope-mounted T-4 and six extra clips. Must have figured on an all-out war. First thing I knew, it felt like somebody hit my shoulder with a baseball bat, and I was down, with the slugs plowing the ground in circles around me. I tried to do something with my rifle, but no go. Kittredge must have had crosseyes or something —couldn't hit the side of a cliff with a howitzer, after the first shot—damn fool stunt, 'scope-mounting an automatic—*somebody* should have taught him better— and there I was, passing out from the recoil every time I squeezed off. You never saw such a blind man's shooting match in your life!

"Then out of this gully he'd been imitating an elephant wallowing through, up pops Al! Slaps the old blunderbuss to his shoulder like the man on a skeet-shoot trophy, and starts blasting away at Kittredge's tree like there was nothing up there but pigeons! Tell you, the sight of that came nearer killing me than Kittredge's best out of twenty-five.

"Well, the jerk might have been crazy, but he wasn't up to ignoring a clipload of soft-nose. He swings that lunatic T-4 of his for Al, and this gives me a chance to steady up and put a lucky shot through a leaf he happened to be in back of at the time. He's still out there."

Cot felt his teeth go into his lower lip. Michael Kittredge!

"He shot you from ambush?"

"He wasn't carrying any banners!"

"But that's disgraceful!" Cot's mother exclaimed. She finished wrapping the gauze over the patch bandage on Geoffrey's bicep.

Cot looked at Alister, who was standing beside Geoffrey, his face still shining. "Is that what happened, Alister?" he asked.

Alister nodded.

"Sure, that's what happened!" Geoffrey said indignantly. "Think this's a mosquito bite?"

"You know what this means, don't you?" Cot asked gravely.

Geoffrey began a shrug and winced. "Fool kid with a bug."

Cot shook his head. "The Kittredges may be lax in their training, but Michael knew better. In a sense, that was a declaration of war. If Michael was out there, the rest of his household may not have known about it, but when they find out they'll be forced to support his action."

"So it's a declaration of war," Alister suddenly said, his tones a conscious imitation of Geoffrey's. "What have we been drilling for?"

Geoffrey's eyes opened wide, and the secretive laughter returned to his expression as he looked at his younger brother.

"Not to start a war—or get involved in one," Cot said. "Their gunnery will be sloppier than ours, but their armor plate's just as thick."

"What do you want to do, Cottrell?" his mother asked. Her delicate face was anxious, and her hands seemed to have poised for the express purpose of underscoring the question.

"We've got to stop this thing before it snowballs," Geoffrey said. "I didn't get it before, but Cot's right."

Cot nodded. "We'll have to call everybody in to a meeting. I don't know what can be done about the Kittredges. Maybe we'll all be able to think of something." He beat the side of his fist lightly against his thigh. "I don't know. It's never been done before. But the Kittredges aren't the AU. We can't handle the problem by simply dropping our shutters and fighting as independent units. The whole community would finish in firing on each other. We've got to have concerted action. Perhaps, if the community lines up as a solid block against them, we'll be able to forestall the Kittredges."

"Unite the community!" His mother's eyes were wide. "Do you think you can do it?"

Cot sighed. "I don't know, mother. I couldn't guess." He turned back to Alister. "We're going up to the club. It's the only natural meeting place we've got. I think you'd better break out the car. The Kittredges might have more snipers among them."

He picked his carbine up from the arms rack, and started to follow the busily efficient Alister down to the garage.

"I'll go with you," Geoffrey said. "Only takes one arm to work the turret guns."

Cot looked at him indecisively. Finally, he said, "All right. There's no telling what the Kittredges might be up to along the road." He turned back to his mother. "I think it might be advisable to put the household on action stations." She nodded, and he went down into the garage.

The road was open, and glaring white in the sunlight of early afternoon. The armored car's tires jounced over the latitudinal ruts that freight trucks had worn into the road, and one part of him was worried about the effect on Geoffrey, battened down in the turret. He looked up through the overhead slits and saw the twin muzzles of the 35mm cannon tracking steadily counterclockwise.

Where did it begin, what started it? he thought with most of his mind. The chain of recent events was clear. From the moment that Mr. Holland had discovered him, that night four days ago, event had followed event as plainly and as inevitably as though it had been planned in advance.

If he had not been upset by his meeting with Mr. Holland, he would not have called Drill the following morning. If he had never seen Barbara at her window at all, there would have been nothing for Geoffrey to taunt him with, and no fear of exposure to drive him to the club. If he had not been drinking, Mr. Holland's references to Uncle James would not have cut so deeply. Had there been no Drill, there would have been no quarrel with Charles Kittredge, and even if there had been Drill, Charles's remarks would not have been so objectionable had there been no smoldering resentment from his talk with Mr. Holland.

For, it was true, he had been angry. Had he not been, Charles and Michael would not be dead, and he and his brothers would not now be in the car, trying to stop an upheaval of violence that would involve the entire community. But his anger had not been his responsibility. A breach of Intregity remained a breach of Integrity, no matter what the subjective state of the Party at Grievance.

But where did it really begin? If his mother had ever introduced him to Barbara, would any of this have happened?

He rejected that possibility. His mother had been acting in accordance with the code that his father and the other free men who had settled in this area had evolved. And the code was a good code. It had kept the farmlands free and in peace, with no man wearing another's collar—until Michael Kittredge broke the code.

And so, while he thought, he turned the car off the road and stopped in front of the club.

The porch of the club was already crowded with men. As he climbed out of the car's hatch, he saw that all the families of the community, with the exception of the Kittredges, were represented. Olsen, Hollis, Winter, Jordan, Park, Jones, Cadell, Rome, Lynn, Williams, Bridges—all of them. Even Mr. Holland stood near the center of the porch, his lined face graver than Cot had ever seen it.

He walked toward them. The news had spread

rapidly. He remembered that a lot of households had radios now. He'd never seen any use for one, before. Probably, he ought to get one. As long as the families were uniting, a fast communications channel was a good idea.

"That's far enough, Garvin!" He stopped and stared up at the men on the porch. Lundy Hollis had lifted his rifle.

Cot frowned. One or two other guns in the crowd were being raised in his direction.

"I don't understand this," he said.

Hollis sneered, and snorted. He looked past Cot at the car. "If anyone in the buggy tries anything, we've got a present for them."

The men on the porch drew off to two sides. Two men were crouched in the club's doorway. One held a steady antitank rocket launcher on his shoulder, and the other, having fed a rocket into the chamber, stood ready to slap the top of his head and give the signal to fire.

"I'll ask once more—"

"Looks like you've united the community, boy," Mr. Holland said. "Against you."

Cot felt the familiar surge of anger ripple up through his body. "Against me! What for?"

There was a scattered chorus of harsh laughs.

"What about Chuck Kittredge?" Hollis asked.

"Charles Kittredge! That was an Affair of Integrity!"

"Yeah? Whose—yours or his?" Hollis asked.

"Seems like the day of Integrity has sort of come and gone, son," Mr. Holland said gently.

"Yeah, and what about Michael Kittredge?" someone shouted from the back of the crowd. "Was that an Affair of Integrity, too?"

259

"What about those two brothers of yours shooting the kid out of a tree?" someone else demanded.

"Geoffrey's in the car with a wounded arm right now!" Cot shouted.

"And Mike Kittredge's dead."

There was a babble of voices. The burst of sound struck Cot's ears, and he felt himself crouch, fists balled, as the knot of fury within him exploded in reply.

"All right," he shouted. "All right! I came up here to ask you to stop the Kittredges with me. I see they got to you first. All right! Then we'll take them on alone, and the devil can have all of you!"

Somehow, in the storm of answers that came from the porch, Mr. Holland's quiet voice came through.

"No good, boy. See, when I said 'against you,' I meant it. It's not a case of them not helping you—it means they're going to start shelling your place in two hours, whether you're in it or not."

"No." The word was torn out of him, and even he had to analyze its expression. It was not a command, nor a request, nor a statement of fact or wonder. It was simply a word, and he knew, better than anyone else who heard it, how ineffectual it was.

"So you'd better get your family out of there, son." The other men on the porch had fallen silent, all of them watching Cot except for the two men with the rocket launcher, who ignored everything but the armored car.

Mr. Holland came off the porch and walked toward him. He put his hand on his shoulder. "Let's be getting back, son. Lots of room at my place for your family."

Cot looked up at the men on the porch again. They

were completely silent, all staring back at him as though he were some strange form of man that they had never seen before.

He shuddered. "All right."

Mr. Holland climbed through the hatch, and Cot followed him, slamming it shut behind him and settling into the driver's saddle. He gunned the idling engine, locked his left rear wheels, and spun the car around. With the motor at full gun, the dust billowing, the armored car growled back down the road.

"I heard most of it, Cot," Geoffrey's tight and bitter voice came over the intercom. "Let's get back to the house in a hurry. We can dump a ton of frag on that porch before those birds know what's hitting them."

Cot shook his head until he remembered that Geoffrey couldn't see him. "They'll be gone, Jeff. Scattered out to their houses, getting ready."

"Well, let's hit the houses, then," Alister said from behind the machinegun on the car's turtledeck.

"Wouldn't stand a chance, son," Mr. Holland said.

"He's right. They've got us cold," Cot agreed.

What had happened to the code? His father had lived by it. All the people in the community had lived by it. He himself had lived by it—he caught himself. Had tried to live by it, and failed.

Cot stood in the yard in front of Mr. Holland's house. It had taken an hour and a half of the time Hollis had given him, to get back to his house and move his family and a few belongings to Mr. Holland's house. There had been a strange, uncomfortable reunion between Mr. Holland and his grandmother. He had kissed his mother just now, and raised his hand as she turned back at the doorway. "I'll be all right, mother," he said. "There are a few things I'd like to attend to."

"All right, son. Don't be long."

He nodded, though she was already inside.

Geoffrey and Alister had gone in before her, taking care of their grandmother and the younger children. Cot smiled crookedly. Alister would be all right. He hoped Geoffrey wasn't too old to adapt.

Mr. Holland came out.

"I'd like to thank you for taking us in," Cot said to him.

Mr. Holland's face clouded. "I owe it to you, boy. I keep thinking this wouldn't be happening if I hadn't chivvied you along."

Cot shook his head. "No—one way or the other, it would have happened. That's rather easy to see, now."

"You coming inside, Cot? I'd like to introduce you to my daughter."

Cot looked at the sun. No, not enough time.

"I'll be back, Mr. Holland. Got a few loose ends to tie up."

Holland looked over the low, barely visible roof of Cot's house. A small dustcloud was approaching it from the other side. He nodded. "Yeah, I see what you mean. Well, you'd better hurry up. Don't have more than about twenty minutes."

Cot nodded. "I'll see you." He dropped the carbine into his hand and loped across the yard, not having to worry about the dog now, cutting through the scrub underbrush until he was just below the crest of a rise that overlooked his house. He flattened himself in the high grass and inched forward, until his head and shoulders were over the crest, but still hidden in the grass.

He'd been right. There were three men just climbing out of a light guncarrier.

Well, that's what our grandparents were, he thought. *Looters.* He slipped the safety. *And our parents had a code.* And, now his brothers had a community. *But I've been living a way all my life, and I guess I've got Integrity.*

He fired, and one of the men slapped his stomach and fell.

The other two dove apart, their own rifles in their hands. Cot laughed and threw dirt into their faces with a pair of shots. One of them bucked his shoulders upward involuntarily, as the dirt flew into his eyes. Cot fired again, and the shoulders slumped. *Thanks for a trick, Jeff.*

The other man fired back—using half a clip to cut the grass a foot to Cot's right. Cot dropped back below the crest, rolled, and came up again, ten feet from where he had been.

Down by the house, the remaining man moved. Cot put a bullet an inch above his head.

He had about ten minutes. Well, if he kept the man pinned down, the first salvo would do as thorough a job as any carbine shot.

The man moved again—a little desperately this time —and Cot tugged at his jacket with a snap shot.

Five minutes, and the man moved again. He was shouting something. Cot turned his ear forward to kill the hum of the breeze, but couldn't make out the words. He pinned the man down again.

When he had a minute of life left, the man tried to run for it. He sprang up suddenly, running away from the weapons carrier, and Cot missed him for that reason. When the man cut back, he shot him through the leg.

Damn! Jeff would have done better than that!

The man was crawling for the carrier.

Over at the Kittredges, the first muzzle-flashes flared, and the thud of guns rolled over the hills.

Cot put a bullet through the crawling man's head.

He'd been right. The Kittredges' gunnery was poor. The first salvo landed a hundred yards over—on the crest of the ridge where he was standing with his rifle in his hand.

CHAPTER EIGHT:

This happened many years after the plague, at about the same time things were beginning to run down in the Great Lakes region and the Seventh Republic there tried to buy time with a legend. But this happened toward the south:

I

Jeff Garvin moved through the loosened window like a darker shadow in the night, and his feet made no sound as he touched the floor. He grinned quietly as he closed the window behind him and adjusted his eyesight with near-animal ease to peer at the darkness of the room.

He was in the dining room. He took quick stock of the doorways and chose the one most likely to lead to the kitchen. He moved toward it without hesitation, holding his rifle with his right forefinger on the trigger while he nudged the door gently open. He'd been right—it was the kitchen, and he stepped noiselessly into it.

He located a storage cabinet, and began to fill his

pack, grimacing because most of the food was home-canned in glass jars. He'd have to be careful with those, if he got in a fight. He packed them as carefully as possible, stopping to listen carefully after each barely audible *tink!* of their touching. When he had a full load, he slipped the pack onto his shoulders and picked up his rifle again. He crossed the kitchen, opened the door, and stepped back out into the dining room.

"Whoa, feller," the voice said, and the rifle was jerked out of his hand. He saw the glint of faint light on the barrel of a shotgun, and stopped still, the spring of his muscles sagging into dissolution. He squinted at the shadowy figure, feeling a despair wash through him, and knew that was it, this was the end, a thousand miles and five years away from home. He had fought and tracked his way this far, over the cold plains and through the long nights, with men against him all the way, and this was where he had finally come to the end of it all.

A girl had caught him. A girl with a shotgun. He grinned at the thought and let her see the grin where she sat in the semicircle of people who were looking at him. He liked the way she didn't try to avoid it, but kept looking at him—looking, not staring the way the rest of the women were doing at the wild outlaw.

"What's your name, mac?" the man who seemed to be running things asked.

"Jeff Cottrell," he said with the right amount of hesitation. He'd found out long ago that Garvin wasn't a popular name in some places. He had no idea if it was the same way here, but there was no use taking chances with a dull knife or a slow fire.

"What were you doing in the Boston house?"

He looked at the man expressionlessly, wondering what sort of local quirk of justice demanded particulars of a man about to be executed out of hand.

"Stocking up," he said, willing enough to play along.

The man nodded. "Been out on the plains a long time?"

That was a trick one. Nobody could do it very long without raiding a lot of towns, and a man who raided a lot of towns was bound to run into times when he didn't come and go without leaving some of the citizenry bleeding. On the other hand, if he gave them some ridiculously short figure, they'd simply lose patience with him and get it over with now.

"Being cagey about it, huh?" the man said. "All right, we'll let that one go." He didn't seem particularly disturbed.

"How many people have you killed?"

"My share," he answered instantly. It was a foregone conclusion anyway.

The man took it without any surprise, and started another question, but the girl cut him off.

"Don't see any point to carrying this business on any longer," she said, standing up.

Whew! I didn't think it'd be you that yelled for blood first, Jeff thought.

"Maybe you're right, Pat," the man admitted. He turned to the rest of the crowd—the town's entire adult population, probably—and directed his next question at them. "How do you people feel about it?"

There was a scattering of nods, and a few people said "Pat's right," or things to the same effect. Jeff braced himself.

The man turned around and looked at him. "We've got a proposition."

Jeff felt the air rush out of his chest. "You've got a *what?*" he asked completely astonished.

The man smiled tightly. "This is something we decided on a while ago. This is a farming town," he explained. "Every one of us has enough to keep him busy all day and half the night. We can't keep up any sort of adequate guard against people like you; and people like you are a nuisance. So we've got a standing offer to every one of you we catch that doesn't flunk the little oral examination. Goes like this: we'll let you draw food and clothing from the town supplies and give you a place to stay. In return, you keep the neighborhood cleaned out of light-fingered tramps like yourself."

"I'll take it," Jeff said.

The man held up his hand. "Let's not get hasty, feller. There's a catch, far as you're concerned. One of us goes with you everywhere you go around town. He carries a gun. You don't. When you go out hunting, we take shifts and send *two* people with you. You get your rifle outside the town limits, and turn it back in before you get inside 'em again. If we catch you heading out, we shoot you down as a sort of generalized favor to all the other towns around here."

"I'll still take it."

"Funny," the man said, "they all do, at first." There was a ripple of cold grins through the crowd, and Jeff didn't waste a thought on wondering why the position was currently empty.

The man stepped up and held out his hand. "We might as well get to know each other. You're bunking with me. My name's Pete Drumm."

Jeff nodded thoughtfully. It was a hard, tough hand.

"Ever ride a horse before?" Pat asked.

Jeff shook his head and looked carefully at the bay hitched to the porch upright.

The girl sighed. "Well, Mister, that's a tired horse. He's been tired for the past five years. So even if you're lying, don't expect to get very far very fast. Get aboard him."

Jeff shrugged and walked over to the animal. He slipped the reins loose and climbed cautiously into the saddle, feeling his thigh muscles stretching into unaccustomed lengths and resigning himself to con- siderable—and probably laughable—soreness if he kept this up very long. Fortunately, the horse did no more than twitch his tail.

Pat looked up and grinned. "No, you're never been on a horse before," she said. "You look as though you expected to wet your pants any minute."

He stared at her for a minute, then burst out laugh- ing in the first genuine amusement he'd felt in weeks. Damn, he *liked* that girl!

She swung up into her own saddle, and they walked slowly through the town while Pat kept up a running commentary. "That's Becker's place. Got a wife, four kids. The kids sleep downstairs, so they can pretty much take care of themselves. That place next to them is Fritch's. Old Fritch lives alone, but he's a sly one. He's got traps all around the place. Wouldn't hurt to look up this way every once in a while, though."

By the end of the afternoon, he had a fairly clear picture of the town's layout. It was much like all the

others he'd seen on the plains—the houses close together for protection, with fields running out in all
directions. It was late fall now, and the fields were
bare, but he could picture how it would look in the
summer: green and prosperous, tough as the grass that
constantly fought the prairie wind. He spotted a string
of bare poles marching toward the horizon, and
nodded at them.

"Telephone line," the girl explained. "Branch out
of Kansas City. Some easterners were through here last
July, hooking up with the St. Louis exchanges. They'll
be stringing wire in the spring. All the old stuff blew
down long ago, of course." Abruptly, she turned in
the saddle and looked at him. "What's it like, back
East?" she asked, laughing wryly. "Funny, how we're
all part of the same lousy mess, and there's the big
difference between city people and small-town farmers.
But Pete tells me it was always like that."

She seemed genuinely interested. To make conversation, at first, and then out of some long pent-up well
of talk as he forgot himself, he began telling her
about life back in New Jersey, about what the people
were like, and about his family. She listened intently,
asking a question here and there, occasionally making
a surprisingly levelheaded comment. By the time they
reined up in front of her house, she knew a great deal
about him, and not even his screaming muscles and
aching knees were enough to kill his odd feeling of
relaxation.

But one thing he never quite let leave his mind;
some way, somehow, he had to find a way to escape.

By the time he had been in Kalletsburg a week, he
knew how he was going to do it. It was the only way

that would work, with these people. It might take a year. Perhaps two. But when the time came, he would leave. And he found himself toying with the idea that it just might be possible to take Pat with him.

He rolled over in his bunk and clasped his hands behind his head, staring up at the lamplit ceiling.

There was no use trying to beat the system of watchers they had set up. Even when it was only Pat who was with him, there was a pistol holstered to her belt, and Drumm had meant what he'd said about his going unarmed. *That* had been an uncomfortable feeling to shake off in itself. His rifle was so much part of him that he had grown accustomed to its weight to balance him. He found himself misjudging the height of his shoulder, or overestimating the muscular effort needed to lift his arm. He'd felt awkward and clumsy without it, and in this short time, hadn't quite gotten over it yet.

But he could get used to it, and get used to having it back, when the time came. Because the town's weak spot was its smallness. He was in constant contact with everyone. In a while, they'd be completely accustomed to the sight of him. If he talked to them, and listened to what they had to say, he'd gradually become one of them. In time, too, he might start working a small field of his own. Perhaps he'd build a house. Give them a hundred signs that he was here to stay—tied to the town in the same way they were.

And then, one night, he'd disappear, and they'd be left to look for a new sheriff. And, as he'd considered before, it was just barely possible that Pat might be willing to go along with him by then.

He grinned quietly.

"What have you got to be happy about?" Drumm

271

asked. Jeff's grin widened. At the moment, everybody in town tacitly accepted, small-town fashion, that Pat was Drumm's girl.

"Oh, nothing special," he said. He lay awake for a few minutes longer, and then went quietly to sleep.

Winter came, and during its first weeks, as the plains outlaws were driven to stock whatever miserable shelters they had managed for themselves, Jeff was busy day and night. He'd spent his last winter in a cave cut into a riverbank, and he knew what the thought-processes were that rose from the sort of life. By October, he'd nailed four figurative hides to the barn door, and then the snow blocked everything off until the desperate, half-starved men began floundering toward the town in mid-December. Meanwhile, he spent his time talking to Pat or Drumm.

Drumm was as interested in his past as Pat had been, for an entirely different reason. He showed Jeff the boxed sheafs of paper covered by his father's precise, economical handwriting.

"*A Study of the Effects of Personal Arms on Conventional Theories of Modern Government,* by Harvey Haggard Drumm, with a bow to Silas McKinley,*" Jeff read, and looked up at Pete in curiosity. "*A History of Theodore Berendtsen's Northern Campaign,*" he read from the label of another box, "With Additional Personal Notes."

"Dad was in on that one," Pete explained. "He was a corporal under one of Matt Garvin's sons."

Well I'll be triple goddamned! Jeff thought. He looked at another box of manuscript, labeled *The Care and Feeding of the Intellectual Militant.*

"And you're hanging on to these in hopes of getting them to a printing press sometime?" he asked.

"Better than that," Pete said. "I'm trying to add to them. That's why I'm so interested in your story. I want to write it down. I want to be able to have other people learn from it. See, we're doing all right, down here. Things starting up, even without Berendtsen's people having gone through here. Because my father came through here."

"Just writing books?"

"Just writing books, and telling people what was in them, and about how in the East things *were* getting better. It makes a big difference when you know somebody's found a way out of the hole, even if you haven't, yet. You keep looking. You don't just curl up and die. I guess that's the best excuse for Berendtsen and his bully-boys. They had to live so my father could talk about the way things were getting started. But we're past that time, now. And I'm damned glad." Pete looked at Jeff with shrewd appraisal in his eyes. "I wouldn't want to see any more gunmen trying to keep going, around here."

"I guess not."

"Yeah."

"What ever happened to your father, anyway?" Jeff asked. He didn't like the way the conversation was going.

Pete smiled softly. "I don't know. I guess I was about ten or twelve when Ryder's bunch came through here, heading for Texas. My mother had just died, and my older brother, Jim, was big enough to run our place with my help. Pop was a rotten farmer anyway, so he talked it over with us, and when

Ryder's bunch pulled out, he packed up all the blank paper he could carry and went off with them. I sort of wanted to tag along, but Pop stepped on that idea hard. He was right, I guess. Ryder wasn't doing any fighting he could avoid, but it was still a hard life.

"Worked out best in the end, too, when Jim got killed by one of you boys. If I'd of gone, there wouldn't have been anybody left to work the place."

"What difference would that make, if you weren't here to see it?"

Drumm shrugged uncertainly. "I know. But I *am* here. It just—I don't know, it just feels that way."

Jeff tried to imagine that trait of character that would make a man think in those terms about a tract of land much like any other tract, anywhere. But he had to give up on that.

Bit by bit, he told Drumm the story of what his life had been like, beginning with his father's death and carefully ending with Alister's marriage to Barbara, and his departure from home. He had to watch himself to make sure he didn't let his real name slip, but otherwise he was able to let the story run almost automatically.

For some reason, a comment that Pete made on Cot's death stayed with him. He found himself thinking about it at unexpected times and places.

"I'm sorry he died," Pete said, "because I'm sorry for anybody who dies. But I'm glad for his sake he did. A man shouldn't outlive his times." He looked up and speared Jeff with his glance. "Once he's decided for certain on what his times really are."

Jeff couldn't seem to shake the words loose.

* * *

When he'd been there a year, his patient plan reached its first goal. He had kept up his duties faithfully, and had stayed away from the telephone wire crew, talking to them only when he encountered them by accident, and not trying to send out any messages or ask for help of any kind. It would have been a futile move in any case, for his kind of man had no friends, and no hope of help, but, more important, he had known the townspeople were watching.

They gave him credit on a small plot of land, and he found time enough during the day to work it. He had to be awake most of the night, but he worked his land as hard as anyone worked theirs, while Pat showed him how. His face pinched while his shoulders broadened, and the thin layer of winter fat ran off him in muddy streams of perspiration. When he caught a raider stealing his young corn, he shot him through the elbow of his gun-arm.

That complete unpremeditated move tipped the scales in his favor, he realized later. The one man who still rode out with him was confidently careless about enforcing the original rules, and if he hadn't wanted Pat so much by then, he could have shot him and left any time he chose. He debated it briefly, but realized that Pat would never go with him on that basis, and stuck to his original plan.

Wait a year, he told himself. In a year, they'd practically let him carry the town out on his back.

That fall, he started building his house. Left to himself, he might have thrown up a one-room shack of some kind, but he had enough offers of help to make a bigger project possible. Moreover, if he built a place large enough for a family, there was something as good as a display poster to advertise his intention of settling down. He realized how right he'd been when he caught Pat's mother and father looking at the two of them over the dinner table and exchanging sly glances.

It seemed to help in his long campaign to wear Pat down, too.

And finally, when the next spring came, he knew it was time. He slept in the house alone, riding in and out of town with his rifle in his saddle boot any time he chose. He called everybody in the town by their first names, and he seldom had to eat his own cooking. The people of Kalletsburg had forgotten he was a raider, an outlaw.

Even Pete Drumm had forgotten, for he was as sour toward him as he would have been toward any other equal who was winning the contest over Pat.

Only me, he thought. *I haven't forgotten.*

He waited until the moon died, and picked a night when it was cloudy enough to rain, piling packs on one of his two horses and working on his rifle until even its slowly deteriorating barrel shone without a trace of pitting. Then he waited patiently, until he was sure Pat's parents would be asleep. He sat in his darkened house and counted slow time. Finally, he moved.

He walked his horses quietly to a stand of cottonwood near the Bartons' house and hitched them there, moving the rest of the way on foot. Without a trace of having lost his old skill, he went into the shed and saddled Pat's horse, and then circled the house.

And he came, inevitably, to the dining room

window, which was still the easiest. *Well,* he thought, *it's a full circle.*

Grinning with cold mirth, he slid through the loose window and stood once more in the Bartons's dining room at night.

He fumed inwardly in response to a by now automatic reflex. He'd told Arnold a dozen times if he'd told him once to fix that window. But the old man just smiled and insisted that Jeff was all the protection he needed.

He shook his head angrily. Well, this'd teach him.

"Look boy," Pat said from the darkness, "the only bathroom in this house is *still* next to the dining room. Can't you learn?"

He sagged against the wall.

Pat came over to him and took his hand. "You must want something awful bad to keep sneaking in here. I hope it's me."

"I—" And all of a sudden, he couldn't say it. He felt foolish, caught here, and somehow awkward, and completely ridiculous.

"I—" he began again, and felt something break open inside him. "Damn it," he said bewilderedly, "I was going to ask you to take off with me. But I can't *do it!* I can't *leave* this goddamn town!"

Pat reached out and held him, her hand tousling his hair fondly. "You damn fool," she said, "of course you can't! You're civilized."

II

And this happened in the north:

Joe Custis stepped out of the dead commander's hut into the flickering shadows from the cookfires. There was a rifleman posted about ten yards away, and Custis looked at him thoughtfully. Then he called, in a voice pitched to reach the man and no farther. "Hey—the boss wants some light in here!"

The man grunted and went to one of the near fires for a sliver of burning wood. He carried it back, shelding it carefully with his hands. "First no lights, and now lights," he grumbled as he stepped through the doorway. He reached up to a shelf where an oil lamp was sitting, and stopped dead as he dimly saw Henley on the floor and the commander lying across the desk. "Now, who the hell'd be dumb enough to kill the commander right in camp . . ."

Custis whipped the flat of his hand across the side of the man's neck. He caught the burning light carefully, crushed it out on the floor. Then he stepped outside again, gently closing the door behind him. He walked slowly away until he was fifty feet away from the huts, in the shadows, and then he turned toward

278

the fire where he had seen Jody working. He had the knife in his belt under his shirt, and as he walked he rolled up his bloody sleeves. His skin gathered itself into gooseflesh under the night wind's chill.

When he was fairly close to the fire, he changed his pace until he was simply strolling. He walked up to the fire, listening for the first sounds from the hut on the other side of the camp. "Jody."

She looked up, wiping the wet hair off her forehead with the back of a hand. "Hi, soldier! Come for supper?"

He shook his head. "Still want to come to Chicago?"

She straightened up. "Just a minute."

She stirred the food in the pot, let the spoon slide back into it, and picked up her water pail. "Ready," she said.

"Let's go."

They walked toward the spring. Out of the firelight, she touched his forearm. "You're not kidding me?"

"No. You know how to get down to where the car is?"

"Yeah." She put the water pail down. "Come on."

As they walked up the rise to the galley entrance, she gripped his hand. "Anything go wrong, Joe? You get hurt, or something?"

"No."

"There's blood on your shirt."

"Henley's."

"You sure?"

"He spilled it. It belongs to him."

She took a deep breath. "There's gonna be hell to pay."

"Can't help it. It worked out that way." He was trying to remember the exact positions the grenadiers had been in.

They came to where the two machinegun pits covered the trail into the valley, and one of the men there heard them walking. "Who's that?"

"Me. Jody."

The man chuckled. "Hey, Jody! You bringin' me my supper?" The other man laughed out of the darkness.

"Not right now, Sam," Jody answered. "I got somebody with me."

There was more laughter in the shadows among the rocks, and then they were past. They made their way down the mountainside, walking as quietly as they could on the loose rock, and then Custis heard a man's shoes scrape as he settled himself more comfortably in his position.

"We're there," Jody whispered.

"Okay." Custis oriented himself. After a minute, he was pretty sure where he was in relation to the car, and where everyone else would be.

"What now, Joe?"

"You walk on down. Let 'em hear you. Talk to 'em."

"You sure, Joe?"

"Yeah. It'll be okay."

"You're not gonna leave me?"

"I told you I'd take you, didn't I?"

"All right, Joe." Her fingers trailed over his forearm. "Be seeing you."

"Give me twenty minutes," he said, and slipped off among the rocks.

He moved as noiselessly as he knew how, the knife

ready in his hand. Once he stumbled over a man. "Scuse me, Buddy," he mumbled.

"Okay, pal," he man answered. "Take one for me."

Farther down the mountains, he heard somebody say loudly: "Hey, it's Jody! C'mere, Jody, gal." He could feel the ripple of attention run through the men among the rocks. Equipment rattled as men leaned forward, sick of this duty and glad of something to watch, and maybe join in on.

Now he was behind one of the grenade teams. He inched forward, found them, and after a minute he was moving on.

The men where Jody was were laughing and tossing remarks back and forth. He heard her giggle.

He found the next team craning forward to look down into a cup behind some rocks where a small fire had been built on the side away from the car. When he was through, he looked over the edge and saw Jody standing in the middle of a bunch of men. Her head was thrown back, and she was laughing.

When he'd left the third emplacement, and was working toward the fourth, he heard the sound of a slap. A man yelled: "Hey, girl, don't you treat me like that!" The rest of the men were laughing harshly.

The fourth team was easy to handle.

Working on the fifth, he missed the last man. It was a tricky business, getting the first with one sure swing and then going for the other before he could yell. This time the man rolled sideways, and there was nothing for Custis to do but kick at his head. He hit the man, but didn't even knock him out. The man slid off the rock, yelling, and Custis scrambled as fast as he could to throw the box of grenades one way, the rifle another, and jumped for the car.

"Lew! Open up! I'm coming in!" he bellowed as the night broke apart.

Rifle fire yammered toward him as he ran, ricochets screaming off the rocks. The car's motors began to wind up. It was still as dark as the bottom of a bucket, and then Hutchinson fired the car's flare gun. The world turned green.

Custis slammed into the starboard track cover, threw himself on top of it, and clawed his way over the turtledeck. He rapped his knuckles quickly on the turret hatch, and Robb flung it back. Custis teetered on the edge of the coaming. The car's machineguns opened up, hammering at the rocks. Custis heard a man screaming: "Where's the damned grenades?"

Then he heard the girl shouting: "Joe."

He stopped. He looked back toward the sound of her voice. "Oh, Christ!" he muttered. Then he sighed. "What the hell," and shouted down into the turret: "Cover me!"

He jumped down off the battlewagon, his boots resounding on the foreplates before he hit the ground. He pitched forward, smashing into the gravel, then threw himself erect and ran toward the spot.

Rifle fire chucked into the ground around him. He weaved and jumped from side to side, floundering over the rocks. Hutchinson fired the next flare in the rack, and now the world was red, laced by the bright glow of the car's tracers as the machineguns searched back and forth in their demiturrets. He heard the tracks slide and bite on the gravel, and the whole car groaned as the bogeys lurched it forward.

The girl was running toward him, and there were

men back in the rocks who were sighting deliberately now, taking good aim.

"Joe!"

"All right, damn you!" He scooped her up and flung her toward the car ahead of him, feeling a crack of fire lace across his back. And then the car was practically on top of them. Lew had his driver's hatch open, and Custis pushed the girl through. Then he was clambering up the side of the turret and into the command seat. "All right," he panted into the command microphone. "Let's go home."

The hatch dropped shut on top of him. He fell into the car, landing very hard on his side. Lew locked a track and spun them around. The inside of the car sounded like a wash boiler being pelted with stones.

Robb looked at him, patting the breeches of his .75s. "Open fire, Joe?"

"No! No—leave the poor bastards alone."

He looked over toward the girl. "Hey, Jody," he grinned.

The halftrack lumbered down the last slope, spraying stones out from under its tracks as it took a bite of the prairie grass. Custis jammed his hands against the sides of the hatch and scowled out at the plains ahead, where Chicago lay beyond the edge of the green horizon. He didn't turn his head back. He was through with the mountains.

He was going to Chicago. He thought about the jagged holes in State Street's asphalt. He shivered a little.

Also available in Methuen Paperbacks

C. J. Cherryh

Chanur's Venture

The latest volume in the Chanur saga.

Pyanfar Chanur thought she had seen the last of
Tully, the lone human who had so disrupted the
peace of Meetpoint Station and gained the Chanur
clan the enmity of half a dozen races as well as their
own. But in this striking sequel to the Hugo-
nominated *Pride of Chanur*, Tully is back, bringing
with him a priceless trade contract with human
space. A contract which would mean vast power,
riches, and a new hornet's nest for the Pyanfar and
The Pride!

'This is a rousing good tale, and Cherryh's feisty
hani are the most believeable alien characters to
come down the SF pike in a long time . . . These
swaggering, vain, tough-talking, hani heroines make
Chewbacca look like a pussycat' *Kliatt*

Clifford Simak

A Heritage of Stars

Thousands of years in the future, Thomas Cushing
is haunted by the history of his ancestors. His quest
is to regain humanity's lost heritage, and he sets out
to find the fabled Place of Going to the Stars, from
which ancient technological man left earth to travel
among the alien civilizations of the galaxy. As he
travels he gathers about him a selection of weird and
wonderful beings – a group of stalking shadows;
Meg, the hilltop witch and a shivering ghostlike
snake. Along with Rollo, the last surviving robot,
Cushing and his companions embark on an exciting
and wonder-filled adventure of the far future.

interzone

SCIENCE FICTION AND FANTASY

Quarterly   £1.50

- *Interzone* is the only British magazine specializing in SF and new fantastic writing. We have published:

BRIAN ALDISS	M. JOHN HARRISON
J.G. BALLARD	GARRY KILWORTH
BARRINGTON BAYLEY	MICHAEL MOORCOCK
MICHAEL BISHOP	KEITH ROBERTS
ANGELA CARTER	GEOFF RYMAN
RICHARD COWPER	JOSEPHINE SAXTON
JOHN CROWLEY	JOHN SLADEK
PHILIP K. DICK	BRUCE STERLING
THOMAS M. DISCH	IAN WATSON
MARY GENTLE	CHERRY WILDER
WILLIAM GIBSON	GENE WOLFE

- *Interzone* has also published many excellent new writers; graphics by JIM BURNS, ROGER DEAN, IAN MILLER and others; book reviews, news, etc.

- *Interzone* is available from specialist SF shops, or by subscription. For four issues, send £6 (outside UK, £7) to: **124 Osborne Road, Brighton BN1 6LU, UK**. Single copies: £1.75 inc p&p.

- American subscribers may send $10 ($13 if you want delivery by air mail) to our British address, above. All cheques should be made payable to *Interzone*.

- "No other magazine in Britain is publishing science fiction at all, let alone fiction of this quality." *Times Literary Supplement*

- -

To: **interzone** 124 Osborne Road, Brighton, BN1 6LU, UK.

Please send me four issues of *Interzone,* beginning with the current issue. I enclose a cheque/p.o. for £6 (outside UK, £7; US subscribers, $10 or $13 air), made payable to *Interzone*.

Name _____

Address _____

_____

Science Fiction and Fantasy from Methuen Paperbacks

While every effort is made to keep prices low, it is sometimes necessary to increase prices at short notice. Methuen Paperbacks reserves the right to show new retail prices on covers which may differ from those previously advertised in the text or elsewhere.

The prices shown below were correct at the time of going to press.

☐	413 55450 3	**Half-Past Human**	T J Bass	£1.95
☐	413 58160 8	**Rod of Light**	Barrington J Bayley	£2.50
☐	417 04130 6	**Colony**	Ben Bova	£2.50
☐	413 57910 7	**Orion**	Ben Bova	£2.95
☐	417 07280 5	**Voyagers**	Ben Bova	£1.95
☐	417 06760 7	**Hawk of May**	Gillian Bradshaw	£1.95
☐	413 56290 5	**Chronicles of Morgaine**	C J Cherryh	£2.95
☐	413 51310 6	**Downbelow Station**	C J Cherryh	£1.95
☐	413 51350 5	**Little Big**	John Crowley	£3.95
☐	417 06200 1	**The Golden Man**	Philip K Dick	£1.75
☐	417 02590 4	**The Man Who Japed**	Philip K Dick	£1.75
☐	413 58860 2	**Wasp**	Eric Frank Russell	£2.50
☐	413 59770 9	**The Alchemical Marriage of Alistair Crompton**	Robert Sheckley	£2.25
☐	413 59990 6	**All Flesh is Grass**	Clifford D Simak	£2.50
☐	413 58800 9	**A Heritage of Stars**	Clifford D Simak	£2.50
☐	413 55590 9	**The Werewolf Principle**	Clifford D Simak	£1.95
☐	413 58640 5	**Where the Evil Dwells**	Clifford D Simak	£2.50
☐	413 52000 5	**The Buccaneers of Lan-Kern**	Peter Tremayne	£1.95
☐	413 54600 4	**Raven of Destiny**	Peter Tremayne	£1.95
☐	413 56840 7	**This Immortal**	Roger Zelazny	£1.95
☐	413 56850 4	**The Dream Master**	Roger Zelazny	£1.95

All these books are available at your bookshop or newsagent, or can be ordered direct from the publisher. Just tick the titles you want and fill in the form below.

Methuen Paperbacks, Cash Sales Department,
PO Box 11, Falmouth,
Cornwall TR10 109EN.

Please send cheque or postal order, no currency, for purchase price quoted and allow the following for postage and packing:

UK — 55p for the first book, 22p for the second book and 14p for each additional book ordered to a maximum charge of £1.75.

BFPO and Eire — 55p for the first book, 22p for the second book and 14p for each next seven books, thereafter 8p per book.

Overseas Customers — £1.00 for the first book plus 25p per copy for each additional book.

NAME (Block Letters) ....

ADDRESS..

....